Two Dreams

New and Selected Stories

Shirley Geok-lin Lim

Introduction by Zhou Xiaojing

The Feminist Press
at the City University of New York
New York

Published in the United States and Canada by
The Feminist Press at The City University of New York
311 East 94th Street, New York, New York 10128-5684

First Feminist Press edition, 1997

05 04 03 02 01 00 99 98 97   5 4 3 2 1

Library of Congress Cataloging-in-Publication Data
Lim, Shirley.
    Two dreams: new and selected stories / Shirley Geok-lin Lim.—1st
Feminist Press ed.
        p.   cm.
    Rev. ed. of: Life's mysteries, 1995.
    ISBN 1-55861-164-9 (alk. paper). —ISBN 1-55861-168-1 (p: alk, paper)
    1. Malaysia—Social life and customs—Fiction. 2. Malaysians—United
States—Social life and customs—Fiction. 3. Women—Malaysia—Social life
and customs—Fiction. I. Lim, Shirley. Life's mysteries. II. Title.
PS3562. I459T97   1997
813' .54—dc21   96-52523
                                                                         CIP

This publication is made possible, in part, by a grant from The National
Endowment for the Arts. The Feminist Press would also like to thank Joanne
Markell and Genevieve Vaughan for their generosity.

Typeset by CompuDesign, Jackson Heights, New York..
Printed on acid-free paper by McNaughton & Gunn, Inc., Saline, Michigan.
Manufactured in the United States of America.

Contents

For my mother and her people

Preface

I CONSIDER THIS collection of short stories a *furoshiki*, a kind of patterned handkerchief that a woman folds in pleats and bows to carry a small package—a gift of fruit, for example, or her lunch. It is a shawl, such as another woman at the end of another story threw over herself to cover her shoulders for warmth; a sort of scarf, to cloak a woman's head for modesty, and also a fabric of many colors, spun deliberately for display.

The stories in the collection span the years from 1969 to 1996. The earliest stories were composed when I had just barely turned a woman, neither at ease in a modern world of choices and freedom—including the freedom to end at the bottom of an emotional and social scrapheap—nor able to live gracefully with the moral constraints that had structured Chinese Malaysian women's lives for centuries, before they cracked in the contact with Western ideas, more dangerous than seducers or midnight lovers.

I have been writing in between America and Asia, and in between chores and duties, for over thirty years. I began writing as a poet. Poetry, the liberal taskperson, requires adventuring into critical essay and interpretation, narrative and imagination. The stories collected here happened when I gave myself permission to slip the traces of academe, and to trace instead the deceptive wavering line of "once upon a time."

Once upon a time, there was a country called . . .

In many of these stories, that country lies in the past, in a place that is neither history nor memory, neither family nor nation, but nonetheless a place real to Malaysians—and I hope also to American readers who wish to know what was to be seen and heard and felt in another country in which English and British were as fantastic as Chinese and indigenous, and all made a brew of rich misery and meanings which only storytelling can retrieve.

Some of these stories retell themselves, with new details and with added voices, despite the old ghosts. Looking for women as desperately as I have all my life, I imagine sisters again and again—women who measure each other, betray each other, warm each other with talk and food. So a more contemporary story, "Sisters," rewrites "Mr. Tang's Girls," written almost fifteen years earlier, as, sisterless, I reimagine women of my blood, from my blood, entering the world of the page.

But even imagined women, like imaginary gardens, are constructed within contested geographies. *Two Dreams* takes the forms of post-colonial places: tropical Malaysia and Singapore, into whose narrow estuarine ports Joseph Conrad had sailed in the nineteenth century with visions of Malay-European romances; the lonely American cities that conceal and shelter the Asian immigrant; the spaces in between airports.

I came to cold snowy Boston in 1969. Having lived in the United States for almost as long as I have been writing stories, I have stored-up tales of America yet to write. *Two Dreams* returns to the place where these stories began, imagining a past different from the one that I have lived—perhaps a past that looks forward to a place where the possessive can ring, not like loss but like love.

Shirley Geok-lin Lim
Santa Barbara, California
1996

Introduction

SHIRLEY GEOK-LIN LIM'S *Two Dreams: New and Selected Stories* is a book at once haunting and haunted: haunting, because after you have read the stories, the characters and their lives stay with you; haunted, because the stories hold something both intimate and strange, something so enticing and elusive that you want to return to them to re-encounter the people, re-experience the places, and re-think things over. This effect is similar to what Toni Morrison, talking about her own work, calls "a quality of hunger and disturbance that never ends."[1]

The attraction of Lim's characters lies in their vulnerability and strength, their complexity and ambivalence, as well as in their distinct personalities. These attributes reflect the complicated everyday realities of life in the multiracial, multiethnic, and multicultural societies of Malaysia and the United States. They also characterize the situations of individuals, families, and communities in the process of transition from traditional values of the East to new ideas and lifestyles of the West. In this process, the traditional Eastern values are challenged; but at the same time, Western values are tested and questioned as they are absorbed in another country, or even on their homeground by immigrants.

Much of the drama in Lim's stories is played out in the meeting places of different peoples and cultures, which are also "in-between" spaces of ambivalence and possibility. Indeed, most of Lim's stories grow out of the interactions and conflicts between East and West, between Asia and America. The geographical and cultural tension in

Lim's stories is perfectly captured in the book's title, *Two Dreams*, taken from the story of a woman whose dreams reveal the deep ambivalence she feels toward her two homelands, Malaysia and the United States.

Readers who are familiar with Lim's autobiographical work *Among the White Moon Faces: An Asian-American Memoir of Homelands* will recognize the parallels between Lim's own life and the lives of the characters in such stories as "Hunger," "All My Uncles," "The Good Old Days," and "Transportation in Westchester." In fact, Lim's memoir can serve as a companion book to her story collection, which can be better understood in the context of her life and the places she has lived. Although most of the stories in *Two Dreams* are not based on Lim's life, they are rooted in her life experience in Malaysia and the United States. Lim's own experience as an immigrant in America, and her intimate knowledge of life in both countries, have enabled her to portray Asian and Asian-American characters and their lives, cultures, and communities with accurate details and penetrating observations.

Shirley Geok-Lin Lim was born in the town of Malacca, on the west coast of the Malay Peninsula. Her early life took place during a time of turmoil and change in Malaysia. At the time of her birth, during World War II, her homeland was under Japanese occupation. After the war Great Britain re-established its longstanding colonial rule over the region, but in 1957, Malaysia became an independent state within the British Commonwealth.

Malaysia had long been a multiethnic, multilingual, multireligious society, with a large population of ethnic Chinese (including Shirley Lim) and a sizable Indian minority as well as native Malays. The decades preceding and following independence were marked by tensions— and sometimes violent clashes—between the groups.

Lim's childhood was also marked by turmoil and instability within her own family. When Lim was still a young girl, the failure of her father's business plunged the family into poverty; a short time later, her mother abandoned the family. The only girl among five brothers,

Shirley received little attention from her father, and was for years left hungry, for food as well as affection. She excelled in her studies, however, receiving her early education in English at a Roman Catholic convent school in Malacca. Later she went to the University of Malaya in the capital, Kuala Lumpur, where she received a B.A. with First Class Honours in English. After teaching at the University of Malaya for two years, Lim came to the United States and earned her M.A. and Ph.D. at Brandeis University in Waltham, Massachusetts. She first taught in the New York City area, at Hostos Community College and at Westchester College, SUNY. In 1990 she took a position at the University of California, Santa Barbara, where she teaches English and women's studies. She lives in Santa Barbara with her husband, Charles Bazerman, and son, Gershom Kean Bazerman.

Two Dreams contains nineteen stories written over three decades, from the 1960s to the 1990s. The stories are arranged into three groups, in accordance with the perspectives and central concerns. The first group, under the section title "Girl," consists of six stories, all of which deal with the lives of girls, though their content is not restricted to girl-hood. In "Hunger," for instance, questions concerning the obligations of motherhood, choices between individual freedom and the mother's responsibility for the lives of her children, are implicitly raised. These questions, however, remain under the surface of the story, which centers on the physical, psychological, and emotional experience of the girl protagonist, Chai.

Chai suffers from a double lack—the lack of food and the lack of a mother. Lim weaves the sensation of hunger and the emotion of longing seamlessly into the girl's everyday life through Chai's observations of details. Walking to school with her schoolmate Suleng, Chai notices that Suleng's uniform "was starched and ironed, the creases sharp and straight, the folds thick like her slice of bread and the yellow margarine spread with a fat knife. The starch made Suleng's royal blue cotton uniform gleam, like the fat sugar crystals glistening on the margarine on top of the bread" (25–26). Through the association of images, Lim enables the reader to experience Chai's hunger and loneliness along with her daily activities and surrounding world.

Association of images is also Lim's strategy for moving the narrative from one situation to another. Chai's memories of her mother and her painful feelings over her mother's absence are unexpectedly and spontaneously revealed through images. The bright blue eyes of Sister Finnigan, a teacher at Chai's school, remind her of the gems in the jewelery stores her mother had once taken her to. The colorless diamond stones, "clear as clear, like looking through water and seeing no bottom, no sky, no eyes looking back," reflect both the mother's absence and Chai's keen awareness of it (28). Again, as Chai wanders to the seawall her desolation is rendered by the undercurrents of meaning in Lim's description of the waves as seen through Chai's eyes: "They were blue like the sky brought close to hand, yet they were no-colour when she put her face down to look" (32).

Two of Lim's recurring subjects are women's social position and their relationships with men. These subjects are explored in a variety of forms, and often through the eyes of a girl. "Native Daughter," for instance, deals with gender relationships, especially the relationship between husbands and wives in the patriarchal society of Malaysia, through the perception and experience of six-year-old Mei Sim. Mei Sim's consciousness of gender difference emerges from listening to her mother's conversations with Grandaunty. She finds out that "women were different from men who were *bodoh* [stupid] and had to be trained to be what women wanted them to be. If women were carts, men were like *kerbau* [buffalo] hitched to them" (38). From their conversation, Mei discovers that her mother is talking to Grandaunty about her father's infidelity.

At age six, Mei learns that in a patriarchal society, where men's privilege and interest are protected by law and women are subordinate to and dependent on men, wives must be tactful in their dealings with their husbands. "'The only thing that women have is their cunning,'" Grandaunty advises her mother. "'What do you want, a

faithful man or a man who will support you and your children? . . .
Talk to him sweet-sweet every time he comes home late. . . . Make
him open the purse-strings'" (39). Grandaunty's practical advice,
apparently devoid of any emotional or moral considerations, lays
bare the stark reality of women's vulnerable status even after they are
married to wealthy men. In their disempowered position, women have
to use submissiveness as camouflage, and niceness as a weapon for their
own survival and the survival and benefit of their children. Grandaunty's
attitudes reflect the values of her patriarchal society, which has shaped
the relationships and behaviors of both men and women.

Two other stories of the first group, "Mr. Tang's Girls" and "Life's
Mysteries," further indicate that the family structure is ultimately a
power structure, that male-female relationships are power relationships which condition the characters' emotional and sexual lives.
Though protected by law, individual male power is not as absolute and
stable as the institutionalized patriarchy. Grandaunty in "Native
Daughter," for instance, is the matriarch who dominates her husband
and sons as well as enslaving her daughter. And in "Mr. Tang's Girls,"
each of the four women—a wealthy man's second wife and three
daughters of his second family—knows exactly what to say and how
to act in front of the father in order to get what she wants from him.
Mr. Tang's authority is threatened by his daughters, who have grown
up under Western influence. His oldest daughter's rebellious behaviour and undisguised sexual desire infuriate and disturb him. Shortly
after Mr. Tang announces an arranged marriage for her, she kills him
as he is dozing off. This parricide seems to be indirectly the result
of the mixture of East and West, the ancient and the modern, which
renders impossible the harmony and control Mr. Tang wants to
maintain within a family based on a centuries-old Asian patriarchal
system now infiltrated by modern Western lifestyles and values. In
this and several other stories, Lim seems to suggest that superficially
imported Western ideas and values can be dangerously seductive and
potentially destructive.

However, not everything Western can be categorized in these terms in Lim's stories. In "The Touring Company," a Malaysian schoolgirl's participation as a fairy in *A Midsummer Night's Dream* and her encounter with the actresses and actors from England make a lasting positive impact on her. The world around her takes on a magical new look; her imagination begins to reach beyond the confines of here and now.

The last story in this group, "Sisters," is an excerpt from Lim's novel-in-progress. The story begins with the childhood of two sisters, Yen and Su Swee, and their Western education in English at a Methodist school in Malacca. Their family structure and their relationship with their wealthy elderly father are similar to those of "Mr. Tang's Girls." But in the later story, the sisters are much closer to each other, and the plot that leads to the father's death is quite different. In fact, the story's comic penultimate scene suggests one of the themes Lim will explore in her novel: the paradoxes faced by young Asian and Asian-American women, raised in traditional families but exposed to modern Western values, as they seek to take charge of their own sexualities.

The deeply disturbing and catalytic effects of interactions between different cultures and peoples underlie many of Lim's stories, particularly those in the second group, under the section title "Country." Colonization and intervention by the West has molded the lives of people in Malaysia on different levels. In "Blindness," England and its literature play an important role in shaping the lives and relationships of a Chinese Malaysian family. In "The Bridge," the Western ideas of democracy and justice which a young girl, Gek Neo, has learned at school move her to report to the school principal, Mr. Blake, about some workmen's extortions of money and food from local people, who are too afraid to do anything about it. Ironically, Gek Neo knows that Mr. Blake, a white man in colonized Malaysia, has the power to help the Malaysians who are victimized by local corruption and power. In "Thirst," James Thamby McNair, a Eurasian, gives up his pursuit of medicine to marry a Catholic Sinhalese girl, and elopes with her to Malaysia, where he works as a "lowly dispenser" on a plantation in the jungle. After many years of marriage he becomes estranged from his wife and children, who have adopted their mother's religion and despise and pity their father for his sins and lack of religious faith. McNair turns to alcohol for comfort and eventually gives in to the seduction of the Malaysian gardener's daughter.

Invasions by foreign powers and interactions of different cultures not only condition people's interpersonal relationships and private lives, but also bring changes in the relationships within and between families, as shown in "All My Uncles" and "The Good Old Days." These two stories can be read as companion pieces about the decline of family fortune, the intrigues and conflicts between five households of five sons of a Straits Chinese patriarch in Malaysia. The loss of family wealth in these stories is in a way connected to the Japanese occupation and to the Western practice of litigation, which is adopted by the five families in hope of getting a good portion of an inheritance, but eventually leads them all into debt. Exposed to the forces and practices of Western values, the traditional Confucian harmony, hierarchy, and familial loyalty erode and finally collapse. Lim subtly blends comedy and tragedy in these stories. Out of the shattered past, new social practices and relationships are formed. As the narrator in "The Good Old Days" notes, though her father and her uncles never became rich businessmen as her grandfather used to be, her eldest brother "is now a top lawyer with his own firm in the capital city," her second brother is a successful accountant, and she herself teaches "Economics in the University" (115).

The interlacing narratives within a narrative in these two stories demonstrate Lim's talent in weaving different strands of story line with ease. In particular, Lim excels at integrating women's oral tradition —in this case, the aunts' gossip—into the structure of her written form. The numerous colorful characters in these stories also illustrate Lim's ability to create unforgettable personalities through her descriptive skill and her use of the characters' idiosyncratic English, without allowing their speech to become stereotypical pidgin English.

But Lim also portrays characters and conveys their experience without relying on their speech. In "The Farmer's Wife," Lim's narrative technique and character portrayal are distinctly different from those in her other stories. Throughout the story, silence remains a dominant effect and serves several functions. First, it recreates the atmosphere of a quiet life on an isolated farm. Second, it enhances the dislocation and loneliness of the farmer's wife, an immigrant from Canton, a large city in China. Third, it adds to the foreboding hush and the intense suspense that has been building up as the narrative progresses through the approach of nightfall and the arrival of morning, but without the farmer's return from the market. Finally, the silence, maintained while the farmer's wife is picked up by a white man in uniform and driven to town, reflects the alienation between the colonialists and the colonized people. This alienation and the colonial officer's self-assumed superiority are powerfully conveyed when the silence is broken at the end of the story. " 'Faugh!' the sergeant said to the Englishman. `These are truly foul-smelling, unfeeling, Godless people!' " (119)

In the third group of stories, under the section title "Woman," interactions between people of different genders, races, and ethnicities become even more complex. All the protagonists in these stories are women, but their emotional, psychological, and sexual experiences are shaped not only by a patriarchal system, but also by the tensions between cultures. In "Haunting," a Chinese-Malaysian woman, Jenny, suffers from anxiety and obsession with the sounds of ghosts in her indigenous Malaysian mother-in-law's old house because of the alienation she feels in the household. This alienation is due in part to the language barrier that separates Jenny from her mother-in-law and their servant, who speak only Malay, and in part to the generation gap, which implies a great difference in lifestyle and values as well as in age. In "Conversations of Young Women," Mary, a glamorous and successful reporter, is raped by her Chinese father's friends as a punishment for her insistence on dating an Indian man.

These intersections of gender, race, and ethnicity, which exist in all of Lim's writing, come to the forefront in this third group of narratives. In "Keng Hua," Weng, a thirty-six-year-old single woman with a successful college teaching career, begins to feel something missing in her life. She invites her American colleague, Peter, along with her friend Siew and Siew's husband, to her apartment for a drink. Siew is hopeful that Peter will fall in love with Weng, but Weng has no patience for Siew's sentimentality about love. She takes her affairs lightly and feels no emotional attachment to the numerous men in her life. In fact, Weng has declined Peter's invitations for a date in various forms before. Now she seems to be willing to give it a try despite Peter's ungainly height and bulk, the "roll of fat above his trousers and thickly coiled dark hair over his bare arms, springing up from the back of his hands," and even his white people's body odor, which Peter does not bother to mask with cologne (179). But Peter's rude manner and behavior humiliate Weng; the evening which seems so full of promise turns into a disaster. This incident forces Weng to confront what she has missed in life, and she cries that night.

The implied moment of revelation Weng experiences—and the narrative strategy which leads to this moment—are reminiscent of the epiphanies of James Joyce's *Dubliners*. There are similar moments of epiphany in other stories, including "Another Country" and "Two Dreams." The protagonist in the title story experiences a powerful moment of insight, although the epiphany is implied rather than described. "Two Dreams" begins with Martha's dream of riding on her brother's bicycle on the beach and ends with her dream of her Malaysian friend Harry's lecture, in which "all his students were leaving because the police were beating them on the head." The first dream reveals Martha's feelings of exile in New York and nostalgia for her childhood in Malaysia; the second one displays her horror and disappointment at the Malaysian police's brutality toward the weak and helpless in society and the politicians' indifference to it. These two dreams reflect Martha's ambivalent feelings about the two countries which have been her homes.

The emotional and psychological tensions and conflicts of living as an immigrant in America are also dramatized in "Transportation in Westchester" and "A Pot of Rice." Although the narrator in "Transportation in Westchester," a lonely young Chinese woman who teaches English at a suburban college, witnesses racial division and experiences racial hostility every day on her long hours of commuting between Brooklyn and Westchester, the tension in the foreground of the story is rooted in class divisions. The narrator avoids the companionship of a fellow commuter, Mrs. Callaghan, an elderly African-American woman, whose lengthy monologues bore her, and whose eager friendliness offends her because she realizes that Mrs. Callaghan is "a domestic," and takes her "for one of her own"—that is, one of the poor, unprofessional working class.

Lim's choice of words and tone for the narrator strategically reveals the narrator's naiveté and self-righteousness, and the fact that her education in classical and English literatures has shaped her perception of the world and people. At the same time, Lim also represents an interesting and unforgettable Mrs. Callaghan through her manner of speech—the syntax, cadence, and rhythm of her monologues. But Lim refuses to portray her characters through binary oppositions between good and evil, right and wrong. Despite her apparent snobbishness, there is much to admire in the narrator, who is struggling as an immigrant in New York with endurance, courage, and unshakable determination to get to a place where she will never suffer again from the hunger she experienced in her impoverished childhood, which still haunts her.

In "A Pot of Rice," gender relationships within an interracial marriage are complicated by cultural differences. Su Yu's ritual of ancestor worship in memory of her dead father offends her American husband, who resents not being served first. As in "Transportation in Westchester," a sense of alienation and loneliness accompanies the immigrant character's embrace of America's opportunities and promise for a better life. With the increasing number of Asians and Asian immigrants in the United States, Lim's exploration of multilayered cross-cultural experiences offers a timely, intimate representation of the special internal and external challenges faced by newly arrived Asians and Asian Americans.

Lim occupies a unique position in contemporary Asian-American literature. Much of this literature is by writers who are American-born, and the Asian places, cultures, and lives it depicts are for the most part imagined, invented, and re-created through intertextual appropriations and revisions of Asian myths, legends, and literatures. Lim's stories, embedded in everyday lives in Asia, have something different to offer the reader.

In spite of the difference, Lim's work has much in common with other Asian-American writings, particularly writings by women. Her characters' emotional and psychological state of being in-between two worlds is characteristic of the Asian-American experience, and has provided recurring subject matter in Asian-American literature. The exploratory side of Lim's stories—a delicate and innovative groping after half-sensed realities, mysterious states of mind, and complicated relationships—is reminiscent of the writings of a generation ago by Diana Chang and Hisaye Yamamoto. Lim's representation of Asian women as subjects of their own destinies, like the representation of women by writers such as Maxine Hong Kingston, Amy Tan, and David Henry Hwang, counters the stereotypes of Asian women as exotic creatures and submissive victims. In her sensitivity to issues of colonialism, nationalism, race, ethnicity, gender, and class, Lim's writings are closely linked to the work of Theresa Jak Kyung Cha. The intersections of gender, class, and ethnic and racial tensions and conflicts in the lives of Southeast Asians and Malaysian immigrants in America in Lim's stories mark both a new arrival and a new departure in Asian American literature.

With their predominant concerns with women's issues and experiences, Lim's stories share many qualities with other literary writings by women, particularly by women of color. Because of the differences of race, ethnicity, and class, the preoccupations of these writers of color are bound to differ from those of white European and American women writers. In her introduction to *The Secret Self: A Century of Short Stories by Women* (1995), Hermione Lee identifies speaking to "the secret self" as one of "the particular qualities of women's stories." Lee quotes Katherine Mansfield's ambition for the short story (expressed in a letter written in 1921): "One tries to go deep—to speak to the secret self we all have—to acknowledge that."[2] The notion of "the secret self" waiting to be discovered and confronted is undermined in Lim's stories. In these stories, the self is unstable; it is constantly being reconstructed and reinvented in different ways by conditions and forces which include racial tensions, class divisions, social changes, and the political climate. Rather than trying to reveal a supposed "secret self," Lim's stories—like the stories of many other women of color, including Alice Walker, Toni Morrison, Louise Erdrich, Leslie Marmon Silko, and Sandra Cisneros—are concerned with the process of the making of the gendered, ethnic, colonized and racialized self in a particular society and historical moment. At the same time, Lim's stories explore the possibilities of empowering, reinscribing, and reinventing this self, without failing to confront the vulnerablities and ambivalences involved in this process.

Finally, the hybrid cultures and the multiracial and multiethnic societies in Lim's stories challenge notions of the purity and stability of cultures and identities. In this sense, her work is also part of the emergent world literature of postcolonial migration and diaspora.

Up to this time, Shirley Lim has been better known as a poet and short story writer in Southeast Asia and Great Britain than in the United States. Her first collection of poetry, *Crossing the Peninsula and*

Other Poems, was published in the British Commonwealth in 1980, and received the Commonwealth Poetry Prize for the best first book of poetry. She has written three other collections of poetry, *No Man's Grove and Other Poems* (Singapore: National University of Singapore English Department, 1985), *Modern Secrets: New and Selected Poems* (London: Dangeroo Press, 1989), and *Monsoon History: Selected Poems* (London: Skoob Pacifica, 1994). Lim also published two collections of short stories with Times Editions in Singapore—*Another Country and Other Stories* (1982) and *Life's Mysteries: The Best of Shirley Lim* (1995)—from which many of the stories in *Two Dreams* are drawn. She received an Asiaweek Short Story award in 1982.

In 1990 Lim co-edited, with Mayumi Tsutakawa and Margarita Donnelly, *The Forbidden Stitch: An Asian American Women's Anthology,* which won the American Book Award (1990). Her memoir *Among the White Moon Faces: An Asian-American Memoir of Homelands* was published in 1996 by the Feminist Press, and subsequently by Times Editions in Singapore.

Although she has been well known internationally as a critic of Southeast Asian and Asian-American literature, and although her poetry and short stories have appeared in North American periodicals and anthologies, Lim's fiction has not been available in the United States in book form. Thanks to the Feminist Press, American readers now have access to Shirley Lim's stories. In the haunted house of *Two Dreams,* readers can enjoy exploring the elusive, confronting the irrational, and being surprised by the unexpected.

Zhou Xiaojing
Buffalo, New York
1996

NOTES

1. Toni Morrison, *Conversations with Toni Morrison,* ed. Danille Taylor-Guthrie (Jackson: Univ. Press of Mississippi, 1994), 155.

2. Hermione Lee, ed., *The Secret Self: A Century of Short Stories by Women* (London: Phoenix, 1995), x.

PART 1

Girl

Hunger

ONLY TWO DAYS since Mother left. The freedom seemed forever. More room for running. More time for staying awake, games, play. Was she glad? Was she sad? There was never time for thinking although the day was long, longer as the afternoon drew on and on towards meal time, longest in darkness when the odours of soy, pork, ginger, garlic and sweet cooked rice lingered on and on in the empty rooms downstairs, like a vague ache in her crotch, a burn in her chest, sensations that followed her to the bedroom to lie down beside her in the brown faded dark of the bottom half of the iron double-bunk bed that had been so fashionable only a few years ago.

Mother would be gone three days next morning.

Chai tightened the uniform belt and thought of Suleng. Suleng's mother was a washerwoman, but in her hand Suleng had a piece of white bread spread thick with margarine and sprinkled with sugar. Suleng wasn't in her A class. Suleng was a B class girl, but her uniform was starched and ironed, the creases sharp and straight, the folds thick like her slice of bread and the yellow margarine spread with a fat knife. The starch made Suleng's royal blue cotton uniform gleam, like the fat sugar crystals glistening on the margarine on top of the bread.

She had watched Suleng eat that slice of bread as they walked across the bridge to school a few weeks ago, when she had first moved to Grandfather's house. Even then Chai had been hungry. Mother had given her two *marie-piah* and some boiled water. Brown, crisp, flat, dry, round, pricked, sugary, crackling, each half the size of a palm—you could buy ten *marie-piah* for five cents. She watched Suleng eat her slice of thick, soft, oily bread. She walked beside her and began talking, watching as Suleng put the last wedge in her greasy mouth.

Now Chai waited for Suleng in the middle hall of Suleng's house, and watched as Suleng's mother spread the margarine on the bread. The margarine tub was huge, almost as large as those square tins of fancy English biscuits Mother bought when they had money and lived in the bank that Father managed. Now she didn't even have those two *marie-piah* for breakfast.

Perhaps she hoped Suleng would not be able to finish her bread and would give her the leftover. Perhaps she hoped the washerwoman would offer her a slice. At every house, from every open and half-opened door, she smelled the fresh yeasty dough of white bread, the clean tang of sugar crystals. The morning was full of food, and she was hungry.

By the next week she had stopped walking with Suleng. She could walk faster, easier, without Suleng who strolled lazily munching her bread. Swiftly she passed the half-opened doors from where warm scents of toast and coconut cakes wafted towards her thin chest. She did not care to pause to breathe the full aromas of black coffee, that clear scent of pandan-scented coconut-boiled rice that made her stomach lurch. The houses were rich, concealed behind gold-leafed, carved doors and windows, like her grandfather's house had been, even in her memory, which seemed now so short, so immediate of quick movement and sunshine.

This was freedom. To walk at a fast trot to school, to think ahead to the day, the play, the books, the next day, the play, the books. Not to think of where she was but how she must go. Quickly she crossed the little bridge, breathed the sulphuric smell of putrid riverine sediment. This is not it, she thought. The *angsana* trees were heavy with yellow blossoms. Their tiny petals littered a stretch of the park, the morning air was acid sharp with their efflorescence and decay. Yellow pollen like gold dust dotted the ground. To the right the Straits of Malacca was always blue or grey, colours as steadfast as her heart as she walked rapidly to school. I am steadfast, she thought, exhilarated. I am myself, no one is me, I am alone. She forgot she was hungry, walking between the weight of the blossoming *angsana* and the empty blue space of the morning sky and the Malacca Straits.

So quickly she had forgotten about Mother. Poor Mother who cried that morning in Auntie's house after she had pulled her in as she was passing by on her way to school and had given her a glass of Ovaltine and a slice of bread and marmalade. Very good marmalade, from Sheffield, England. It had strips of bitter peel and was shining clear orange, just the way she liked marmalade. But that was only one morning. Mother wasn't at the window of Auntie's house the next day nor the next, nor the next, and so on. Mother had gone some place, gone away. Now she walked quickly past Auntie's house with its closed gold-leafed, carved windows and doors and tried not to think about the marmalade.

Sister Finnigan was a tall scarecrow. Her eyes were bright blue, little shifting chips of precious star sapphire behind the steel-rimmed glasses. Mother had taken her to many jewellery stores. She had sat in front of the long glassed-in counters and stared at the coloured stones, watery aquamarine, flushed pigeon rubies from Burma, the bland green jade best for carved peaches and Buddhas, and dense yellow tourmaline from Brazil. It was the colourless stones that cost the most: clear as nothing else in the world. No blue, no grey, no yellow, the hardest stone in the world, Mr Koh, the man behind the

5

glass counters with his abacus and little magnifying glass, had told her. No-colour, clear as clear, like looking through water and seeing no bottom, no sky, no eyes looking back, the impossible clear that is still not nothing, that has been chipped and chipped till the planes tilt like crazy mirrors refracting each other and their cross-reflections catch dizzy fire, and what you saw then was this blaze, this spark that sprang up at you and pulled you in. But it was just a stone, a stone with no colour. Now Mother had been gone for weeks she was becoming like that stone, she was becoming no-mother, a memory clear as clear, and Chai knew she was forgetting her, as if Mother had no reflection in the bottom of her memory or in the sky above. Sister Finnigan's blue star-sapphire eyes snapped and pulsed, although not as blue and steadfast as her own heart.

She sat on the floor by the classroom door and sewed a row of back-stitches, hemming handkerchiefs. She had to unpick the first row.

"You're taking too much cloth in the stitch," Sister Finnigan said, turning the handkerchief over to show the way the stitches bunched up on the seamless side. "Pick only a thread," she said, her long white fingers pushing the needle smoothly through the cotton, sliding through a thread of the weave, "and don't pull tight." She turned the cloth over to show where the stitch had closed the seam, not even a faint shadow of the thread showing. "Invisible, it must be invisible," she said.

Try as she would, Chai could not do it. The handkerchief was for her father. Invisible, she thought, pick only a thread, leave smooth. But the needle was huge and clumsy and wouldn't obey her. It broke off the thread of the weave and left cloth scars. Her anxious fingers printed smudges of pencil grey lead and grime. After Mother left, she didn't take a bath everyday, sometimes it was three days before she felt grubby enough to strip and pour buckets of well water over herself. There was no soap and Father rinsed their clothes and dried them on Saturdays and Sundays. Sister Finnigan fixed her chipped blue eyes on her crumpled uniform, the socks she slipped lower each day into the canvas shoes so as to hide the spreading grey heels. So she sat right by the doorway, as far as she could from Sister Finnigan's stinky black robes as Sister perched on her desk showing the eager girls how to turn daisy petals, knot bachelor buttons, cross-stitch a satin oval, and ruffle and gather smocks and aprons. She could only hem a handkerchief, and she could not go beyond the second seam.

Still, sewing was alright. It was better sitting in class an A girl than in the room at night without Father or Mother there. Her brothers slept in a different corner. She never remembered in the afternoon if she had changed into pyjamas or had just fallen asleep in her skirt and blouse waiting for Father to come back. She kept the handkerchief in her desk, she had never finished it, and Sister Finnigan forgot about her poor back-stitches because she memorized the *Book of Luke* and recited each chapter that was asked for perfectly as if she had swallowed the book and had only to open her mouth to find the page and rattle off verse and chapter. Being an A girl in class was much better than being a girl at home.

Father had forgotten about her too. He forgot she walked to school every morning without breakfast, that he hadn't given her money for lunch, and that she hadn't taken her bath before he slipped out each night some place.

She was beginning to forget she was hungry. They must have eaten at night. Something some auntie gave them. In the morning she washed by the well with a bucket of water smelling slightly of sulphur and hurried past the splendid houses of gold-leafed, carved closed doors and across the bridge. It was the bridge that brought her to herself, across to the *angsanas* in the park and the long consoling line of blue and grey Straits water. Once across the bridge she began reciting the *Book of Luke,* long mouthfuls of words. Sister Finnigan loved her for the *Book of Luke.* She had this secret machine inside her that could eat up books, swallow them whole, then give them back in bits and pieces, as good almost as before she ate them.

She didn't look up at the *angsanas* anymore, all their flowers were gone and only dry brown rustling seeds hung down and scattered by her feet. Some auntie, her mother's sister, had told her that the seeds were devils' shoes. The auntie had peeled the tough fibrous brown covering and showed her the tiny shoe-shaped seed. "Don't you put any in your pocket," Mother's sister said. "The devil will come to your house looking for his shoes." She had been afraid when the auntie told her this, and she had put that little shoe in the pocket of her pyjamas that night. Mother was still with them then, she had not been hungry, only naughty. She fell asleep frightened that the devil would come, but the next morning the shoe was still in her pocket and then the pyjamas had been washed and the shoe disappeared.

Things disappeared all the time now. First it was Mother, then her doll with the round blue eyes over which pink plastic lids tufted with tough bristle-lashes could fall as you pushed her head down. She had forgotten about her doll in the freedom which Mother's disappearance brought. All those hours of afternoon play by the river's muddy flats, the grubbiness between her toes that nobody scolded her for. Then she saw her cousin Ah Lan carrying the doll. Ah Lan said it was her doll, but she recognized the red blemish on one upper arm which she had always pretended was a vaccination mark. It was her own doll, with shining yellow stringy hair springing in clumps from the hard plastic head, and the straight fat legs that could move only from the hip like the German soldiers in the old war movies. She was sad the doll no longer belonged to her, it had been her doll and she never saw it again after that afternoon she asked Ah Lan to show her its upper arm and pointed out the red patch on it. And Second Auntie, Ah Lan's mother, didn't allow her to play in her rooms any more.

But Chai went to school every day. Sister Finnigan loved her. Chai sat in the front row and read all the books. One day, after recess, it was so hot she felt faint. She thought she saw Sister spread out her arms. The black robe fell like a cloak from Sister's arms, it ballooned

8

like a cape, like furry black wings, and Sister rose towards the ceiling, her face still calm and smiling, the blue eyes glinting like pieces of sky. There was a little dribble of saliva by the corner of her mouth; she had fallen asleep and Sister Finnigan was still leaning against the desk reading a passage about the Seven Years' War. She had felt really hungry then, as if she would die if she didn't have something to eat immediately, but she knew she wouldn't. She hoped Sister Finnigan would not catch her sleeping in class, so she stretched her eyes wide open and rolled the pupils around like marbles to keep awake. Instead she felt nauseous. She kept her eyes on the page and tried drinking in the words. The next period was library hour and she knew there were all kinds of adventure books in the cupboard she hadn't read yet, so if she could wait till then she would be able to forget about being hungry.

It was getting harder to play in the afternoon. She was tired and weak a lot. She waited every evening for Father to come home from work. Then Second Auntie gave them their meal. Her brothers ate so much rice, three plates full of rice. She couldn't eat that much. Her stomach hurt after the food, although she had been waiting all day to eat.

She waited in the morning as she walked past the park with its long green sweep of grass lying beside the pulsing Straits waves. Now it was a kind of loneliness. She sang to herself as she walked, and kept her head down as she passed the crowded areas where other children who went to other schools were noisily crowding around the ice-cream man, the Indian peanut seller, the pushcart on which the peddler was quickly grilling peanut waffles. The fruitsellers had baskets of golden langsats, egg-shaped crimson rambutans, spiky with dark hair. They had split open dark red juicy watermelons dotted with shiny black seeds, gleaming yellow jackfruit, plump and ribbed, and light green guavas with pink seedy hearts. She kept her head down as she past, only lifting it high to sing to herself when she was safely alone under the umbrella *angsanas*.

But she still had to go through recess every day. She waited till the girls had rushed out and pushed their way to their favourite stalls. Some bought fried noodles or sardine sandwiches or rice cakes. Others had brought bread and jam and spent their money on syrupy ice drinks or sweets. She waited in the classroom till she thought they had finished eating, then she went out to play with them.

Only after she got home did she feel hunger. Her stomach made so much noise crying for some food that she shouted louder as she played to hide its noise. Her brothers played more and more in the streets. They ran further and further beyond the house. They always came home before Father did, before it became night. Away from their house and the other gold-leafed covered doorways, the streets were narrow and the houses crowded and small. She was running down the narrow street going home when the old man waved at her. He was very old and thin, an opium smoker, she thought, like her uncle in the big house. She hurried after her brothers; she was so hungry, she didn't wave back.

The old man was sitting on a bench outside the small house the next afternoon.

Her brothers had found some seahorses in the Straits water beside the seawall. They knew it was dangerous to walk that far out on the seawall, but a whole crowd of children had gone anyway. She was timid at the close sight of so much water. The seawall was about eight feet high and the Straits came up almost to the top of the wall. On the landward side of the wall it was all steaming mud. Wrinkled mudskippers leapt from mudhole to mudhole like her bad dreams in the morning; they were grey like the mud come alive, and they had loose flaps of warty skin, flopping open mouths and waggling tails; they were creatures from the stinking revolting mud. Immediately on the other side of the wall was the clear Straits waves, so bright in the burning afternoon sun that it hurt her eyes to look at them too long. They were blue like the sky brought close to hand, yet they were no-colour when she put her face down to look.

10

Her brothers had found a Players Cigarette tin and had tied a string through a rusted hole in its side. They had thrown the tin into the water and dragged it alongside as they walked along the seawall. Then they found two tiny seahorses swimming in the tin when they fished it out.

The seahorses swam bravely up, their horseheads held up high. From their curving flanks fringed fins fluttered like mermaids' fans. She fancied they were ladies dressed for a ball; there they would dance and never ask about dinner the way she would never ask her aunties about food. She was a machine like the sea, churning her own salt, licking the sweet salty flavour of her body in secret at night when hunger woke her. The seahorses waltzed, strange tiny women in a tinful of water. She wanted them thrown back into the huge sea, she wanted to keep them to show Father, she wanted them to wink at her, she knew them very well. But they curled like grey grubs and died, floating in the leaking tin, ugly things.

She was running away from her brothers who had caught and killed the seahorses and who wanted to stay by the wall to catch more of them. Whatever for? They would only sail for a few beautiful moments, then turn on their sides like capsized boats, only they were already in the water, and die. So there. She wasn't staying to watch that. Then she saw the old man sitting on the bench just like yesterday. Only this time he had a giant guava in his hand, as big as her two hands, and he was smiling. She could see he didn't have a tooth in his mouth, he was so old, he must be somebody's grandfather.

He waved the guava, saw her stop, held it out to her. It was light green, ripe, that's when they're the sweetest. She knew because of the times Mother had taken her to Grandmother's house and she had picked the fallen guavas in the garden. Now Mother was gone, and she would never visit Grandmother's house. Had Grandmother died and no one told her? But that was because she was only eight. Grandmother's guavas were never so large. She wanted it not to bring home to Father but to eat it like she ate all those little sweet guavas in Grandmother's guarden when Grandmother was alive.

The old man handed her the guava and tugged at her to follow him. The front room was empty and dim, it didn't look like anyone lived there. He put his hand under her dress and stroked her front. She didn't think anything of it. He was shivering, the folds of his face matching the folds of his arms. She didn't know skin and flesh could drip and drape like spotted grey cloth over a body. He put one hand through her sleeve and twisted her nipple. It didn't hurt, but she moved away, then ran out.

The next day, he was sitting by the bench waiting for her. This time he had a ten-cent coin, all shiny and new, and she stayed just a little longer while he stroked her arms and chest, his eyes shut mysteriously. But when he called to her the day after, and the days following that, she ran past without looking. He had only money to give her, and the ten-cent coin did not make up for the terrible pleasure of ignoring his pleading eyes and wavering hand.

Native Daughter

"TA' MALU!"

Mei Sim wriggled at her mother's words.

"You no shame! Close your legs."

Mother was standing five steps below the landing, the soft straw broom in one hand and her head level with Mei Sim's shoulders.

Mei Sim stared down her legs which she had spread apart the better to balance her body as she half-lay on the smooth wooden landing and thought her thoughts to herself. Up came the broom and it thumped against her knees. She pulled them together and tugged at her short skirt.

"What you do here all day? Go ask Ah Kim to give you a bath." Her mother's round pretty face was troubled. She had had a perm just last week, and the fat curls sat like waxed waves over her brow, wrinkled with vexation. "We're going to visit Tua Ee. And don't sit with your legs open there. She think I bring you up with no shame."

"Ya, ma." Mei Sim sidled past her mother's solid body down the stairs, glad for something to do. Every day was a problem for her until her brothers came home from school at three when they would shout at her to go away but still could be persuaded to give her a piggyback ride or to let her hold their legs in a wheelbarrow run. The house was empty and dull until then, containing only chairs, tables, beds, cupboards, photographs and such like, but no one to play with.

Ah Kim was scrubbing her brother's school uniform on the ridged washboard. Drub, drub, drub, slosh, slosh. Mei Sim squatted beside her. Ah Kim's stool was only a few inches high and she had her legs thrust straight in front with the wooden board held firmly between. Her *samfoo* sleeves were rolled up high and the pale arms were wet and soapy up to the elbows. Taking the chunk of yellow laundry soap in her right hand, Ah Kim scrubbed it over a soiled collar. Then, seizing the collar in a fist, she pushed the cloth vigorously up and down the ridges. Her knuckles were red and swollen, but her face was peaceful. "You wait," she said, not turning away from the washboard. "I wash you next."

Bathtime was directly under the tall tap in the corner of the open-roofed bathroom. Mei Sim was just short enough to stand under the full flow of water pouring in a steady stream from the greenish brass tap while Ah Kim scrubbed her chest, legs and armpits with Lifebuoy. She was six and would soon be too tall for this manoeuvre. Soon, Ah Kim said, she would have to bathe herself with scoops of water from the clay jar in the other corner of the bathroom. Dodging in and out of the water, Mei Sim thought she would not like to have to work at her bath.

Mother dressed her in her New Year's party frock, an organdy material of pink and purple tuberoses with frills down the bib and four stiff layers gathered in descending tiers for a skirt. She picked a red and green plaid ribbon which Ah Kim threaded through her plaits and, her face and neck powdered with Johnson Talc, she waited for the trishaw, pleased with herself and her appearance.

Mother had put on her gold bangles, gold earrings, and a long heavy chain of platinum with a cross as a pendant. Her *kebaya* was pale blue, starched and ironed to a gleaming transparency under which her white lace chemise showed clearly. Gold and diamond *kerosang* pinned the *kebaya* tightly together, and the gold-brown sarong was wrapped tightly around her plump hips and stomach. She had to hitch herself up onto the trishaw and, once seated, carefully smoothed the sarong over her knees. When Mei Sim climbed in, Mother gave her a push to keep her from crushing her sarong.

Grandaunty's house was all the way in Klebang. Usually Father took them there for visits in the evening after their meal. It was enough of a long way off for Mei Sim to always fall asleep in the car before they reached home.

The trishaw man pedalled vigorously for the first part, ringing his bell smartly at slow crossing pedestrians and hardly pausing to look before turning a corner into another narrow road. At Tranquerah he began to slow down. There was much less motor traffic, a few bicycles, and now and again a hawker's cart got in his way. Green snaky veins zigzagged up his calves. His shaven coconut-round head was dripping with sweat. He didn't stop to wipe it, so the sweat ran down his forehead and got into his eyes, which were deep-set and empty, staring vaguely down the long road.

After a while, Mei Sim grew bored with watching the trishaw man pump the pedals. She leaned forward to stare at the houses on both sides of the road. What interesting things to see that she had missed on their evening car rides! Here was a small stall with bottles of *cencaluk* and *belacan* neatly mounded on shelves. She glimpsed through an open door a red and gold altar cloth and bowls of oranges and apples before a dim sepia portrait. Two *neneks* in shabby sarong and *kebaya* sat on a long bench by the covered front of another house. Each woman had a leg pulled up under her sarong, like one-legged idols set for worship. Here was a pushcart with a tall dark *mamak* frying red-brown noodles in a heavy *kwali*. How good it smelled. Mei Sim's stomach gave a little grumble.

Now they were passing the Baptist Gospel Hall where on Sunday evenings she had seen many people standing in rows singing sweetly. In the morning glare the shuttered windows were peeling paint and a crack showed clearly on the closed front door which had a huge chain and lock on it.

"Hoy!" the trishaw man shouted. The wheels swerved suddenly and bumped over something uneven. Mei Sim hadn't seen anything.

Her mother gripped her arm and said aloud, "You *bodoh*. Almost fall off the trishaw. Sit inside all the way."

"What was that, ma?"

"A puppy dog."

She turned her head to peer behind but the canvas flaps were down.

The trishaw man was talking to himself in Hokkien. A small trail of saliva was trickling down the side of his mouth. Mei Sim could only hear mumbles like, "Hey … *yau soo*… chei …"

"What is he saying, ma?" she whispered.

"Never mind what he say. He angry at puppy dog, bring him bad luck."

Mei Sim looked at the bare brown legs again. They were moving much more slowly, and the mumbles continued, sometimes louder, sometimes quieting to a slippery whisper. Her mother didn't seem to mind the trishaw's pace or the man's crazy talk. She had been frowning to herself all this time and turning the three thick bangles round and round her right wrist. Her agitated motions made a jingle as the bangles fell against each other, like chimes accompanying the slow movements of the trishaw pedals.

They were on a deserted stretch of Klebang before the sandy rutted path on the left that led to Grandaunty's house and the shallow sloping beach facing the Malacca Straits. Wood-planked shacks roofed with rusty galvanized iron alternated with common lots on which grew a wild profusion of morning glory, *lallang*, mimosa and pandan bushes. A few coconut and areca palms leaned in jumbled lines away from the hot tarmac. The sky was a blinding blue, barren of clouds, and arching in a vast depth of heat under which the dripping trishaw man mumbled and cursed. The bicycle lurched

16

forward and the attached carriage, on which Mei Sim crouched as if to make herself lighter, moved forward jerkily with it.

"Aiyah! *Sini boleh,*" her mother said sharply, and almost at the same moment the man's legs stopped and dangled over the wheels. She pushed Mei Sim off the sticky plastic seat and stepped down carefully so as not to disarrange the elaborately folded pleats of her skirt.

The man took a ragged face towel from his pocket and mopped his face. Mrs Cheung clicked the metal snap of her black handbag, zipped open an inner compartment, extracted a beaded purse from it, unbuttoned a flap and counted some coins which she clinked impatiently in one hand, waiting for him to take the change. She poured the different coins onto his calloused palm, then walked up the path without a word. Mei Sim stood for a moment watching him count the coins and, at her mother's annoyed call, ran up the narrow lane just wide enough for a car to go through.

Waddling ahead of her, her mother was singing out, "Tua Ee, Tua Ee." A wooden fence, newly whitewashed, separated Grandaunty's house from the lane which suddenly petered out into a littered common compound shared with some Malay houses on low stilts. Beneath the houses and through the spaces between the concrete blocks on which the wood stilts were anchored, Mei Sim could see the grey coarse sand grading to a chalky white for yards ahead, clumped by tough beach grass and outlined at stages by the dark, uneven markings of tidal remains, broken driftwood, crab shells, splinters of glass, red-rust cans and black hair of seaweed.

Grandaunty came out through the gap in the fence in a flurry of *kebaya* lace. Her gleaming hair was coiffed in a twist, and a long gold pin sat on top of her head, like a nail on the fearsome *pontianak,* Mei Sim thought.

"What's this?" she said in fluent Malay. "Why are you here so early without informing me? You must stay for lunch. I have already told that prostitute daughter of mine to boil the rice, so we have to

17

cook another pot."

Grandaunty had four sons, of whom she loved only the youngest, and a daughter whom she treated as a bought slave. She was not a woman for young girls and gave Mei Sim no attention, but she tolerated Jeng Cheung as the niece whose successful marriage to a rich *towkay's* son she had arranged ten years before.

Mei Sim's mother visited her at least once a week with gifts of fruits, *pulut* and *ang pows,* and consulted her on every matter in the Cheung family's life. At six, Mei Sim was allowed to listen to all their discussions; she was, after all, too young to understand.

It was in this way she learned what men liked their women to do in bed, how babies were made and how awful giving birth was. She knew the fluctuations in the price of gold and what herbs to boil and drink to protect oneself from colds, rheumatism, heatiness, smallpox, diarrhoea or female exhaustion.

It was in the this way she found out that women were different from men who were *bodoh* and had to be trained to be what women wanted them to be. If women were carts, men were like *kerbau* hitched to them.

This morning she settled on the kitchen bench behind the cane chairs on which her mother and grandaunt were sitting close to each other sharing the *sirih* box between them, chatting and scolding in Malay and snatches of English, and she listened and listened without saying a word to remind them of her presence.

"... and Bee Lian saw Hin at the cloth shop ... she told me he's been going there every afternoon when he's supposed to be at the bank ... that slut is probably taking all his money, but I haven't said a word to him, I thought maybe you can help me. What should I say to him, oh, that swine, useless good-for-nothing, I scratch his eyes out. Better still if I take a knife and cut her heart. These men always walking with legs apart, what does he want from me? Three children not enough, but she is a bitch—black as a Tamil and hairy all over. I keep myself clean and sweet-smelling, a wife he can be proud of. So itchified, never enough, always wanting more, more. That's why now he won't give me more money, say business bad. Ha, bad! We know what's bad. I'll get some poison and put it in her food, and all my friends talking behind my back. She's making a fool of me, but what can I do? I tell them better than a second wife, not even a mistress, just loose woman smelling like a bitch any man can take, so why not my Peng Ho."

It was Father Mother was complaining about! Mei Sim rubbed her ears to clear them of wax, but quick tears had risen and clogged her nostrils, so her ears were filled with a thick sorrow. She knew all about second wives. Hadn't Second Uncle left his family to live in Ipoh because their Cantonese servant had bewitched him, and now he had three boys by her and second Aunty was always coming to their house to borrow money and to beg for the clothes they'd outgrown for her own children? And little Gek Yeo's mother had gone mad because her father had taken another wife, and she was now in Tanjong Rambutan where, Mother said, she screamed and tore off her clothes and had no hair left. Poor Gek Yeo had to go to her grandmother's house and her grandmother refused to let her see her father.

Mei Sim wiped her nose on her gathered puff sleeve. Grandaunty had risen from her chair and was shaking the folds of her thickly flowered sarong. Her Malay speech was loud and decisive. "All this scolding will do you no good. Men are all alike, itchy and hot. You cannot stop him by showing a dirty face or talking bad all the time. You will drive him away. The only thing that women have is their cunning. You must think hard. What do you want, a faithful man or a man who will support you and your children? Why should you care if he plays with this or that woman? Better for you, he won't ask so much from you in bed. No, you must be as sweet to him as when you were first courting. Talk to him sweet-sweet every time he comes home late. This will make him feel guilty and he will be nicer to you. Make him open the purse-strings. Tell him you need money for prayers at Hoon Temple to bring luck to his business. He will appreciate you for your efforts. Some men have to be bullied like your uncle, but …"

She stopped to take a breath, and Siew Eng, her skinny dark daughter, crept up beside and whispered, *"Na' makan, 'mak?"*

"Sundal!" Grandaunty shouted and slapped her sharply on her thin bare arm. "Who asked you to startle me? You know how bad my heart is. You want me to die?"

Siew Eng hung her head. Her *samfoo* was faded and worn at the trouser bottoms, and the thin cotton print didn't hide her strange absence of breasts. She was already sixteen, had never been sent to school but had worked at home washing, cleaning and cooking since she was seven. All her strength seemed to have gone into her work, because her body itself was emaciated, her smile frail, and her face peaked and shrivelled like a *ciku* picked before its season and incapable of ripening, drying up to a small brown hardness.

Mei Sim had never heard her cousin laugh, had never seen her eat at the table. She served the food, cleaned the kitchen and ate standing up by the wood stove when everyone had finished.

Mother said Siew Eng was cursed. The fortune teller had told Grandaunty after her birth that the girl would eat her blood, so she wouldn't nurse or hold the baby, had sent her to a foster mother, and had taken her back at seven to send her off to the kitchen where she slept on a camp bed. Mei Sim was glad she wasn't cursed. Her father loved her best, and Mother bought her the prettiest dresses and even let her use her lipstick.

"Now your uncle …" Grandaunty stopped and her face reddened. "What are you waiting for, you stupid girl? Go serve the rice. We are coming to the table right away. Make sure there are no flies on the food."

Her daughter's scrawny chest seemed to shiver under the loose blouse. "Ya 'mak," she mumbled and slipped off to the kitchen.

"Come, let's eat. I have *sambal belacan* just the way you like it, with sweet lime. The soy pork is fresh, steaming all morning and delicious."

Grandaunty gobbled the heap of hot white rice which was served on her best blue china plates. She talked as she ate, pinching balls of rice flavoured with chillies and soy with her right hand and throwing the balls into her large wet mouth with a flick of her wrist and thumb. Mother ate more slowly, unaccustomed to manipulating such hot rice with her hand, while Mei Sim used a soup spoon on her tin plate.

"Your uncle," Grandaunty said in between swallows of food and water, "is a timid man, a mouse. I used to think how to get male children with a man like that! I had to put fire into him, everyday must push him. Otherwise he cannot be a man."

"Huh, huh," Mother said, picking a succulent piece of the stewed pork and popping it into her mouth whole.

"But Peng Ho, he is an educated man, and he cannot be pushed. You must lead him gently, gently so he doesn't know what you are doing. Three children, you cannot expect him to stay by your side all the time. Let him have fun."

"Wha ..." Mother said, chewing the meat hard.

"Yes. We women must accept our fate. If we want to have some fun also, stomach will explode. Where can we hide our shame? But men, they think they are *datuks* because they can do things without being punished. But we must control them, and to do that we must control their money."

Mei Sim thought Grandaunty was very experienced. She was so old, yet her hair was still black, and her sons and husband did everything she told them. She was rich; the knitted purse looped to her string bag under her *kebaya* was always bulging with money. Father had to borrow money from her once when some people didn't pay for his goods, and she had charged him a lot for it. He still complained about it to Mother each time they drove home from Grandaunty's house.

"But how?" protested Mother, a faint gleam of sweat appearing on her forehead and upper lip as she ate more and more of the pork.

Grandaunty began to whisper and Mei Sim didn't dare ask her to speak up nor could she move from her seat as she hadn't finished her lunch.

Mother kept nodding and nodding her head. She was no longer interested in the food but continued to put it in her mouth without paying any attention to it until her plate was clear. "Yah, yah. Huh, huh. Yah, yah," she repeated like a trance-medium, while Grandaunty talked softly about accounts and tontines and rubber lands in Jasin. Mei Sim burped and began to feel sleepy.

"Eng!" Grandaunty called harshly. "Clear up the table, you lazy girl. Sleeping in the kitchen, nothing to do. Come here."

Siew Eng walked slowly towards her mother, pulling at her blouse nervously.

"Come here quickly, I say." Grandaunty's mouth was dribbling with saliva. She appeared enraged, her fleshy nose quivering under narrowed eyes. As Siew Eng stood quietly beside her chair, she took the sparse flesh above her elbow between thumb and forefinger and twisted it viciously, breathing hard. A purple bruise bloomed on the arm. "I'll punish you for walking so slowly when I call you," she huffed. "You think you can so proud in my house."

Siew Eng said nothing. A slight twitch of her mouth quickly pressed down was the only sign that the pinch had hurt.

"What do you say? What do you say, you prostitute?"

"Sorry, 'mak," Siew Eng whispered, hanging her head lower and twisting the cloth of her blouse.

Only then did Grandaunty get up from the table. The two women returned to the chairs beside the *sirih* table, where two neat green packages of *sirih* rested. Sighing happily, Grandaunty put the large wad in her mouth and began to chew. Mother followed suit, but she had a harder time with the generous size of the *sirih* and had to keep pushing it in her mouth as parts popped out from the corners.

Mei Sim sat on her stool, but her head was growing heavier; her eyes kept dropping as if they wanted to fall to the floor. She could hear the women chewing and grunting; it seemed as if she could feel the bitter green leaves tearing in her own mouth and dissolving with the tart lime and sharp crunchy betel nut and sweet-smelling cinnamon. Her mouth was dissolving into an aromatic dream when she heard chimes ringing sharply in the heavy noon air.

For the briefest moment Mei Sim saw her father smiling beside her, one hand in his pocket jingling the loose change, and the other hand gently steering an ice cream bicycle from whose opened ice box delicious vapours were floating. "Vanilla!" she heard herself cry out, at the same moment that Grandaunty called out, "Aiyoh! What you want?" and she woke up.

A very dark man with close-cropped hair was carefully leaning an old bicycle against the open door jamb. Two shiny brown hens, legs tied with rope and hanging upside down from the bicycle handles, blinked nervously, and standing shyly behind the man was an equally dark and shiny boy dressed in starched white shirt and pressed khaki shorts.

"Nya," the man said respectfully, bowing a little and scraping his rubber thongs on the cement floor as if to ask permission to come in.

"Aiyah, Uncle Muti, *apa buat?* You come for business or just for visit?"

"Ha, I bring two hens. My wife say must give to *puan,* this year we have many chickens."

"Also, you bring the rent?" Grandaunty was smiling broadly, the *sirih* tucked to one side of her mouth in a girlish pucker. "Come, come and sit down. Eng, Eng!" Her voice raised to a shriek till Eng came running from behind the garden. "Bring tea for Uncle Muti. Also, take the hens into the kitchen. Stupid girl! Must tell you everything."

The boy stayed by the bicycle staring at the women inside with bright, frank eyes.

Curious, Mei Sim went out. He was clean, his hair still wet from a bath. "What school you?" she asked. He was older, she knew, because he was in a school uniform.

He gave her a blank stare.

"You speak English?"

He nodded.

"You want play a game?" She ran out into the compound, motioning for him to follow.

Mei Sim had no idea what she wanted to play, but she was oh so tired of sitting still, and the white sand and fallen brown coconuts and blue flowers on the leafy green creepers on the fence seemed so delicious after the crunch, crunch, crunch of Grandaunty's lunch that she spread her arms and flew through the sky. "Whee, whee," she laughed.

But the boy wouldn't play. He stood by the sweet smelling *bunga tanjung* and stared at her.

"What you stare at?" she asked huffily. "Something wrong with me?"

"Your dress," he answered without the least bit of annoyance.

"What to stare?" Mei Sim was suddenly uncomfortable and bent down to look for snails.

"So pretty. *Macam bunga*"

She looked up quickly to see if he was making fun of her, but his brown round face was earnestly staring at the tiers of ruffles on her skirt.

"Want play a game?" she asked again.

But he said, "My sister no got such nice dress."

Mei Sim laughed. "You *orang jakun*," she said, "but never mind. You want feel my dress? Go on. I never mind."

He went nearer to her and stretched out his hand. He clutched at the frills around the bib, staring at the pink and purple tuberoses painted on the thin organdy.

"Mei Si-i-m!" Her mother's voice brayed across the compound. There was a confusion as the boy rushed away and the woman came

24

running, panting in the sun, and pulled at her arm. "What you do? Why you let the boy touch you? You no shame?"

Grandaunty stood by the door, while the dark man had seized his son by the shoulder and was talking to him in furious low tones.

Mei Sim felt tears in her mouth, and wondered why she was crying, why her mother was shaking her. Then she saw the man pushing his rusty old Raleigh through the gate, without the hens, still holding the boy by his shoulder. She saw the look of hate which the boy threw at her, and she felt a hot pain in her chest as if she knew why he must hate her. A huge shame filled her and she was just about to burst into noisy weeping when she saw her mother's red, red eyes. "He did it, he pulled at my dress," she screamed, stretching her body straight as an arrow, confronting her lie.

Mr Tang's Girls

KIM MEE CAUGHT HER SISTER smoking in the garden. It was a dry hot day with sunshine bouncing off the Straits. The mix of blue waves and light cast an unpleasant glare in the garden whose sandy soil seemed to burn and melt under her feet. Everyone stayed indoors on such Saturday afternoons; Ah Kong and Mother sleeping in the darkened sunroom and the girls reading magazines or doing homework throughout the house. Kim Mee had painted her toenails a new dark red colour; she was going to a picnic in Tanjong Bidara on Sunday and wanted to see the effect of the fresh colour on her feet bare on sand. The garden behind the house sloped down to the sea in a jungle of sea-almond trees and pandanus. A rusted barbed-wire fence and a broken gate were the only signs which marked when the garden stopped being a garden and became sea-wilderness. A large *ciku* tree grew by the fence, its branches half within the garden and half flung over the stretch of pebbles, driftwood, ground-down shells, and rotting organisms which lead shallowly down to the muddy tidal water. It was under the branches hidden by the trunk that Kim Li was smoking. She was taken by surprise, eyes half-shut, smoke gently trailing from her nostrils, and gazing almost tenderly at the horizon gleaming like a high-tension wire in the great distance.

"Ah ha! Since when did you start smoking?" Kim Mee said softly, coming suddenly around the tree trunk.

Unperturbed, without a start, Kim Li took another puff, elegantly holding the cigarette to the side of her mouth. Her fingers curled exaggeratedly as she slowly moved the cigarette away. She said with a drawl, "Why should I tell you?"

"Ah Kong will slap you."

She snapped her head around and frowned furiously. "You sneak! Are you going to tell him?"

"No, of course not!" Kim Mee cried, half-afraid. There were only two years' difference in age between them, but Kim Li was a strange one. She suffered from unpredictable moods which had recently grown more savage. "You're so mean. Why do you think I'll tell?" Kim Mee was angry now at having been frightened. In the last year, she had felt herself at an advantage over her eldest sister whose scenes, rages, tears, and silences were less and less credited. The youngest girl, Kim Yee, at twelve years old, already seemed more mature than Kim Li. And she, at fifteen, was clearly superior. She didn't want to leave Kim Li smoking under the cool shade with eyes sophisticatedly glazed and looking advanced and remote. Moving closer, she asked, "Where did you get the cigarette?"

"Mind your own business," Kim Li replied calmly.

"Is it Ah Kong's cigarette? Yes, I can see it's a Lucky Strike."

Kim Li dropped the stub and kicked sand over it. Smoke still drifted from the burning end, all but buried under the mound. "What do you know of life?" she asked loftily and walked up the white glaring path past the bathhouse and up the wooden side-stairs.

Kim Mee felt herself abandoned as she watched her sister's back vanish through the door. "Ugly witch!" She glanced at her feet where the blood-red toenails twinkled darkly.

Saturdays were, as long as she could remember, quiet days, heavy and slow with the grey masculine presence of their father who spent most of the day, with Mother beside him, resting, gathering strength in his green leather chaise in the sunroom. Only his bushy eyebrows, growing in a straight line like a scar across his forehead, seemed awake. The hair there was turning white, bristling in wisps that grew even more luxuriant as the hair on his head receded and left the tight high skin mottled with discoloured specks. Now and again he would speak in sonorous tones, but, chiefly, he dozed or gazed silently out of the windows which surrounded the room to the low flowering trees which Ah Chee, the family servant, tended, and, through the crisp green leaves, to his private thoughts.

They were his second family. Every Friday he drove down from Kuala Lumpur, where his first wife and children lived, in time for dinner. On Saturdays, the girls stayed home. No school activity, no friend, no party, no shopping trip took them out of the house. Their suppressed giggles, lazy talk, muted movements, and uncertain sighs constituted his sense of home, and every Saturday, the four girls played their part: they became daughters whose voices were to be heard like a cheerful music in the background, but never loudly or intrusively.

Every Saturday they made high tea at five. The girls peeled hard-boiled eggs, the shells carefully cracked and coming clean off the firm whites, and mashed them with butter into a spread. They cut fresh loaves of bread into thick yellow slices and poured mugs of tea into which they stirred puddles of condensed milk and rounded teaspoons of sugar. Ah Kong would eat only fresh bread, thickly buttered and grained with sprinkles of sugar, but he enjoyed watching his daughters eat like European mems. He brought supplies from Kuala Lumpur: tomatoes, tins of devilled ham and Kraft Cheese, and packages of Birds' Blancmange. Saturday tea was when he considered himself a successful father and fed on the vision of his four daughters eating toast and tomato slices while his quiet wife poured tea by his side.

"I say, Kim Bee," Kim Yee said, swallowing a cracker, "are you going to give me your blouse?"

The two younger girls were almost identical in build and height, Kim Yee, in the last year shooting like a vine, in fact being slightly stockier and more long-waisted than Kim Bee. Teatime with Ah Kong was the occasion to ask for dresses, presents, money and other favours, and Kim Yee, being the youngest, was the least abashed in her approach.

"Yah! You're always taking my clothes. Why don't you ask for the blouse I'm wearing?"

"May I? It's pretty, and I can wear it to Sunday School."

Breathing indignation, Kim Bee shot a look of terrible fury and imploration to her mother, "She's impossible ..." But she swallowed the rest of her speech, for she also had a request to make to Ah Kong who was finally paying attention to the squabble.

"Don't you girls have enough to wear? Why must you take clothes from each other?"

Like a child who knows her part, Mother shifted in her chair and said good-naturedly, "Girls grow so fast, Peng. Their clothes are too small for them in six months. My goodness, Kim Yee's dresses are so short she doesn't look decent in them."

"Me too, Ah Kong!" Kim Mee added. "I haven't had a new dress since Chinese New Year."

"Chinese New Year was only three months ago," Ah Kong replied, shooting up his eyebrows, whether in surprise or annoyance no one knew.

"But I've grown an inch since then!"

"And I've grown three inches in one year," Kim Bee said.

"Ah Kong, your daughters are becoming women," Kim Li said in an aggressive voice. She was sitting to one side of her father, away from the table, not eating or drinking, kicking her long legs rhythmically throughout the meal. She wore her blue school shorts which fitted tightly above the thighs and stretched across the bottom, flattening the weight which ballooned curiously around her tall skinny frame. Her legs, like her chest, were skinny, almost fleshless.

They were long and shapeless; the knees bumped out like rock-outcroppings, and the ankles rose to meet the backs of her knees with hardly a suggestion of a calf. In the tight shorts she didn't appear feminine or provocative, merely unbalanced, as if the fat around the hips and bottom were a growth, a goitre draped on the lean trunk.

Everyone suddenly stopped talking. Mother opened her mouth and brought out a gasp; the sisters stopped chewing and looked away into different directions. Kim Mee was furious because Ah Kong's face was reddening. There would be no money for new clothes if he lost his temper.

"And you, you are not dressed like a woman," he replied without looking at her. "How dare you come to the table like a half-naked slut!" He had always been careful to avoid such language in his house, but her aggressive interruption aroused him.

"At least I don't beg you for clothes. And what I wear is what you give me. It's not …"

"Shut up!" he roared. "You …"

"Go to your room," Mother said to Kim Li before he could finish. Her voice was placid as if such quarrels were an everyday occurrence. If Ah Kong's bunched-up brows and protruding veins all balled up like a fist above his bony beak put her off, she didn't show it. "Peng," she continued, sweet-natured as ever, "maybe tomorrow we can go over the cost of some new clothes. The girls can shop for some cheap materials, and Ah Chee and I will sew a few simple skirts and blouses. We won't have to pay a tailor. They'll be very simple clothes, of course, because it's been so long since I've stitched anything …" So she chatted on, rolling a cosy domestic mat before him, and soon, they were spreading more butter and drinking fresh cups of tea.

Kim Li did not leave the table till Ah Kong's attention was unravelled; then she stretched herself out of the chair, hummed, and sauntered to her room, casual as a cat and grinning from ear to ear. Her humming wasn't grating, but it was loud enough to reach the dining room. What could Ah Kong do about it? He had again slipped into silence, drowsing along with the buzz of feminine discussion, acknowledging that, Sunday, he would once again open his purse and drive off in the warm evening to their grateful goodbyes.

But there was Saturday night and the evening meal late at nine and the soft hours till eleven when his girls would sit in the living room with long washed hair reading *Her World* and *Seventeen*, selecting patterns for their new frocks. And by midnight, everyone would be asleep.

There was Ah Chee snoring in her back room among empty cracker tins and washed Ovaltine jars. He had acquired her when his second wife had finally given in to his determined courting and, contrary to her Methodist upbringing, married him in a small Chinese ceremony. The three of them had moved in immediately after the ceremony to this large wooden house on Old Beach Road, and, gradually, as the rooms filled up with beds and daughters, so also Ah Chee's room had filled up with the remains of meals. She never threw out a tin, bottle or jar. The banged-up tins and tall bottles she sold to the junkman; those biscuit tins stamped with gaudy roses or toffee tins painted with ladies in crinoline gowns or Royal Guardsmen in fat fur hats she hoarded and produced each New Year to fill with love-letters, bean cakes, and *kuih bulu*. Ah Kong approved of her as much as, perhaps even more than, he approved of his wife. Her parsimonious craggy face, those strong bulging forearms, the loose folds of her black trousers flapping as she padded barefoot and cracked sole from kitchen to garden, from one tidied room to another waiting to be swept, these were elements he looked forward to each Friday as much as he looked forward to his wife's vague smile and soft shape in bed. Ah Chee had lived in the house for seventeen years, yet her influence was perceivable in only a few rooms.

Ah Kong seldom looked into Ah Chee's room which, he knew, was a junk heap gathered around a narrow board bed with a chicken wire strung across the bare window. But, at midnight, when he rose to check the fastenings at the back door and the bolts on the front, he looked into every room where his daughters slept. Here was Bee's, connected to her parents' through a bathroom. A Bible lay on her bed. She slept, passionately hugging a bolster to her face, half-suffocated, the pyjama-top riding high and showing a midriff concave and yellow in the dimness. Across the central corridor Kim Yee stretched corpse-like and rigid, as if she had willed herself to sleep or were still awake under the sleeping mask, the stuffed bear and rabbit exhibited at the foot of her bed like nursery props, unnecessary now that the play was over. He sniffed in Kim Mee's room; it smelt of talcum and hairspray. The memory of other rooms came to mind, rooms which disgusted him as he wrestled to victory with their occupants. But no pink satin pillows or red paper flowers were here; a centrefold of the British singers, the Beatles, was taped to one wall and blue checked curtains swayed in the night breeze. Kim Mee slept curled against her bolster. In a frilly babydoll, her haunches curved and enveloped the pillow like a woman with her lover. He hated the sight but didn't cover her in case she should wake. There was a time when he would walk through the house looking into every room, and each silent form would fill him with pleasure, that they should belong to him, depend on his homecoming, and fall asleep in his presence, innocent and pure. Now the harsh scent of hairspray stagnated in the air. Its metallic fragrance was clammy and chilled, a cheap and thin cover over the daughter whose delicate limbs were crowned with an idol's head aureoled and agonized by bristling rollers. Again the recollection of disgust tinged his thoughts, and he hesitated before Kim Li's room. He didn't know what to expect any more of his daughters, one spending her allowance on lipstick, nail polish, Blue Grass Cologne, and this other somehow not seeming quite right.

Kim Li was not yet asleep. With knees raised up, she sat in bed reading in the minute diagonal light of the bedlamp. He stopped at the door but could not retreat quickly enough. She turned a baleful look. "What do you want?"

"It's twelve o'clock. Go to sleep," he said curtly, feeling that that was not exactly what he should say; however, he seldom had to think about what to say in this house, and his self-consciousness was extreme. Suddenly he noticed her. She had cut her hair short, when he couldn't tell. He remembered once noticing that her hair was long and that she had put it up in a ponytail which made her unpretty face as small as his palm. Tonight, her hair was cropped short carelessly in the front and sides so that what might have been curls shot away from her head like bits of string. She's ugly! he thought and turned away, not staying to see if she would obey him.

He stayed awake most of the night. This was true every Saturday night for many years. Sleeping through the mornings, drowsing in the lounge-chair through the afternoons, and sitting somnolent through tea and dinner hours, his life, all expended in the noise, heat, and rackety shuttle of the mines during the week, would gradually flow back to being. The weakness that overcame him as soon as he arrived at the front door each Friday night would ebb away. Slowly, the movements of women through the rooms returned to him a masculine vitality. Their gaiety aroused him to strength, and his mind began turning again, although at first numb and weary.

He was supine and passive all through Saturday, but by nightfall he was filled with nervous energy. After his shower he would enter his bedroom with head and shoulders erect. His round soft wife in her faded nightgown was exactly what he wanted then; he was firm next to her slack hips, lean against her plump rolling breasts; he could sink into her submissive form like a bull sinking into a mudbank, groaning with pleasure. Later, after she was asleep, his mind kept churning. Plans for the week ahead were meticulously laid: the lawyer to visit on Monday; the old *klong* to be shut and the machinery moved to the new site; Jason, his eldest son, to be talked to about his absences from the office; the monthly remittance to be sent to Wanda, his second daughter, in Melbourne; old Chong to be retired. His mind worked thus, energetically and unhesitatingly, while he listened to his daughters settle for the night, the bathrooms eventually quiet, Ah Chee dragging across the corridor to bolt the doors, and soft clicks as one light and then another was switched off. Then, after the clock struck its twelve slow chimes, he walked through the house, looking into each room while his mind and body ran in electrical fusion, each female form in bed renewing his pleasure with his life, leaving each room with a fresh vibrancy to his body. So he would lie awake till the early hours of Sunday, calm yet vibrating strongly, breathing deeply, for he believed in the medicinal value of fresh night air, while his mind struggled with problems and resolved them for the next week.

Tonight, however, his sleeplessness was not pleasurable. Old, he thought, old and wasted his daughters had made him. He couldn't lie relaxed and immobile; the bodies of women surrounded him in an irritating swarm. He heard Kim Li slapping a book shut, footsteps moving towards the dining room; a refrigerator door opening and its motor running. "Stupid girl!" he muttered, thinking of the cold flooding out of the machine, ice melting in trays, the tropical heat corrupting the rectangles of butter still hard and satiny in their paper wrappers. But he didn't get up to reprimand her.

All day Ah Kong would not speak to Kim Li. This wouldn't have appeared out of the ordinary except that she sat in the sunroom with him most of the morning.

Kim Bee and Kim Yee escaped to church at nine. In white and pink, wearing their grownup heels and hair parted in braids, they looked like bridesmaids, ceremoniously stiff with a sparkle of excitement softening their faces. The Methodist Church was ten minutes' walk away. Mother no longer went to church, but her younger daughters went every Sunday, since it was still their mother's faith, and were greeted by women their mother's age, who sent regards but never visited themselves. The pastor was especially nice to them, having participated in the drama eighteen years ago.

She's a stray lamb. Those were barbaric times after the Japanese

34

Occupation; otherwise, she would probably not have consented to live in sinful relationship as a second wife. And, although I suppose it doesn't matter who the sin is committed with, Mr Tang is a well-known, respectable man. Her situation is more understandable when you know how careful and correct Mr Tang is with everything concerning himself and his family. It's a pity he is so Chinese, although, of course, divorces weren't as acceptable until a few years ago, and, even now, one shouldn't encourage it. Yet, if only he would divorce his first wife, she could return to the Church and the children ... They're lovely girls, all of them, although the oldest hasn't been to service in a while, and the second seems excitable. The two young ones are so good, volunteering for the Sunday School Drive, singing in the choir (they have such sweet tones!) and so cheerful. A little anxious about the Scriptures. They want to know especially what has been written about the day of Judgement, which isn't surprising seeing ... Now, if Mr Tang weren't a pagan, he couldn't maintain this terrible life, keeping two households in separate towns, but, of course, he's old-fashioned and believes in the propriety of polygamy. Pagans have their own faith, I have no doubt, and Christ will consider this when the Day comes, but for the mother ...

For Kim Bee and Kim Yee, Sunday service was one of the more enjoyable events in a dull weekend. Fresh as frangipani wreaths, they walked companionably to church, for once in full charge of themselves. They radiated health and cheerfulness from the hours of imposed rest, from their gladness at meeting the friends their parents never met but still approved of, and from the simple encouraging emotions of welcome, love, and forgiveness which welled up in hymns, and which were the open subjects of the pastor's sermon.

"Love, love, love," sang the choir. "Our Father, Our Father," they murmured and flooded their hearts with gratitude, with desire. Radiant, they returned from church at noon, in time for lunch and, later, to say goodbye to Ah Kong who drove back to Kuala Lumpur every Sunday at two.

All morning Kim Li sat cross-legged on the floor next to Ah

Kong's chair. Now and again she attempted to clip a toenail, but her toes seemed to have been too awkwardly placed, or, perhaps, she had grown too ungainly; she could not grip the foot securely. It wasn't unusual for the girls to sit on the floor by Ah Kong's feet. As children they had read the Sunday comics sprawled on the sunroom floor. Or mother would bake scones, and they would eat them hot from the oven around their father. It was a scene he particularly savoured, a floury, milling hour when he was most quiescent, feeling himself almost a baby held in the arms of his womanly family. This morning, however, Kim Li's struggles to clip her toenails forced his attention. Her silent contortions exaggerated by the shorts she was wearing bemused him. Was she already a woman as she had claimed last evening? Ah Kong felt a curious pity for her mixed with anger. Yes, he would have to marry her off. She moved her skinny legs and shot a look at him slyly as if to catch him staring. If she weren't his daughter, he thought, he could almost believe she was trying to arouse him. But he couldn't send her out of the room without admitting that she disturbed him. Once he had watched a bitch in heat lick itself and had kicked it in disgust. He watched her now and was nauseous at the prospect of his future: all his good little girls turning to bitches and licking themselves.

Leaving promptly at two, Mr Tang told his wife that he might not be coming next Friday. He had unexpected business and would call. He didn't tell her he was planning to find a husband for Kim Li. Complaisant as his wife was, he suspected she might not like the idea of an arranged marriage, nor would the girls. By midweek, he had found a man for Kim Li, the assistant to his general manager, a capable, China-born, Chinese-educated worker who had left his wife and family in Fukien eleven years ago and now couldn't get them out. He'd been without a woman since and had recently advised his Clan Association that he was looking for a second wife. Chan Kow had worked well for Mr Tang for eight years. What greater compliment to his employees than to marry one of them, albeit one in a supervisory position, to his daughter? Chan Kow was overwhelmed by the proposal. He wasn't worthy of the match; besides, he was thirty-three and Mr Tang's young daughter may not want him. But he would be honoured, deeply honoured.

Ah Kong called Mother with the match sealed. Would she inform Kim Li and have her agreeable for a wedding in July, the next month, which was the date the fortune teller had selected as propitious for the couple? When he arrived on Friday night, he was surprised and relieved to find the family unchanged by his precipitous decision. "You did the right thing," his wife said late at night after the girls had gone to their own rooms. "My goodness, I was afraid Kim Li would yell and scream. You don't know the tantrums she can throw. Well, she took it so calmly. Wanted to know his name, his age, what he looks like. The girls were quite upset. Kim Mee is so sensitive. She was crying because she was afraid you will arrange a marriage for her also, and I couldn't say a thing to her. But you should have seen Kim Li. She was so excited about it. Started boasting that soon she was going to be a married woman and so on."

Ah Kong grunted.

"I told her a married woman has all kinds of responsibilities. She's lucky she'll have a husband who'll take care of her, but she will have to learn to get along with him. Well, she didn't like that. She wants to let her hair grow long now, and she needs some new dresses and nightclothes, of course. And we have to shop for towels and sheets for when she goes to her own house ..."

"Spend whatever you like," Ah Kong said, and his wife fell silent. He had never said that before. She began calculating all she would buy for the other girls and for the house as well as long as he was in a generous mood.

"When am I going to meet the lucky man, ha, ha!" Kim Li asked the next morning, appearing suddenly in the sunroom. Startled, he opened his eyes with a groan. He thought he might have been asleep and had wakened on a snore. "When am I going to meet this Chan Kow?" she repeated loudly. His wife came hurrying in from their bedroom next door. He said nothing and closed his eyes again. "Ah Kong, I want to meet my husband-to-be. Maybe I can go to Kuala Lumpur with you and have a date with him, ha, ha!" Behind his shut eyes, he sensed her looming figure; her voice had grown strident.

Without opening his eyes, he said, "In an arranged marriage, the woman doesn't see the man till the day of the wedding. You can have a photograph of Chan Kow if you like."

"No, I want to go out with him first."

"Kim Li, you're having a traditional wedding. The man cannot go out with the woman until after they're married," the mother said in a mild tone. "You mustn't spoil the match by acting in a Western manner."

The other three girls huddled by the door listening to the argument. Kim Mee felt a great sympathy for her sister. It wasn't fair of Ah Kong to rush off and pick a husband for Kim Li. What about love? It was true that Kim Li was stupid and had been rude to Ah Kong, but this wasn't China. She wouldn't accept such an arranged marriage even if it meant that she had to leave home and support herself. She looked at her sister curiously. Imagine, she would be married next month! In bed with a stranger, an old man who only speaks Chinese! Kim Mee couldn't think of a worse fate.

Kim Li left the sunroom scowling; her mother couldn't persuade her that she didn't have a right to a few dates with Chan Kow. She didn't appear for tea, and all through Sunday, she was languid. She walked slowly through the rooms as if she were swimming underwater, lazily moving one leg and then the other, falling into every chair on her way, and staring blankly at the walls. Ah Kong ignored her; she was as good as out of the house.

When he came back next Friday, Kim Li had gone through a total change. "I'm a woman now," she had said to her sisters and began using Kim Mee's make-up every day. She pencilled her eyebrows crudely, rubbed two large red patches on her cheeks and drew in wide lips with the brightest crimson lipstick in Kim Mee's collection. After every meal, she went to her room and added more colour. Blue shadow circled her eyes, and her clumsy application of the mascara stick left blotches below her lids like black tear stains. She teased her short hair into a bush of knots and sprayed cologne till it dripped down her neck. Kim Mee didn't complain. Her sister who roamed up and down the house peering into every mirror and rubbing the uneven patches on her face had all her sympathy. To be married off just like that! No wonder Kim Li was acting crazy.

Ah Kong stood at the door afraid. No, he could not possibly allow Chan Kow to meet his daughter before the wedding, this painted woman who was smiling at him provocatively from her bedroom door. He could not understand from where Kim Li had picked up her behaviour. In her blue shorts with her wide hips tilted, she presented a picture he was familiar with and had never associated with his home. No, his wife was always submissive, a good woman who could never suggest an immodest action. Was there something innate about a woman's evil that no amount of proper education or home life could suppress? It was good she was marrying soon, for her stance, her glances, her whole appearance indicated a lewd desire. He turned his eyes away from her and stayed in his room all night.

Lying in bed on Saturday morning, he asked the mother to take the girls to town. "I've work to do, and they are too noisy," he said. He was very tired. That he had to lie to his wife with whom he'd always had his way! He felt this other half of life falling apart. The shelter he had built for eighteen years was splintered by the very girls he supported, by their wagging hips and breasts.

"I don't wanna go," Kim Li was yelling. "I'm setting my hair."

"You must come along." Mother was patient. "We're shopping for your trousseau. You have to pick your clothes. Then we're going to the tailor shop and you have to be measured."

"All right, all right. I'm going to be a married woman, ha, ha! Do you wanna know about my wedding night, Kim Mee? You have to be nice to me. I'll have all kinds of secrets then."

Only after the front door shut behind their chatter did Mr Tang go to the sunroom where Ah Chee had pulled down and closed the louvres. Next to his chair she had placed a plate of freshly ripened *cikus*. Because it grew so close to salty water, the tree usually bore small bitter fruit, but this season, it was loaded with large brown fruit which needed only a few days in the rice bin to soften to a sweet pulp. Stubbornly refusing to throw any out, Ah Chee was serving *ciku* to everyone every day. Mr Tang slowly lowered himself on to his green leather chaise. Using the fruit knife carefully, he peeled a fruit. It was many years since he had last tasted one. Juice splattered on to his pyjamas. He spat out the long shiny black seeds on the plate. His hands were sticky with pulp, but he kept them carelessly on the arms of his chair and let his head drop back. Gradually the cool dark room merged into his vision, Ah Chee's banging in the kitchen faded, and the silence flowed around his shallow breathing, flowed and overcame it until he felt himself almost asleep.

A body pressed against him softly. It was his wife's rolling on him in their sleep. He sighed and shifted his weight to accommodate her. The body was thin and sharp. It pressed against him in a clumsy embrace. He opened his eyes and saw Kim Li's black and blue eyes tightly shut, her white and red face screwed up in a smile. His heart was hammering urgently; he could feel his jaws tighten as if at the taste of something sour. "Bitch!" he shouted and slapped her hard. Kim Li's eyes blazed open. He saw her turn, pick something, and turn to him again with her arms open as if in a gesture of love or hope. Then he felt the knife between his ribs. Just before he fell into the black water, he saw the gleaming fish-eyes of the fishwoman rise from the *klong* to greet him.

Life's Mysteries

SHE WAS CRYING FURIOUSLY. Large tears rolled down into her mouth and splashed onto the table. Her eyes hurt, and she blinked hard to keep them clear of the tears so she could see the knife. She rather enjoyed their taste; they were warm, sweet, and slightly salty, like good preserved plums. The tears fell into the bowl of onions.

"Mui-mui! Give me the knife. You are making the onions dirty."
Ah Phan took the bowl from the table and placed it in the sink.

Swee Liang wondered how tears could make onions dirty. Were they the same as sweat which you had to wash off immediately? If sweat dried on your skin, it left a dead white spot which only sulphur and lime juice could clean. That was why some people were completely white, Ah Phan had told her. They didn't wash themselves, and gradually, the sweat spots spread and turned them dirty white. Swee Liang no longer believed this story. The Geography teacher had explained about different races. Caucasians were white, Negroids black, and she was a Mongoloid and yellow. When Swee Liang repeated this information, Ah Phan, who had never been to school, made an angry face and said she had never heard she was a Mongoloid. She was a Cantonese and could prove it.

There were many questions she wished to ask Ah Phan, but now she was ten, she was afraid to do so. Lately, Ah Phan had been short-tempered; Mui-mui was old enough to know these things by herself, she had said sternly. Swee Liang hoped she meant that if she waited, the answers would come. Besides, Ah Phan certainly didn't know everything in the world; she had no idea of geography at all.

Still, she wished she dared to ask Ah Phan why she called her 'Mui-mui'. To Mother and Father, she was Swee, and in school, she was known as Swee Liang, but Ah Phan, who had been their servant from the time she was born, always addressed her as 'Mui-mui'. She could only suppose that Ah Phan once had a daughter named Mui-mui whom she had to leave in order to care for *her*. When she was younger, she had felt sad for the lost daughter and wondered whether Ah Phan regretted leaving her, but she never told Ah Phan her thoughts.

"How can tears make onions dirty?" She hoped Ah Phan wouldn't remember her age and scold her for her question.

"Aii! Tears are bitter things. They come from bad feelings. If someone eats your tears, he will also have bad feelings. Do you want your father's friends to eat your tears?"

"No. Can we wash them away?"

"Luckily for you, yes. Now give me the knife before you cut yourself."

Ah Phan was preparing a special meal because Uncle Bala was coming to dinner with a Siamese girlfriend. Swee Liang had heard Father telling Mother about it. He didn't tell her that Uncle Bala's girlfriend was from Siam, but Mother had made a point about it to Ah Phan and Auntie Alice. They had both laughed as if it were a joke to be Siamese, but Mother seemed angry.

Her mother was a pretty woman with a soft round face, round brown eyes, a clear fair skin, and curved pink lips. When she went out with Father to the cinema or for drives, she made her eyes up with blue and green colours. Then she looked very faraway with black-pencilled eyebrows and dark red mouth.

Her mother cried easily. Sometimes, although Swee Liang could-n't see her, she could tell from her voice that she was crying. "Is it my fault if you don't have a son?" she had heard her say one night, and she knew from the way the voice trembled and breathed that her mother's eyes were reddening, that tears were gathering on the corners and forming on the lashes and would soon be falling.

She admired her mother's ability to cry. Whenever she heard the first in-drawn breath in her presence, she would look up quickly to see if she could glimpse the tears as they brimmed to the surface of the shiny brown eyes. She saw her mother as a wonderfully sad woman, a heroine like the saint among the lions in the holy picture that Sister Pauline, her Scripture teacher, had given her last year. When her mother beckoned to her, her languid motion and drooping smile reminded her of the white woman calmly facing the giant lions, her arms full of white lilies, and, like the lions, Swee Liang felt a desire to run and sit by her mother's feet.

She was different from her mother, she knew. She wasn't pretty, her face was long and narrow, her eyes black and slanted, and her hair straight and short. She thought she was more a boy than a girl. Last month, *The Straits Times* reported that a man had undergone a sex-operation in Denmark. The papers showed a photograph of him wearing a low-cut dress. His curly hair, pouting lips and pencilled eyes appeared almost like a woman's. When she read the news, she became excited. If Father and Mother want a boy so much, perhaps I can have a sex-operation, she thought. She locked her bedroom door, stripped herself and sat naked on the bed to examine her body. She was as fleshless as a cricket, Mother often said, and Swee Liang wondered what the Danish doctors could possibly cut off her body to change her to a boy. But she didn't know how to go about getting the operation, and gradually she lost interest in the idea.

Her mother was disappointed in her. She accepted that it must be so, for she was nothing at all like her. Ever since she could remember, their relatives and friends had found the differences remarkable. "She doesn't look a bit like you!" they said with astonishment. "Looks more like her father." She was grateful they found a resemblance to her father, for she knew more than they did how truly different she was from her mother. She didn't enjoy combing her hair or cleaning her face or going to the tailors or shopping on Batu Road or visiting her mother's friends. She loved to smell her mother's face cream; it was shiny white and smelled of flowers and sugar. She loved it when her mother returned from the hairdresser's with her hair standing up from her pink face in fat round curls. But she refused to cream her face or to perm her hair. And she could never cry. Except when she peeled onions or when a speck of dust got into her eye.

Uncle Bala had thought it was funny when she skinned her knee falling over Bats, their cat, as she was running out to meet him and she didn't cry as she looked at the pulpy mess oozing blood. "Swee's a tough girl," he said to Father who was trying to put Mercurochrome on the knee without looking at the scrape. In fact, where her mother would cry, Swee Liang often found herself laughing as if surprised by pain.

"Swee grows prettier every day," Uncle Bala said, fishing for a snow-pea with his chopsticks.

"She's grown taller this year. I was afraid she would be a shorty, but she's taller than her grandmother already." Her father was happy and chatty this evening and gave her a great deal of attention. He was drinking Guinness Stout. At one point during the meal, he pushed his chair closer and poured a little glass of Stout for her. He was usually restrained and allowed her mother to do most of the talking, but whenever Uncle Bala came over, he was like a young man, full of jokes, attention, and slight caresses.

"Where are you from, Miss Lee?" Mother had asked when Uncle Bala first introduced his girlfriend.

"She doesn't speak any English, Poh, so don't expect her to reply.

She's very shy, aren't you, Miss Lee?" Uncle Bala jostled her elbow and the young woman smiled without saying a word.

"How do you talk to her then?" her mother asked with a quick rise in her voice.

"She speaks a little Hakka," Uncle Bala said. He laughed as if he had made a joke. "I can speak Hakka, Cantonese and Hokkien. I never have any trouble communicating."

"You also speak Malay and English, Uncle Bala."

"Oh yes, I do! And don't forget I'm Tamil. I speak first-class Tamil."

Swee Liang was curious about Miss Lee. She appeared only a few years older than her, and, unlike her mother, Miss Lee was not wearing any make-up. Her face was pale and thin; it seemed paler in contrast to her thick black hair cut in bangs above her forehead and falling in a curve to her shoulders. She was dressed in a sleeveless shift made of shiny yellow fabric. It had a little dip for a collar, and her bones stuck out in a shiny way below her neck and from her shoulders. She wasn't much larger than Swee Liang. Her father kept staring at Miss Lee as if she were doing something strange. All the time Miss Lee was at the table, she smiled and looked straight ahead of her, eating only a little chicken with small delicate movements of her jaw and taking little sips of orange squash.

Uncle Bala talked with his mouth full of roast pork. He didn't care that his lips were greasy with fat. "This is first-class *char siew,* Poh! You know why I like coming to your house? Because you have an A-one cook. If you get a younger servant, I'll take Ah Phan away from you. Nowadays, black-and-white servants are hard to find."

"Is Ah Phan a black-and-white servant because she wears black and white *samfoos,* Uncle Bala?"

"Oh yes, but do you know why she wears black and white *samfoos?* She's a member of a society of women from China who've sworn never to marry. The black and white *samfoo* is their trade uniform."

Swee Liang frowned in concentrated fascination.

Glancing at her mother, Uncle Bala continued, "These women give all their money to their *kongsi,* and when they become too old to work, the *kongsi* takes care of them. It will even pay for the funeral." He laughed. "Now which woman can be sure her husband will do those things for her?"

"Why do they join the society?" Swee Liang felt Uncle Bala wasn't being serious enough.

"Who knows? Maybe they hate men. I've heard that black-and-white *amahs* hate us. They may have been unwanted women. Perhaps their fathers almost drowned them when they were born. Perhaps they are too ugly to marry."

"But Ah Phan isn't ugly, Uncle Bala."

"Oh yes, sometimes they improve with age. But then, they are too old to marry. Still, it is sad. *Amahs* are rare nowadays. Women don't want to become servants any more; they all want to work in the factories."

"The factories exploit the girls," her father said. "They get less pay than servants, and they have to pay for their food and room. The management doesn't care for the girls when they get sick. It's a bad exchange." He leaned over his bowl and shook his head at Miss Lee.

"It's this thing called freedom," Uncle Bala said, looking at Miss Lee. "Once the people get a taste of it, they never get enough. They don't care if they have no future. They have their friends in the factory, they can go out at night and dress as they please. It's all the fault of the West. Freedom is a terrible thing. We are all suffering because of it."

"Has Ah Phan any children?"

Uncle Bala showed his big white teeth and laughed. "Not unless they are ... I'm sure she hasn't."

But Swee Liang didn't hear him. She was watching her mother who was beginning to cry. The tears fell on her lap silently and slowly.

"Please, Poh!" her father said, putting down his chopsticks.

"You men. It isn't freedom. It's men. She has freedom, but what about me?"

"Poh!" her father repeated loudly. But she was leaving the room already and didn't look back.

"Tell your mother I'm driving Uncle Bala to town," her father said. "And tell Ah Phan to lock the door."

Miss Lee didn't seem to notice that anything was wrong. She smiled at the two men who hurried her, obediently picked her handbag from the front table, and went out of the door without saying anything to Swee Liang.

"Good-night, Swee," Uncle Bala said and tugged at her hair gently.

She woke up once when the night outside the window was turning ashy. Someone was walking in her parents' room; the footsteps sounded like thuds of a heartbeat echoing from the ceiling.

In the morning, Swee Liang heard the car roaring into the porch next to her room. She went to the window and watched her father unlock the front door. The door had a metal gate which pushed aside with a loud creaking and rattling. Still in her pyjamas, she ran out of her room to greet him, but he was in the bathroom brushing his teeth. She wandered into the kitchen. Her mother was sitting at the table drinking a cup of tea while Ah Phan was scrubbing a saucepan. Staring into her cup with a crumpled puffy face that was yellow from lack of sleep, she had become an old woman. Her hair was uncombed and sprang up in screws of curls which left white swaths of scalp showing.

"What are you laughing at?" she said to Swee Liang who was waiting, astonished, by her chair.

"I saw Father coming home. Where was he last night?"

Her mother's eyes were pink and dry. She looked with hatred at her daughter. "Always so many questions. Ah Phan, you tell her." As her mother left the kitchen clutching her robe around her chest,

Swee Liang noticed that her feet, usually hidden in gold-embroidered slippers, were bare.

Ah Phan stood by the sink rinsing the pan which was now shining aluminium again. Observing her black-and-white back, Swee Liang knew Ah Phan wouldn't tell her. She knew also that she would never ask and that her father's whereabouts and her mother's outburst would remain, forever, for her, another of life's mysteries.

The Touring Company

THE AFTERNOON SUN striking against the curtains surged noiselessly round. It was a hot day. A few steps out on the heated road and she had retreated to the negative discomfort of her room. Somewhere, she thought passionately, are wet, cool, running, deep sleep, ease. She looked out of the window at clouds hanging torpidly over the red, white and green of bungalows. In the sun's glare they blew out protruding bellies and turned languid somersaults which took much time to complete.

There was no time to watch them all. She returned to her assignment: Oberon and Titania moved lightly through the fantasy coolness of their midsummer's night and purple-blue woods. By contrast her body felt heavy, her flesh already sagging on the bone, while sweat ran in uncomfortable pools in hidden joints and hollows. The play had a strange glamour for her, always. Elusive sprites, lovers' quirks, fumbling tradesmen and bureaucratic authority fell to the quality of night, the distortion of shadow and dream. Reading the volume of criticism on it, her eyes marking nimbly each point of character, structure and language, her mind went to sleep. Once too, she had been Mustardseed, a ten-year-old schoolgirl in stage make-up, in gauze and wings, combing Bottom's rough hair which smelt of horse. It was perhaps then that night first took on its weight of glamour for her which even the long and hot days could not entirely dispel, as if she had been enthralled those few nights, or was it awakened; and all the nights after, and the days, she had been asleep in disenchantment.

The arrival of the Shakespearean Touring Company was the most exciting thing to happen in the school in a long time. The girls talked about it all during Recess and under cover of their books. A few lucky girls had caught a glimpse of some of the actors when the Reverend Mother was showing them round the school. There was a pretty lady with long yellow hair, a handsome young boy, and a big lumbering man. Their presence transformed the school. The *angsana* trees in the front lawn appeared to droop more darkly over the fence, the sunshine outside was dustier and brighter.

Next morning, at Chapel, she looked up to where the tabernacle was and prayed fervently. Not for anything. The quiet building, the slow dancing light of the oil lamp, and the statues caught in prayerful gestures whispered on all sides of her. But she would not be contained and looked up intently towards the altar, dancing inside. So she was not especially surprised when the Reverend Mother came into class, interrupting their reading of Moses on Mt Sinai. The Company needed four fairies for their staging of *A Midsummer Night's Dream*. Surely among this brood of cheery children are four lovely fairies? Everyone smiled and nodded. It was a happy day. She kept her eyes on the principal's black coif. The morning was burning bright. Even the dark *angsana* trees were leaf-green and the lawn was green with sunlight. It was decided she was to be Mustardseed and they were to meet the players at eight that night.

She had never been out so late at night. Cycling through Old Church Street, she heard swallows twittering in the eaves of Christchurch. The streetlamps were dim-yellow, hardly lighting any large space along the narrow road. The road along the park was wider, running past the Old Fort gate and its companion flame-of-the-forest. The schools on the left were unlighted and deserted. By the time she reached the school hall, she was hungry, having come without dinner, and a little frightened. The school corridors were unfamiliar; the holy pictures hanging along the walls and the crucifix above the halldoor were newly strange with menace brought on by shadow.

Thou hast by moonlight at her window sung,
With feigning voice, verses of feigning love;
And stolen the impression of her fantasy.

The greater part of the hall was empty. A small crowd was gathered below the lit stage. Some were talking loudly. The figure on the stage, with a hand outstretched, continued with what he was saying, his voice raised above the others. A few stood listening to him.

"Daphne, Daphne, where are you?" a huge, bearded man was calling.

She had hardly arrived at the noise and movement when someone frowned vaguely at her direction.

"Oh here you are dear, well we must do something about the fairies now, mustn't we, where are the others, oh yes, come along now, we shall have to learn a dance, can you do a little something, skip about you know, Joan, Joan, come along now and give this fairy a copy."

This agitated mouth which made a pink hole in the pale face took charge of her. She was now a fairy chanting "Lulla, lulla, lullaby, lulla, lulla, lullaby."

Some distance away from their circle, the burly man was shouting furiously, "Daphne, Daphne." She saw Daphne stepping out of the unlighted wing; her yellow hair swung in the arc of the stagelights.

"Yes, yes, yes," she laughed, pirouetting. "I forgot something." Her skirt ballooned and collapsed around her white thighs.

Everyone paused in what he was doing to look at them. The

vague mouth stopped moving and looked too at the stage, then called out clearly, "Dear, I've finished with the fairies. Do you want to try them out now?"

When he turned round, his eyebrows were in a straight line. "All right. Over here, everybody."

The children huddled together on stage. The lights were too bright. She remembered how her eyes smarted. Also, how angry the bearded man was, walking up and down the breadth of the hall and striking the air, "No more of your tricks, Daphne."

No one paid much attention to the fairies. She could stare at Daphne who smiled on her and showed her where to stand. Beautiful lady with yellow hair, she laid down on the dusty stage floor and stretched her arms out, saying, "What angel wakes me from my flow'ry bed?" She could not understand half of what was said, only that the words were beautiful as they were spoken by that sweet mouth. Lying on her bed that night, she thought she loved Daphne and wished to be like her. Daphne laughed at everyone except when she was acting. Even the bearded man smiled when she took his hand.

Backstage, on the night of the performance, everyone was talking and stepping out of the way. As she ran up to take a peep at the audience, her fairy's tutu made her clumsy, and she tripped over Titania's bank of paper flowers. Bending to examine the stiff net for tears, she saw Daphne standing behind the prop. Someone's hand was on her white dress. It was the handsome one called Lysander, talking softly. No one was looking so she twitched the curtains aside and laughed to see the teachers sitting in the front row like boarders at Sunday Mass. Then she was abashed at her excitement when Daphne, who had come up behind her, laughed in her ear. She was to hurry to the dressing-room. Didn't she know that even fairies wore make-up on stage?

Running carefully down the stairs, she found her way blocked by the bent back of the bearded man. He was shouting at Lysander who was standing a few steps further down, and did not hear her coming. Or rather, he appeared to be shouting because his voice was angry, but the words were indistinct. She knew by then that he was the director which Daphne said meant that he should be angry with everyone all the time. All the players kept silent when he shouted except Daphne who laughed at everyone anyway. She herself was frightened of him, and when he drew back scowling for her to pass, she stumbled against Lysander. Lysander was friendly and indifferent to the fairies, and she was grateful when he turned and caught her from falling. For a moment, she saw his face close-to, before he turned away to face the director again. His eyes had showed no consciousness of her presence. The handsome face was frowning and behind the mouth, the teeth were set tight. She ran all the way to the dressing-room wishing she could kick the director for frightening her and for making everybody unhappy.

During most of the performance, she and the other fairies stood in the wings out of the way. They each wished secretly that she was playing Puck, or at least, that Joan were more friendly. They envied her her green tights, and because she had eyebrows drawn up to her forehead. She was twelve years old and she overawed them all. When it was their cue, the stagelights did not hurt their eyes any more. They danced and sang loudly, and though there were mosquitoes, none of them dared scratch herself. Only once was she distracted. Daphne was leading the way offstage, where the director was waiting, smiling at them. Someone else stood some way behind him. Only the pale face could be seen in the shadow of the backstage. It seemed almost asleep, like an old ivory head, and so beautiful she did not recognize who it was immediately. As Daphne sweetly intoned her last lines,

> *And when she weeps, weep every little flower,*
> *Lamenting some enforced chastity.*
> *Tie up my love's tongue, bring him silently …*

she saw the carving break. A pinkish hole flowered out, disfiguring the oval, and its creamy perfection darkened. Before the face turned away, she recognized the lady who had taught them the dance and knew that she was crying. She put her hand out to tell Daphne this, for perhaps, Daphne would know why and would run to comfort her. Then the curtains drew shut, there was loud applause, and the director was talking to Daphne about some other thing.

At the end of the play, Daphne was given a bouquet of flowers. The children curtsied and the Reverend Mother nodded to them from the audience. Later she came backstage when they were having their make-up removed and patted them on the shoulder, saying they had performed creditably and had been good children. The players seemed to be running everywhere so that the little dressing-room was crowded, warm and noisy with everyone talking and laughing and nobody listening. Outside, the patch of playground was crisscrossed with light coming from the back-entry to the stage, and from the dressing-room. Here and there the light showed the fence of morning glory with its purple flowers now shut tight, the shaky seesaw with one end lifted to the sky, and made humps of shadow on the uneven level of coarse grass and sand. It was the first time she was in school grounds so late in the night. She looked around her at the room crowded with all sorts, sizes and shapes of people, cluttered with heaps of costumes on chairs, and make-up stuff falling onto a floor littered with soiled tissues, paperbags and newspaper wrappings. The excitement of the last three days left her. In its place, she felt the strangeness of these people, travelling from one unknown town to another, shuttling with their metal trunks down unknown roads. Almost as if forever, she saw them travelling through countries and peoples, shut among themselves in dressing-rooms and backstages, talking, angry, crying, laughing. She would never meet them again. Not Daphne, who was nowhere to be seen, nor the director, who came up and smilingly dismissed them with a tin of sweets each, nor the crying lady with the beautiful pale face, who even now was

54

kneeling quietly in the corner packing the costumes away and did not look up to say goodbye. Outside, walking to the bicycle-stand, she saw the stained glass of the chapel flicker with colour, and remembered wonderingly the tabernacle flame burning alone in the shut building.

She summarized the last paragraph of the chapter she was reading, squashing her writing to fit in the blank margin left on the sheet, then looked through the page. How perceptive the writer is, she thought, and yet, how absurd. No, no amount of writing, however intelligent, can contain the play. She was overcome by nostalgia. The tin of butterscotch had lasted two weeks. She had eaten a sweet a day, religiously, and each time, she had recalled the bright, exciting time among those strange, energetic men and women. Even now, she loved butterscotch. And somehow, since then, she had always been open to the night, and to its changes on people and things. Its total darkness brought out the colours of light, lamplights, roomlights, carlights, streetlights, trafficlights, neonlights, lights through curtains. Sometimes, in the day too, she lapsed into these strange musings and she would grow sulky and restless. She walked up to the window and looked out across the road to the hills. Perhaps, she thought, she should have a bath. In a few hours it would be dark. He was coming to fetch her, and they would kiss under the trees and talk about their life together. If she could only tell him how, for her, the plants and flowers, the houses drawn against the night and seen from outside, the black roads, were beautiful, but left her disturbed, reaching forward to where he and the place were not.

She did tell him, but diffidently, not passionately as she thought she would. He was silent. She knew then that the critics were right after all. That fairies were the other side of madness and as much beings of darkness as she had taken them to be magical and delightsome creatures. She lay back smiling on the grass and let the moon stare into her eyes, separated from him by his silence till the sound of his unhappiness reached her and she turned back to him.

Sisters

WHEN YEN WAS SEVEN, she took Su Swee to the Methodist School playground and placed her on the swing. Su thought the swing was a dumb hairy animal, its plank seat hanging unbalanced on fraying hemp a loose swinging head suspended by ropes of frizzy hair. "Swing, swing!" Yen chanted, pushing the dangling seat into the air, and Su felt the rush of a large animal against her cheeks. It rustled its mysterious paws in her hair. She smelled its breath up close in her nostrils—something sharp, ammoniacal, like the fumey air from the caustic soda bottles in Ah Voon's storeroom—before she wetted herself. "Aiiyah," Yen scolded, "good for nothing, scaredy cat!"

"Not so little, already five, how you marry if cannot keep your pee in?" Ah Voon grumbled when she changed Su out of her soiled clothes.

"Swing, swing," she mumbled, trying to keep the new word in her mouth a little longer. At five Su believed words were a kind of magic, conjuring ways to protect her from Ah Voon's rough caretaker's hands; when Yen and Su talked—Yen more talk and Su ear—words invaded invisibly, placing unseen, powerful beings into their everyday life.

56

Later, Su found that words could still the irregular mobile dancing visions that so terrified her, wordless, behind closed eyelids, and steady the motes into PRINT, that became STORY and MEANING.

Su remembered the day when Yen first came home from Methodist School speaking a strange new language called English. Wah, a new magic in the world, and one better for being black magic to Ah Voon, who could only scold them in noisy Hokkien, crackling like strings of firecrackers. Not listening, the sisters spoke more and more English— elegant, chirpy, difficult—to each other, leaving Ah Voon ignorant of their wicked ways.

Yen brought back new words for Su each day. Separate words like colored fragments, falling, shifting, breaking out in dreamy shapes inside a kaleidoscope. Or like dried plastacine figures, brittle, snapping as Su forced them out. *England. Asia. China. America. House. Father. Mother. Baby. Man. Woman. Brother. Sister. Dog. Cat. House. Tree. Bird. Aeroplane. Sky. See. Run.*

Yen laughed because the words scratched Su's throat and crumbled into messy pieces as she tried to repeat them. But Su didn't mind her laughter. Su liked the way the sounds scattered, pulling her out of Ah Voon's lap and into places Voon couldn't follow.

Su didn't mind Yen even when she kicked and bit, screaming no words until her face turned pink, then purple.

It was the wind entering into her, Ah Voon explained, a bad wind unbalancing her body's hot and cold and making her sick. Mama said she was just a no-good eldest sister.

Su knew Yen only wanted her to grow up faster so they could play better together.

Because of Yen's biting, Mama didn't send Su to Methodist School. Instead she went to the Government School. Su liked Government School because Yen had taught her English words and how to swing.

Two Dreams

The earth under the school playground's ten swings was scraped hard by hundreds of pairs of canvas shoes bumping on it every day. At recess, Su's classmates crowded into the tuckshop for curry puffs and sticky sweet orangeade. She planted her feet on the grassless dried hollow and pushed off alone on the swing. Once in the air she stood on the seat, pumping the swing higher and higher until it was flashing above the ixora bushes, higher than the young coconut palms by the toilets; until she was almost a bird rushing through the warm air, if she would only let go. Swooping up and falling down, hands gripping the woven hemp, air humming under feet, addicted to flying but more afraid of tumbling off—and so, at last, slowing down, out of breath and hungry.

Then the hot blue sky reeled by as she ran with the other children, without Ah Voon or Mama shouting, Don't be a tomboy! Don't get burned in the sun! Don't fall down! Don't get dirty! Don't sweat! She joined the othe children singing and dancing. Marching with them down the lines of uniforms, chanting "Oranges and lemons, say the bells of Saint Clemons," she shivered with delicious fright as they approached the executioner couple, fearing yet longing for her turn, yelling in one big voice, "Here comes the candle to light you to bed, here comes the chopper to chop off your head!"

Later Su found books. Neither Mama nor the teachers who were always lecturing her about running-around play said anything against hours of reading, although books carried her higher than the swings in the playground. Looking up from the page, her eyes saw teachers farfar-far away, inconsequential specks on a moonscape, through the reverse end of a flying telescope. Other characters in books—barbaric, hunch-backed, miserly, alien, all familiar—she saw close, so close she whiffed their frightened sour-vinegar armpit sweat, the salt in their monstrous unwashed hair, as if holding her right up against them, chest to chest, they forced her to stare into their pained irises and breathe their choking, phlegmy, secretive breaths.

In this way Su became a good student. Taking in, learning, chewing, imagining words, words, words every day in Government School. Vocabulary lists, spelling lists, dictionary tests, adjectives and adverbs, synonyms and antonyms, prefixes, suffixes, roots, gerunds and participles, verbs and proverbs, nouns and pronouns, and pronunciation. Days filled with word-eyes, sprouted vines branching into paragraphs that rooted in her scalp and sent long-legged taproots into her brain, grew arteries shooting oxygen, life, blood into her frontal lobes. The months rustled in thickets of pages, clumps, whole strands of chapters and treatises, massive historical forests of books, shelves on shelves of paper, pulp and ink and paste, ancient timber to wander in, in the one-room library hardly anyone ever entered except her.

Of all the thousands of words she learned, she liked the words of her name best even though they weren't English words.

"Wing Su Swee" was the last name teachers called from their rollbooks, like a favorite sweet kept for last, or an almost-forgotten story.

Wing for Ah Kong and Mama. For Yen and herself. For Peik, so different that Yen and Su often forgot they had another sister.

Su, her name, like an ending sigh. *Su-su,* meaning "milk" in Malay, which the Malay girls, teasing, called her.

Swee, "beautiful" in Chinese, everything lovely and sweet to Mama.

Her name was both Malay and Chinese, and in Government School it became English.

She became possessive of her family name as she grew older and discovered no other Wings in town. There were hundreds of Wongs. Humdrum name. Wong, all wrong, Su hummed to herself. Thousands of Tans, Lims, Lees, Chins, Chans, Chias. But only one Wing family. Magic name, easy to associate with feathers and flutters and flight, bird freedom—starlings, magpies, kingfishers, rice-birds, even the grackles and crows which flew in and out of raggedy eaves in the narrow streets just before sunset, calling the sun down.

What was the good of magic if it didn't do something?

At seventeen Su became impatient for something to happen, something breaking out of the promise of their winged family name.

Then Ah Kong died. Ah Voon, who did not attend the funeral in Singapore, hearing about it, said it was wickedly unnatural not to cry. Su supposed she would have cried monsoon rains if it had been Mama who died. Ah Kong was a different kind of family.

Pastor Fung used to tell his parishioners it was a fairy tale, Ah Kong having three daughters. Even what Mama asked them to call him was part of the fairy tale. Ah Kong. Chinese for royalty, king, your highness, the grand vizier in *A Thousand and One Nights*, patriarch, sir, grandfather, daddy, papa, father, all rolled into one name. Or King Kong, as Yen complained.

That was the creepy part of being a Wing. Ah Kong was old enough to have been their grandfather, so old he had hair growing out of every aperture—nostrils, ears, curling over his lips. Su sometimes wondered where else. The individual hairs grew longer and whiter year by year. They pushed out of his ears like white smoke, getting more solid every year. Or like long skinny ancient worms poking out to sniff the air.

Next to him Mama looked like a girl. He must have been seventy, and she only thirty or so, skin slippery soft, and dimples gently creasing her cheeks. Whenever she laughed, she looked like an older sister.

We must be grateful to the powerful for giving us life, she said.

But they didn't have to love him.

Every week, for Saturday nights and Sunday mornings, Ah Kong came to stay with them. His visits were short. The girls walked on his back with bare feet, pulled his toes till they crunched, and read their exercise books aloud until he fell asleep in the evenings.

Good girls did those kinds of things for their fathers, Mama said.

Ah Kong stopped talking to Yen one evening after he leaned close to her to say something and the white hairs sticking out of his nose-holes tickled her cheek.

"Aiiyah! Don't come so close, Kong-kong!" she cried out, slapping at her cheek. "Your hair is so itchy! Itchified!" She was fourteen.

He was offended. Girls must never call their fathers itchified, it means the wrong thing.

Yen was always getting into trouble with Ah Kong. It wasn't because she couldn't get her words right. They were right for her. But she didn't pay attention when she spoke, and words came carelessly out of her, hot sputtering oil that could hurt.

Ah Kong didn't speak to her again for a long time.

Mama said Yen was stupid all the time. Su disagreed. Yen had so many thoughts that she seemed forever mixed up, in one huge confusion.

About Su, Mama said she was too clever for her own good, because Su could see and be two ways at the same time, like the little girl in the poem Yen read to her from her first-year English book in school: "And when she was good, she was very very good, but when she was bad she was horrid." Whenever Mama reminded Su of the poem to shame her, she thought she was better off being two ways than Yen, who seemed only one way.

Ah Kong liked Little Peik the best because she had the sweetest tongue of them all. By the time Peik was three, she knew when to be quiet and exactly what to say to him.

Take the last Saturday Ah Kong came home. When he came out of the shower, Peik had the Tiger Balm by his chaiselongue, "Ah Kong, you so tired, I massage you now."

Peik was the one whose feet pattered on his back most often, kneading him with clean bare soles. Ah Kong lay groaning while she pounded his shoulders, double-fisted.

Then she brought out her best class drawings, papers smoothly encased in plastic folders. "Ah Kong, see, I keep these pictures for you!"

She copied photographs of American cars and cities that appeared in *Life* and *National Geographic,* the only magazines that Ah Kong subscribed to for the girls. Yen and Su saved their money for *Seventeen* and *Vogue,* which they hid under their beds. Ah Kong hated to see pictures of modern women, actresses and models showing off lipstick and mascara and short skirts.

That Sunday morning, before Ah Kong drove back to Singapore, Peik gave him his glass of warm ginseng tea. "Kong-kong, come back next week," she repeated parrotlike, a tape recorder for a mouth.

When the lawyer read the will, Ah Kong had dictated, "To my daughter Peik Wing who gave me twice the pleasure of her sisters, I bequeath a double share."

It didn't matter to Su, because he left each of them enough to be independent.

Besides, he had ten other children in Singapore, and they received much more than the daughters did. They were his first wife's children, the legal family, the Wings Su had hardly met, except at Jason's and Wanda's weddings and at Ah Kong's funeral.

Su wasn't sad when Ah Kong died. What was the good of being a Wing if you couldn't fly?

She had thought and thought so much about it.

The strangest thing about their family was the difference between their name and their lives. Ah Kong kept them tied to him. They were his fledglings, he the eagle with hawk nose and white hair feathers, driving his Mercedes SL 270 across the Johore Causeway between Singapore and Malaysia every weekend.

Ah Kong had more than two nests. At Jason's wedding when Su and Yen and Peik met their sisters and brothers, the legal Wings, many of them older than Mama, one of their brothers told them Ah Kong had been called the Timber King of Indonesia. He had lived in Sumatra,

Sarawak, and Borneo when he was younger and had minor wives in each place, but because he didn't marry these women their children had never been introduced to his legal family.

Mama said she knew better. She held out for a Chinese ceremony even if a civil wedding was impossible, so her daughters were Ah Kong's recognized second family.

At Jason's wedding they had to address Jason's mother as First Mother, but they kept forgetting to call Mama Second Mother. First Mother told Mama they were badly trained daughters.

"Imagine that!" Mama said. "With her youngest daughter living with an American diplomat—unmarried!—imagine her saying my daughters are badly brought up!" Mama didn't like to gossip. Still, she had a way of getting things known.

Yen and Su never told Mama how Ah Kong died. Because she was never suspicious, Mama forgot what were secrets and what were not, and she often got Yen and Su into trouble with Ah Kong. After Su confided in her about a boy she liked or about some poor exam results and she promised not to tell, she was sure to mention it to Ah Kong over supper on Saturday. One night when Ah Kong slapped Su for going to a dance without his permission and she complained Mama had broken her promise, he retorted, "Your mother is simple as rain water. I married her for one reason—for her virtue. You should learn from her if you wish to find a good husband." That terrified Su.

Ah Kong was the only person in their family who could fly. The sisters were allowed to leave Malacca twice—each time to travel to Singapore. A few years after they met Ah Kong's first family, they were told to come for their Seventh Sister's wedding.

Yen wore a new red dress for Wanda's wedding reception at the Equatorial Hotel. She had hemmed the pouf skirt up without telling Mama, and even in the expensive hotel lobby full of white women tourists in bare sundresses she looked amazing, as if she was wearing a tutu and had wandered on to the wrong stage, or as if her legs had sprouted inches overnight.

Mama didn't show any embarrassment. Being the Second Wife, she had warned them, she was accustomed to mean gossip, and she had already anticipated rudeness from First Mother's children and grandchildren, some of whom were meeting them for the first time.

Yen was disgracing the Wing family, they said, pulling long faces at Mama.

The next weekend Ah Kong greeted them with a dirty face, white eyebrows scrunched up like dishrags. Peik showed off the pillow case she was embroidering for him with peonies and phoenixes, Chinesey images he liked, but the fancy stitching didn't help improve his mood.

"Yen," he said after dinner. They were all surprised, for he hadn't spoken directly to her for years. "Yen," he repeated. "You are completing your exam this year?"

"Yes, Ah Kong." Yen looked at Mama for help.

"What plans do you have?"

"Plans?"

"Yes, what do you plan to do after sixth form?"

"Sixth form?"

"Don't repeat after me like an idiot! Your mother was already married with two daughters when she was your age. A woman cannot be too careful about her plans when the time comes. I was watching you at Wanda's wedding. It seems to me I should be making some plans for you if you haven't any of your own."

Yen gave Mama another look and opened her mouth.

Before she could speak Mama said, "Goodness, Ah Kong, of course you must make plans for Yen. She not yet nineteen and know nothing of the world, and her exam results maybe not successful, she maybe not lucky, able to continue in university, maybe a secretarial course in Singapore or even London the best thing for her, so hard three daughters, how to help them later in life. . . ."

"I'm thinking of an arranged marriage for Yen," Ah Kong interrupted.

"What!"

"Don't be rude, Su," Mama said softly. "Apologize to Ah Kong."

"Sorry," Su mumbled. Ah Voon padded to the table with a plate of gold-yellow *sooji* cake famous among Mama's friends. Su bolted a square down to comfort herself.

"Yen, thank Ah Kong for thinking of your future," Mama prompted. Curious Su stared at Yen. Yen never liked reading Barbara Cartland and Harlequin Romances. So sissy, she sneered at Su's taste, preferring Raymond Chandler and Mickey Spillane—tough guys. I want to be tough, she said to Su one night when they caught each other sneaking into the kitchen for Ah Voon's love-letter biscuits.

"Yi, I don't care! I don't believe in love," Yen said. "Like you and Mama, uh? You also had arranged marriage."

Mama kept her eyes down.

"If not love, what difference does it make? Anyone can do."

"We have a family reputation to maintain. Not anyone can marry a daughter of mine." Su could see Ah Kong was steaming. "It may not be easy to find a husband for you."

"Will Yen be able to choose?" Su had to ask it.

"There will be no time," Ah Kong stared at her suspiciously. "The fortuneteller says Chap Goh Mei is the auspicious time for her to marry. That is in a few months. I have two prospects; the one from Sarawak is more willing."

"What's the hurry, Ah Kong? I'm not going to go bad, you know. Hah hah! Now I'm not so sure what my plan is. You have already made plans for me before you asked me. That's not right!"

Reading so many detective novels, Yen had grown an extra-vigilant mind. "What's behind all this?" she nagged, harassing Mama and Ah Voon after they had cleaned her room or rearranged her things. Once she asked the question there was no putting her off. It was as if she just set her mind down, gone on strike.

"Right? Right? A daughter has no right. Ignorant girl! Have you done any work in your life? Made any money? You've been a parasite all your life, living off my body, this body which gave you life," Ah Kong smacked his chest. The liver spots on his cheeks throbbed like purple thumbprints.

"Now, Ah Kong, Yen not disobeying you, you know her tongue always put in wrong place, we talk more about it next week, Peik has letter commendation from Mrs. Winny Chew, you know, her Sunday school teacher, she want you to read it."

Peik said Mama was truly the meek of the earth. But Su agreed with Yen that what Mama wanted was to inherit the earth. In Ah Kong's will he left her plenty of money. To my good and obedient wife, he said, even after death, and Mama was still obeying him, exactly the way she did when he was alive.

Su took her share of Ah Kong's money—blood money, she said to Yen—and went to America.

Where should her wings carry her?

Mama said not New York and not San Francisco, because they were wicked cities—Sodom and Gomorrah Pastor Fung called them when she went to him for advice.

"Only to study," he added. "A young girl must be protected. In a quiet college far away from big cities."

Su had thought all America was the same.

"You see Paul Newman in the East and in the West and he looks just the same," Yen agreed. "Boy oh boy oh boy! You're gonna have fun!"

They talked like Americans when they were alone together, a game they began after seeing *West Side Story* on television. A good movie; the actors talked with twisted mouths, and the boys and girls rumbled and kissed.

Su picked Colgate College because it was in New York. Besides, it was the only college to accept her application.

Mama and her friends thought she had done the funniest thing.

Everyone they knew apparently had a tube of Colgate toothpaste in their bathrooms. "Colgate! Ah, she learning to brush her teeth there?" Auntie Mei-mei asked, rolling her eyes. Her classmates thought Su was going to dental school. "Why you want to be dental hygienist?" they asked. "Lousy job, looking down people's stinky mouths. All those rotten teeth!"

Ah Kong had been prowling around the house that Saturday night, the week after he began arranging for Yen to marry a stranger in Sarawak. Yen had told Su she had seen him peeking into their bedrooms, but Su never believed her until that Saturday.

Su was angry that he was shipping Yen off like that, simply because she had worn a short skirt to Wanda's wedding. As Mama liked telling everyone, their half-sister Weena had been the mistress of a U.S. attaché in Singapore for years before he married his American fiancée. Ah Kong never made a stink about it. Being mistress to an American Embassy official was acceptable to First Mother and her children—they were proud of Weena because Paul Frazer took her to diplomatic parties and she got to shake the hands of visiting dignitaries like the Sultan of Brunei and assorted rajahs. "Face clean, backside dirty," Mama giggled, explaining First Mother's attitude. Su couldn't understand why Ah Kong would act as if Yen's mini-skirt episode had tarnished her virtue.

She could not rouse Yen to indignation.

"Oh, who cares?" she said chirpily. "Where am I going to meet a man anyway in sleepy old Malacca? I don't want to continue studying, and marriage must be okay. So many million women marry and do okay!"

Yen had no idea about herself and what she wanted. She was like Mama, but without the check on her tongue Mama practiced in front of Ah Kong.

When Su told Mrs. Brecker, her high school English teacher, that her oldest sister was having an arranged marriage, Mrs. Brecker was horrified. "Why, that's like the dark ages!" she exclaimed. "You poor girls. Has your mother told your sister anything about sex?"

Sex? Poor Mama would have burst before she could pronounce the word. Su dropped her eyes in embarrassment that Mrs. Brecker would use the word in front of a student.

On Friday after class, flushed, determined, Mrs. Brecker gave Su a package for Yen. She had it wrapped in newspaper as if it were a fish from the wet market. "Tell your sister she should open this only in the privacy of her room!" she admonished.

Su's fingers traced the outline of a large oblong book beneath the newspaper wrapper. She stifled her curiosity until she and Yen were alone in the evening.

"Can I look?" she pleaded as Yen opened the package.

At first she was disappointed. It was an old book, more worn than even the books you would buy from the second-hand bookstalls along the Central Market alleyway which sold paperbacks the Australian backpackers left behind in the YMCA. The pages were yellow and frayed, and the bent cover showed a boring black and white picture of women holding up a poster, "WOMEN UNITE," and in red the title proclaimed, *OUR BODIES OURSELVES.*

"It's a book by women," Yen turned the pages, "so I guess it isn't a dirty book."

All through Saturday, with Ah Kong lounging around the house, Su could not talk to Yen about her book, although she was sure Yen was reading it in secret, quiet all day, a smirk appearing through supper hinting at some bubbling inside. Thinking of Yen reading the book, she couldn't sleep, and at about midnight she sneaked out of her room.

Sure enough, when she pushed open Yen's door, Su saw her sitting in bed, knees up, reading.

"Let me read a little," she whispered.

"No, no, I'm at an exciting part."

"It isn't fair! You have the book only because of me."

"Well, come into bed with me. We'll read together."

Yen was reading a passage about that part of a woman's body, the vagina. They stared at the photograph of a mirror reflecting a woman's bottom.

"Hey, let's do an examination!" Yen said, excited. "We can use the reading lamp instead of a flashlight, and a compact mirror."

"I get to look first." Su wasn't going to be the shy one.

"Cannot. I'm getting married first, so more important for me to know about the labia and all that. Here, you take the compact. Now, squat on the bed and open your legs wide, I'll bring the reading lamp close, and we can see what we look like there."

Would Su dare? She lifted the nightgown around her waist. Whichever way she turned, nervous, the cloth shifted, blocking the light, until she pulled it over her head and squatted on the bed.

It was difficult to see anything in the small compact mirror. She tried angling it different directions, and Yen twisted the gooseneck so the lamp turned, shining upward. It came into view. Two pink things, frilled, a little tongue, as well as a small opening, an indentation in her bottom. It flashed in the mirror, a stranger's face, bearded, with lips and mouth, having hidden down there all her life.

"Let me see, let me see," Yen urged, craning her head down. Then Su looked up and saw Ah Kong at the door.

How to gauge how long he had been watching them? She wanted to dive under the blanket, her flesh suddenly rising in hard cold pimples. Yen raised the lamp to shine on his face, the white hairs in his nostrils moving because he was breathing hard.

"Filth!" His mouth was shaping rather than speaking sounds, English Chinese sounds Su had never heard him make before. "Sisters sluts perverts mother . . . you have no shame no fear . . . I . . ."

Grabbing her nightgown, Su pulled it down over her head just in time to see Yen sticking her tongue out at him. That must have done it because he left at once, and they could hear him stumbling against something in the kitchen.

Su wanted to run to Ah Kong to beg his forgiveness. She wanted to show him the book, to show him they were simply learning about their bodies. But she didn't move. Ah Kong would never understand such a book. For him it could only be a dirty book.

"Go away!" Yen ordered, irritated. "If you hadn't come into my room we wouldn't be in this trouble. Just wait. Ah Kong will find a way to punish you also."

A faint light glowed where Ah Kong had opened the refrigerator door. Su thought of going into the kitchen to say something, then remembered he had just seen her squatting naked, breasts tingling with cold, bottom raised, an ugly abnormal frog. Covering her face with the bedsheet, she knew she would stay awake all night wishing she were dead. But she must have slept, because she didn't hear Ah Voon screaming until Mama shook her.

At her usual time, 5 A.M., Ah Voon went to the kitchen. There she found Ah Kong lying beside the refrigerator. Standing in front of the open door, he had had a massive heart attack. *Myocardial infarction,* Dr. Hong told Mama, what you expect in a man his age, except he had seemed healthy—particular in diet, regular in habits, someone who took care of his body.

Frigid air had been pumping out of the refrigerator all night, and Ah Kong's body was doubly cold and rigid when Ah Voon found him, the tiny fridge doorlight spotlighting his twisted face.

"Aiiyah, what an unlucky way to die! He didn't look like a man, more like a ten-thousand-demon," she repeated, "hard like wood, his eyes open, glaring at Tua Peh Kong, the Underworld God. I always say cold water is bad for the body. Why he want a cold drink at night?"

Mama never ever knew he had come to Yen's room. He hadn't had a chance to tell her what he had seen, and how were Yen and Su to say that Ah Kong died because he caught them looking into a mirror?

PART 2

Country

All My Uncles

WE KNOW CHILDHOOD is ending when the fantastical longing to believe anything, anything, begins to lose ground to the stupefying fact of observation. So it was with the stories of my third aunt, a solid pudgy personage, a true Chinese woman in black silk trousers and blue side-buttoned blouse whose thinning hair, so fine you could see the pale scalp shining beneath, was combed rolled in a tight bun and stuck to the head with a long thin pin. Our mother having left us some time before, third auntie had the responsibility of feeding the six of us, my brothers and myself, together with her own numerous children, my cousins too many to name or remember. She was a stout, lazy woman blessed in having older daughters whom she ordered around to do the marketing, cooking, and cleaning. I was nine years old, young for domestic work and good only for carrying her youngest boy, Johnnie, from room to room all afternoon and evening and for listening to the women.

In the large narrow house, my aunts had separate apartments upstairs. But they met every day in the kitchen on the ground floor to prepare their separate evening meals. As they waited for the rice to boil, peeled garlic clumps, and picked scratchy bony spines from *ikan bilis,* they talked, a mixture of complaints, gossip, familial hypochondriacal details on voiding and child-carrying, birth-labour and cures of root herbs, and endlessly, constantly, talk of the past, the wealth when grandfather was alive and managing the hardware stores, rubber plantations, vegetable farm, three carts, and five bullocks to pull them.

My hip sore from Johnnie's two-year-old weight, I stood silently listening for these stories while the women snapped ribs of *bak choy,* fried vegetable bits in a stinging steam, set plates of food on their separate round wooden tables, and while the children ate scrabbling their bowls with chopsticks. We were the last to eat because we didn't have a jealous mother sheltering the very nutrients in every rice grain to make us grow. It wasn't that third auntie was stingy or unfeeling; we ate enough to not suffer hunger. But we were fed as an afterthought, on soup cooled from her children's satisfaction and on the last scrapings of rice which had turned crusty and brown like congealed plaster-of-paris. Much like the poor man in the fable my brothers and I waited by the kitchen fires sniffing the complex spicy smells from our aunts' dinners and watching our cousins' merry eating till it was our turn to devour our meal, a tepid grease more flavoured for being all that was left. Our feet were numb and swollen from waiting. Meanwhile the women's stories filled us with images of the past, bright busy years to oppose our stale one-room apartment unfurnished and crowded with bedding. What I know of my family's history comes from those smoky evenings when the loud stories covered over the strange nervous rumblings from our insides.

Third auntie, because she never had to leave her chair to tend to the cooking, was the indisputable matriarch. She was the only fat woman in the house. Her round face above the many soft chins was pretty; it was fair, unmarked by pocks. A black mole bobbed just above the right upper lip. She had strong white teeth, an unwavering smile, and best of all a throaty chuckle that could go on and on till you had to smile with her. She was an attractive fat woman, and she continued to attract her husband (who gave her nine children), most of her sisters-in-law, and all of the children to whom her good humour was like the gooey treacle sold from buckets on the streets. You would nibble just a little at a time. It was so sweet you never wanted to stop eating it, and when you finally licked the last dissolving drop from its stick you were desolate, desperate at finding the brown sugar all gone and at the perfidy of your own rash greed. Shifting her baby boy from one tired hip to the other I stayed by her chair staring open-eyed at her insinuating chuckles, her wonderfully odd, brief family stories.

Why did we have no second uncle? Simply, second uncle was caught breaking curfew by the Japanese and beheaded. When the Japanese troop bivouacked in Malacca, the commandant set 5 p.m. as the curfew. Second uncle was the adventurous one among the six sons, the clever, restless, disobedient son who was on his way to study medicine at Raffles College before the war broke out. Of course he stayed out late to defy the Japanese edict; he was also probably on his way to a brothel. All of the sons were lecherous young men; only second uncle refused to marry young. His body was found floating on the muddy river-mouth with the head attached by a frail skin membrane. Grandfather was stricken by his death and in a year he turned distracted, withdrawn, old. Third auntie repeated the story often. It never ceased to make us shudder. As she told it everyone would gradually grow solemn. We would be quiet for a quivering moment in the sudden evening, all fifteen or twenty of us; then the stir-frying would start up with a clanging of metal or the chopsticks rattle again against the rice bowls. There was something about the flatness of the story, the swift plain recital of act, punishment, family consequence which always convinced me it was true. It was true in a way that living in Hereen Street was true. It made real the sensation of hunger. When I looked out through the narrow window of our room later that night, it made real the funeral darkness of the town and the blurred yellowness thrown by the low streetlamp, the only

77

light anywhere that I could see, burning its small hole into my eye.

The other war story I liked was about banana money. After the Japanese troops overran Malaya, they began to press their own currency. Straits dollars, the British currency, was forbidden; they could not be used to buy anything. Grandfather hid his Straits dollars for years, believing that the British would eventually return, then decided to exchange them secretly for Japanese imperial currency. These were handsome bills faced with pictures of full-leafed banana trees bearing large combs of bananas and numbers printed from 5 to 10,000. A few months after his exchange British soldiers landed on the Northeastern beaches, the Americans bombed Nagasaki, and the Japanese Emperor surrendered. Even the bottle-man would not accept Japanese banana money. Grandfather was left with trunks full of brand-new green, pink, yellow, gentian, purple paper which couldn't buy him anything. Each time third auntie told this story I remembered the cane hamper full of Japanese dollars which I played with when I was five and mother was with us and we were all living together on the second floor of father's Bata store.

At five I knew what it was like to be rich. The stacks of bills, my playthings, had dollar numbers I could read. The notes crackled with a kind of stiffness and crispness that the child respected as money. When the hamper with its wealth disappeared, I wasn't upset; I had known it could buy all kinds of comic books, toffees and tea sets. That grandfather was made immeasurably poorer because he bought banana money with real Straits dollars was a new story. It was part of the story of the Japanese Occupation, with my aunts and uncles eating tapioca instead of rice, the babies having worms because there was no milk, families quarrelling irrevocably over which had been given unfairly a larger ration of sugar. This was a new story against which the joy of having thousands of dollars to buy the biggest jars of sweets from the Cold Storage diminished. It was so straightforward it had to be true. Trying to break up the hard panes of rice scrapped from the bottom of the pot, I knew third auntie told the best stories because they were truthful.

The other absent uncle was fourth uncle, a man who had the worst life imaginable. He had married a woman below him in station, for love, a farm-woman who bullied him, berated him publicly, would do nothing for him, made his life miserable, was miserable in the house, finally left him to return to the farm, and would not come back despite his humiliation, his appeals, his threats. Among the sons he was the weakest, weaker than the woman who cared nothing for him. He drank caustic soda which burned his mouth, throat, and stomach. He lived for a few agonizing months. Even then his wife refused to visit him, and he died a slow drawn-out death. The story could not horrify us. How we hated fourth auntie!

Each time third aunt paused at the conclusion for us to consider the tragedy, first auntie snatched at the rest of the tale in a propulsive harsh abusive Hokkien: "The cursed woman's behaviour was learned from water buffaloes. She is a dead pig, a sow with no understanding of human ties. It is a good thing she is barren so there are no ten thousand devils to claim kinship with us."

First aunt had fallen from the position of matriarch since, pitifully, she had only one son and one daughter; but she made up for the scarcity of her womb and for her skeletal frame by a voice whose pitch and volume could be felt from the front altar room to the outhouses at the back. In her capacity for long scoldings she remained first among the sisters-in-law. Her straight bony body and starved face were crossed by thick hairy brows which marched ahead of her in a crowd of Chinese women whose brows, normally sparse and faint, were further suppressed when they were shaved off during the wedding ceremony. "I, first aunt, handfed fourth uncle every day because the evil bitch refused to do her duty!" she said, still angry after twelve years. "I have a soft heart," she shouted over and over again, but we never trusted her jarring banging voice, the breastless emaciated body, those waving heavy browlines. So I could not believe first aunt's story; as her tirades prolonged, out of weariness I almost felt sympathy for the stubborn rebellious wife. I longed to be persuaded of her wickedness, but her story failed me.

These were the evenings when I looked forward to father returning from work, staying up sometimes to midnight so I could stroke his arms before falling asleep. Why was fourth uncle weak? Why caustic soda? At nine I wanted the abrupt melodrama, clashing clarities. The deep narrow merchant's house was slowly cracking: the screens of delicately etched glass around the interior courtyard were almost all broken. Barrels of tar stored in the second courtyard were snapping loose; black viscous ooze, uncovered in the hot mornings, slipping down the sides inch by inch to crawl over the tiled flooring, an ugly mess that could never be cleaned up, from which the pale green and flowered porcelain tiles were never to be recovered. The story's irresolution was not to be imagined.

Four uncles, four aunts and their children lived in the house that year: first uncle and first aunt, third uncle and third aunt, my father, the fifth son, and sixth uncle and his two wives. Of course, third auntie could not tell us stories about these people for we were all their children. Of my first and third uncles, I knew them as remote opium smokers. Much of the day they kept together in a windowless room at the centre of the house. They lounged on bolsters on the cool mahogany floor separated from each other by an oil lamp whose low-burning wick was enclosed in a glass funnel. Now and then, one would pass the pipe to the other. The pipe, about two feet long and two inches in diameter, was a seamless carved piece of wood with a small metal aperture in its middle. Rickshaw-pullers, herb-doctors, town clerks brought shiny black opium balls, like rat droppings wrapped in dried bamboo leaves, into the house. These opium balls were impaled on thin metal skewers, then roasted carefully above the oil lamp's flame till they gave off a pungent smoke, much like fried coffee beans, only deeper and oilier—as if the scent of a sackful of coffee beans had been fried and condensed into a nugget. The roasted pellet was then dropped on the cupped metal aperture. The smoker, lying sidewise relaxed in Roman fashion, would inhale its mysteriously vanishing fumes. Inhaling, the two men made a loud snoring noise. Their centre room even with doors closed spread an influence of dream, drowsiness, illicitness throughout the apartments.

First and third aunties talked of opium-hunger and opium shit, but these were descriptive terms with no intention in them. When they spoke, away from each other's company, their stories to explain why their husbands lay together in opium stupor were uninteresting, barely credible gossip. "It was third auntie," whispered first aunt, "who first began giving opium smokes to Wee Hong. She was afraid he would take a second wife. To keep him in her bed, to turn his mind away from cabaret girls, third auntie turned him to opium pleasures. But the Chinese doctor recommended opium for your first uncle. He had sprained his back in the shop, but he couldn't lie still; he was worried about the business. The opium cured his back."

In her private apartment third auntie told us, "First uncle was very angry when grandfather would not let him run the shops by himself. He was too impatient, a bad businessman. Your grandfather gave him opium to keep him happy. You see how he leaves the business alone now and lets people cheat us every day. Third uncle, you know, has a tubercular infection. See how thin he's become! The opium stops the chest pains; he needs it."

It wasn't certain if they heard each other's stories retold by a third person. They had only each other to listen to, for, as my tenth birthday approached, my uncles stayed in the opium room almost all day, and the smoke, heavier and constant now, was drifting even to the lower floor. In the sooty kitchen the dark opium taste mingled with the taste of wood ashes, soy sauce, and lard. We could hear men snoring all day from ten in the morning to when we pulled our blankets over our heads and closed our ears.

One evening third aunt sent me to look for Johnnie. He was running by himself round and round the courtyard. "Go away!" he yelled. I was no longer responsible for carrying him. It wasn't long after third auntie's last baby learned to run that father found a house for us. It was a three-roomed bungalow two miles from the town. I thought we had moved to the farm because there were trees in front of the house and bamboo canes grew around the drains at the back. When the monsoon came the rain banged on the zinc roof and kept us awake. I attended a Catholic missionary school, read English books, and somehow, suddenly, forgot how to speak Hokkien. Third auntie seldom visited us. The last time she came, her neck was all puffed up and grizzled by goitre, her hair was greyer, and she had lost so much weight we did not recognize her. She had stories of her daughters' marriages, her increasing swamp of grandchildren. Clearly her sons still cherished her. But I didn't enjoy her stories any more.

By then she was a widow. The last of her brothers-in-law living were Father and his youngest brother who looks so much like him that I have the sensation I am seeing my father each time I meet him. Third auntie never told me a story about either man, perhaps because with one I am so familiar that I could tell her a hundred stories about him and another hundred which I know people must have of him, and with the other, the only son alive today of grandfather's six sons, she would not have dared to tell. I have observed them both myself. Aside from their debonair looks, happy natures, and greedy enjoyment of food, they shared the fact of having each two wives and many children by both. They could not help living, insisted on living, despite the sale of the house, the shops, the plantations, the farmland, as *baba* children. They were men who enjoyed life first and who worked only so long as work did not interfere with their pleasures. They wanted nothing more out of life than to get home early and to play mahjong till two in the morning, to be comfortable in loose pyjamas, and to eat titbits cooked by their wives. I found this observation stupefying, the unscalable wall against which my childish yearning to believe in something must collide, shatter, and re-form— as what?

An older woman now, like my third aunt was once, it is important for me to remember that these men, my uncles, grew up in a non-woman world. My grandmother died when they were mere boys. Their only sister was given away to a rubber merchant's family when she was six months old so that she could be trained as a proper daughter-in-law by her prospective mother. A niece and daughter to these men, I have had to make my way through their reckless impoverishment, trying each time to write stories that may transmute fact into something else believable.

The Good Old Days

WHENEVER MY MOTHER talks about the good old days, I remember Grandfather's funeral. Alive, Grandfather had been an important man, owning two hardware stores, ten houses, one hundred and fifty acres of rubber estate, and three farms. But I hadn't known how important he was till he died and anyone who was anybody in the town came for his burial. The police closed the town roads to make place for the procession as it wound its way through the major thoroughfares. Aside from the fifty-man band blowing dignified oomppahs on polished brass, there were over a hundred banner-bearers, each carrying a tall bamboo pole to which was attached a long piece of coloured cloth. The cloths had been respectfully presented by the town's businessmen, and the names of their shops were emblazoned on the banners in red and gold letters. The lorry loaded with its huge mahogany coffin followed slowly after, decorated with a profusion of wreaths and paper effigies. This was the year that acetate paper was first used in town, and the funeral shop had been inspired by its many possibilities. The effigies of motorcars, multi-storied buildings, even a man in a tailcoat and top hat, were constructed of shimmering purple, aquamarine, emerald, rose and topaz acetate. Grandfather wouldn't have approved. He had been a plain cautious man who dressed simply in black trousers and white open-necked shirts and who preferred eating congee to European cake.

We walked after the hearse in grand fashion, stumbling along in our straw sandals, our heads covered with strawplaited mats, all four of his surviving sons, five daughters-in-law, twenty-five grandchildren, sundry nephews, nieces, cousins, and kinsfolk by blood, by marriage, and by custom. We wore new clothes of the most bitter black. The dye was fresh and pungent and the seams stiff with starch. We rustled like the Saragossa Sea, trampling behind the dead and smelling as foul as a black tide. The women screamed and wailed, the men paced solemnly behind, and we trotted as fast as we could, scratching wherever the straw and clothing itched us. The procession stretched for almost a quarter mile. Grandfather's retainers, employees, tenants, customers, suppliers, government officers he had bribed for business favours, debtors, creditors, hangers-on, all walked with him under the imperturbable tropical sun, some waving palm fans, others reading the newspaper, eating melon seeds, or gossiping.

The trouble began even before the funeral. Grandfather, who spoke no English, had gone to an Indian lawyer who drew up a brief will leaving all Grandfather's possessions equally to his children. The lawyer, of course, had no way of knowing that nothing could be equal in our family. The evening Grandfather died and the coffin was still being hewn, our fathers, his sons, met to discuss how to divide the property.

"We will keep everything the way it is. The profits from the shops, farms, estates, and rents will be divided each month among us," First Uncle, the eldest son, said.

"Who will oversee the businesses?" Second Uncle wanted to know.

"I will continue to do so. You know I've been doing most of the work for the old man in the last five years."

Third Son, my father, didn't like the idea at all. He had been trying to build up his business as a middleman trading in rubber. The shop was not doing well because there was a glut of synthetic rubber and because of the recent American quotas. Father had bought a lot of smoked rubber last year and he couldn't find a buyer for most of it. The land behind our house was piled with tacky rubber sheets which smelled like a mixture of putrefying fish heads, pig swill, and wet copra rotting under canvas. Although Mother didn't complain, Father was obviously unhappy about the rubber stink which filled every room in our house and about the low-class appearance of his yard. Father was a sensitive, dreamy man who should never have gone into rubber trading.

"I want my share of the property. We should sell everything and divide the proceeds among us. A little money every month cannot help me."

"Third Brother is right," Second Uncle said, beaming. "We would like our share immediately. But there are problems with the economy this year. It would be foolish to place the properties on the market. We may have to accept a price less than their value. A better method is to divide the properties among us. First Brother, being the eldest, will have the first choice of the parcels, I the second, and so on. In this way, we can each do what we wish with our share. First Brother can keep his business, Third Brother can sell his share, and I, I haven't decided what to do." Second Uncle was the clever one in the family. Whenever the brothers played mahjong together, he was usually the big winner. No one trusted him.

"Both Second and Third Brothers are right," Fourth Uncle added, "but I must stupidly disagree with Second Brother about the method of division. The properties are not all of equal value. The last person choosing will end up with the least. If we don't sell, then I would prefer to use a lottery system to decide who should choose first and who last. In this way, we can try to be equal as the old man wished it."

At this point, according to Father, the meeting broke up into shouting matches and only the presence of Grandfather's body in the next room prevented them from pushing and hitting each other.

"Greedy and stupid men!" my mother fumed as she spread Planter's Margarine and sugar over our morning bread. "You were right in insisting on your share. Even now, when people are hard up, your father's lands and houses will fetch a good price. Think of all we can do with the money."

"I can rent a warehouse to store the rubber," Father murmured, looking pale and miserable. He had been eating very little and had grown thin and worn because the stink of the unsold rubber, he said, upset his stomach.

"And we can buy a larger house with six bedrooms, one for each child."

We all looked up when we heard this. "I don't have to share a room with Fatty and Piggy?" "Who are you calling fat, you balloon!" "Shut up, midget! I'll get you later." "You boys are so rude." "Ooh! And you're so pretty, ugly!" "Ma, he's pinching me!"

"I have to go to work," Father said and left his coffee on the table. "Can I drink Father's coffee?" "I want it!" "Me too!"

"Quiet! You must show proper respect for the dead. Your *kong-kong* is just dead one day, and you're already acting like monkeys."

But we didn't mind Mother's words; we were all too happy at the prospect of having our own rooms and went off willingly to school that morning.

We came home excited. "Ah Chen told me Second Auntie called Father an ox. She says Father is so dumb he believes the mice will buy his rubber." "Soong says he's not supposed to talk to me. We're ungrateful hooligans and his father doesn't want us to influence him." "I told Ah Leng you called his father stupid and greedy. His mother says we're thieves. She also said Father will murder them just for the money." "Is Father a murderer?"

Father was a hero. No one would blame him for killing Fourth Auntie whom, we agreed, was a stingy poker and a nag. Her *samfoos* hung on her like rags drying on a washboard, she was so flat and ugly.

Father didn't seem a violent man, but one could never tell. We remembered the noodle-man who had a stall down the road, a little man who was remarkable because he had the middle finger missing on his right hand. One night, a few months ago, he chopped up his wife with a cleaver, and who would have thought *he* was a killer as he threw shrimps and fish-balls into the wok for their supper?

After the funeral, First Auntie visited us to make amends. A new enemy had appeared. Fifth Uncle's widow, whom no one had included as a beneficiary, had actually hired a lawyer to claim her share. Mr DeSouza, an established Eurasian lawyer with an office near Government House, apparently promised that her children were entitled to one-fifth of Grandfather's wealth, and the greedy upstart was suing the family.

"I spotted her for a poisonous spider from the first," First Auntie said triumphantly. "Any woman who would go to the cinema with a man before they are married is not to be trusted. And imagine having six children in seven years! No wonder poor Fifth Brother coughed himself to death."

Mother listened with a vexed face. She had always defended Auntie Woo, the only sister-in-law beside her who had received an English education in the Methodist School. They had exchanged *True Romance* magazines and *Heartbreak* comics when Fifth Uncle was still alive and suffering from tuberculosis, and, after his death two years ago, our cousins had often come home with us for lunch. "It does seem wrong to bring family affairs to court," Mother admitted.

"If only her husband can see her unfilial behaviour! He will have no rest and must curse his own children for having this evil witch for mother. Surely she will be condemned to the lowest level in Hell where the God of the Underworld Himself will supervise the demons as they pull her entrails up through her mouth. Which monastery will dare to pray for her spirit which is as ravenous as a man-eater's?" We clung to Mother's chair and hid under the table as First Auntie cursed.

Mother looked more and more guilty. "Perhaps I will ask her children not to eat with us," she finally ventured. "The poor children are forever hungry, for they have little to eat at home. You know, since Fifth Brother's death, they have almost nothing."

We shivered when we heard this. To be hungry and to have almost nothing! No wonder Koh and Seng and their two sisters were happy to help us finish our rice and soup.

"You must do at least that," First Auntie urged. "She's hurting the whole family through her ridiculous suit. May I die if I go to a *Serani* ten-thousand devil to make trouble for my own flesh and blood!"

A *Serani* devil! Mother didn't understand how Little Sister could talk face-to-face with a Eurasian. It was all right to see white people in the pictures where they were either punching or lewdly kissing each other, but to do business with a Eurasian who was, after all, almost a white man! Her financial problems were driving Fifth Auntie mad, Mother told us. We dutifully promised we wouldn't bring our cousins home any longer, but we also vowed among ourselves to take our morning bread to school to share with them during recess.

Two weeks later, we came home from school and found Fourth Auntie, whom Father was going to murder, bravely sitting in the kitchen. She twirled her jade bangles as she talked. Now and again they slid off her bony wrists and she would catch them nervously and push them back. If she pushed hard enough, we thought, the bangles could slide all the way up to her armpits.

"The younger members of the family must stick together," she said passionately. "Second Brother is cunning like a wolf waiting at night for the careless person. He will eat us up one by one unless we band together. You know how dangerous a wolfish nature is. Such people are rapacious. They will eat their own children, they are so controlled by their appetites. Cannibals and murderers!"

We pinched Little Su who had begun to wail at the thought of being eaten, and Ah Beng pulled her under the table from where they could safely observe Fourth Auntie's skeletal feet and listen to her without Mother noticing.

"How did Second Brother find a white lawyer?" Mother asked.

"Only the devils know. He was afraid of the *Serani*, DeSouza, for he knows how the white court has its barbaric laws which favour the red-haired devils. What is more cunning than to hire a red-haired devil to fight in court?"

"But there are no white lawyers in town," Mother countered, furrowing her brow.

"Yes, but he found one in the capital city. This lawyer, Mr Deel, is supposed to be a golf-partner of the Minister, and he goes to the racetracks with the politicians. We have no chance against him unless we fight together."

Mother, however, wouldn't promise to join ranks with her which made all of us glad. Although we were afraid of Second Uncle's wolfish appetite, we didn't care for Fourth Auntie either. She was so tightfisted that she had come to our house without any cakes or fruit for us.

"She's right," Father said. "I'll speak to Fourth Brother tomorrow about getting a lawyer to represent us."

We kept very quiet and raised our heads out of bed in order to hear more clearly. Often, when our parents thought we were asleep, they would have long conversations on scandals, villains, and escapades from their youth. Then, we kept ourselves awake as late as we could, listening to them whispering and chuckling, and, many times, as we tumbled into warm slumber, we would be dreaming already of drowsy grownup stories about half-known actors, gods, and demons alive in our town twenty years ago.

"We'll have to go to C.S. Tan, I'm afraid. He's a good friend from High School days, and he'll charge a reasonable fee for old times' sake, but he has no experience with big sharks. Most of his clients are immigrants from China applying for citizenship. He's become almost as much of a salted cabbage as they."

"But he knows the law, and he understands Chinese families better than a *Serani* or red-haired devil. You're making a good choice," Mother whispered.

We heard the bed creak. "If I had the money, I'd find a white lawyer also."

"Once the case is settled, you'll have the money."

"We won't need a lawyer then! No. With the old man's money, I'll start a grocery business. I'll get rid of the rubber and open a nice shop selling tinned food, dried meat and vegetables, and sweets. Nothing fresh because fresh food rots if it doesn't sell quickly." Father spoke confidently. "Everyone has to eat. It doesn't matter how bad the economy is; people can go without shoes or cars and certainly without books. But everyone has to eat. A grocery shop will do a splendid business."

"How clever of you! Of course, a business selling food can't go wrong."

We secretly agreed with Mother. What a wonderful day that would be when Father finally sells off the rubber and we can again eat our meals without having to hold our noses, we thought. A grocery shop selling sweets! We dreamt about English Toffees, Cadbury Chocolates, chewy Allsorts and yellow Lemondrops. To be surrounded by tall fat bottles of striped Bullseyes, green mints dusted with confectioner's sugar, and gleaming black Licorice! Shelves full of sugar wafers, nougat bars, colourful rock candy, and boxes of chocolate-covered Brazil nuts! Our stomachs began to growl which started Su Ching laughing and Little Su crying, and Mother came out and shushed us.

A few days later, as we were having lunch, Mother hurriedly began to clear the table. "Your First Auntie is coming up the road," she explained. "I hope she's not angry with me because your father went to a lawyer. I'm sure she'll scold me for having such an untidy house. I'll make some tea and Ho Beng will run to the store and buy some biscuits."

First Auntie was more sorrowful than angry. She spoke her mind even before tea was served. "Tell me, why must Third Brother waste his money on a lawyer? Young people act foolishly when they don't save; besides, you don't have that much to throw away. I'm thinking only of your own good. My husband knows that as the eldest son, his rights come first; he isn't concerned. But I'm unhappy to see how estranged we've become."

Mother began to cry.

"You're young," First Auntie continued after drinking her tea. "It's easy to overlook your obligations. But the young must support the old. As the Taoists taught us, the Heavens are carried by the lowly turtle. What would happen if the turtle refused to carry the Universe because it was tired or preferred to do something else? Tua Peh Kong, the Supreme Deity Himself, would no longer be safe. The moon and stars would fall into the ocean, and the sky would crack open and leak its venom on the world."

Mother cried even harder. Little Su clung to her blouse, and Ah Beng and I scowled at the thought of the wicked turtle.

First Aunt scowled back at us. "See how your children learn from your behaviour. Someday, you too will be old, and you'll want your children to carry you. How you'll curse them then if they disobey. May they be dead pigs, vile worms, strangled at birth if they do so."

Mother wiped her eyes with her sleeves, gave Little Su a biscuit, and told us to take her outside to play. As soon as First Auntie left, she took us to visit Fourth Auntie in her large wooden house in Green Lane.

"Didn't she tell you Eldest Brother has hired a lawyer also?"

Mother was sitting in Fourth Auntie's living room, drying her eyes when Fourth Auntie broke the news.

"Here you are, crying because you believe we shouldn't upset our elders, and there she was, the lying lizard, leading you on all the time," Fourth Auntie scolded, looking annoyed at us as we fidgeted on her hard wooden chairs. "What a state you're in, hair uncombed and blouse rumpled, and your children overexcited. And for what? First Auntie is a vulture. These birds can smell a corpse from a hundred miles away and will approach a roof even while the man below is unaware he's dying. You know she can't be trusted."

"A lawyer? Who?" Mother stood up indignantly, and Little Su slid off her lap.

"Old Mr Dass, the same man who drew up Grandfather's will."

"But I thought he died last year."

"No, he was hospitalized for chronic kidney trouble. You know how these Indians are. Either drunk on toddy or near dying."

Mother shook her head disbelievingly. "But everyone knows he's senile. Why, he must be at least seventy years old."

"Eldest Brother had no choice. He's the only lawyer left in town." Fourth Auntie's face grew scrawnier as Mother began to laugh helplessly. We giggled with Mother and tickled each other until we were gasping with laughter at Fourth Auntie who was wriggling her black eyebrows in disapproval.

But Father didn't think we were funny when Mother described the scene to him. "The children don't understand how serious the situation is. C.S. told me it will be at least a year before the case is decided. In the meantime, he's willing to wait for his fees until the estate is settled." Father appeared worried and perplexed. "Perhaps I should work harder at trading rubber. Mustn't be like the hare and the tortoise and count my chickens before they're hatched." He sighed and went to the yard to check the ghostly mounds of rubber sheets glued together under the rising moon.

"Second Auntie's here, Second Auntie's here!" we chorused as we sighted her plump body plodding up the road. It was months since we heard from any of Father's relatives, and we had almost forgotten Grandfather's will. Ah Beng ran to fetch Mother who was watching her favourite Chinese opera on television with the neighbour. Little Su danced towards Second Auntie whose pet she was; we all knew our generous aunt had brought presents. Apples for Mother, dried plums for us, and for Little Su, a whole *kati* of oranges.

Accepting her second cup of tea, she went straight to the point. "Sister," she said calmly, "we must stop this family wrangling. Did you hear that Fifth Brother's widow tried to kill herself yesterday?"

"No!" Mother shooed us away, but we hid behind her chair and crept under the table. "Why would she do such an unspeakable act? Who would care for her children?"

Second Auntie chewed another biscuit and smiled. "Of course, Fifth Brother's widow did not consider these questions before she tried to end her life. Her eldest boy came to my house crying. Apparently she tried to hang herself from a rope tied to the cradle beam, but the rope was too long and she only managed to give herself a good choking. However, she was quite incapacitated and could hardly speak. Fortunately, the children had too much good sense to call the police. What a scandal it would be for our family if the attempt had been reported."

"Why didn't she come to me?" Mother cried. "I would have helped her."

We shrank under the table, for we remembered we had warned our cousins not to come near our house. It was many weeks since we had played with them in school.

"She was foolish to begin the court suit," Second Auntie said, ignoring Mother's tears, "and she deserves to be punished. But she has punished herself already. She couldn't tolerate the family's bad feelings towards her, and neither can my husband. In the last months, he's been suffering from insomnia, and his health is weak. We should reconcile our differences now."

"What can I do, Second Sister?" Mother asked abjectly. "My husband has also been affected. He isn't eating and is as thin as a ghost."

Second Auntie spoke with authority. "We'll tell the lawyers to stop the case, and we'll share the property according to whatever means are agreeable. You'll see. By this time next month, we shall have everything resolved."

But Second Auntie did not understand the depth of Fourth Auntie's suspicions or the extent of First Uncle's and Mr Dass's senility.

They pressed on with the suit, and a few months later a judge decided that the property should be sold to the first reasonable bidders and the money divided equally among the five brothers and their families after payment of legal fees. The bidders paid only a fraction of what the property was worth, and after Messrs DeSouza, Deel, Tan and Dass, together with their clerks and assistants, were paid, the family was left with a debt of $10,000.

Did the family receive anything from Grandfather's will? Well, Father and his brothers never became rich businessmen, but my eldest brother, Ho Beng, is now a top lawyer with his own firm in the capital city; my second brother, Ho Peng, is a successful accountant, and I teach Economics in the University. About once a year, around New Year season, my mother, who lives with me, gets a longing to return to the hometown to visit relatives and to talk about the good old days. And that's when I'm particularly reminded of Grandfather's funeral.

Blindness

MRS HONG'S BROTHER lost his sight when he was fifty-one, the year after he retired. She was teaching the Form III class in Hock Seng Secondary Government School when she was told the news. In the middle of sketching the diagram of a glacial retreat, she heard someone say 'pssst,' startling her into a clumsy scratch on the blackboard. In a grey and purple *sari*, with her grey-black face and inky black hair, Mrs Dorsey, the office clerk, appeared like some unlucky apparition outside the classroom.

"Pssst … Telephone!" Mrs Dorsey whispered, opening her mouth wide and biting her lips so dramatically that every pupil in the classroom heard her message with an eager jump.

Irritably, Mrs Hong picked her bag. The chalk fell from her fingers and shattered on the floor in minute fragments. Immediately she stepped on a piece of chalk which ground noisily into dust under her foot. These mishaps seemed significant to her, for they expressed the sense that she had lost control of the situation.

The girls giggled at the loud sound of the chalk breaking under her foot, but they stopped when she faced them sternly by the doorway.

"Mariann," she commanded, "continue reading on page eighty-four. I will question all of you on glacial formations when I return."

Clutching her bag, she hurried down the corridor followed by Mariann's loud complacent tone and a rising hum of voices. Her irritation increased as she approached the school office: who could be calling her during the school day? All the years they had been married, Mr Hong had never rung her up in school, and her daughter was away in London. She had received a letter from Lillian just yesterday, describing her first winter and enclosing a photograph of Lillian in a dark blue coat leaning against a mouldering stone in an Essex churchyard.

The black receiver of the telephone lay on a stack of papers, silent and foreboding. Mrs Hong knew Dorsey's sharp ears were opened even as she stood at a distance with her back turned, pretending not to listen.

"Hello?" she said firmly into the black mouthpiece.

"Mrs Hong? This is Dr Chen. I have some bad news for you."

"What? Who is this? What are you talking about?"

Her lips fumbled nervously; from the corner of her eye she watched Dorsey watching her curiously.

"This is Dr Chen. I'm calling for your brother, Teik Lock. Your brother came into my office today, he was having problems with his eyes. You should know, he's going blind."

"Hello? What are you saying? Teik Lock? Where is he? How did it happen?"

Mrs Hong could not stutter even when she was most upset. The best she could do was to bark out questions in rapid sequence, like a high-strung Pekinese, shivering slightly as she did so. Her principal wrote once in a testimonial that if Mrs Hong had been a man she would have been a police inspector because she attacked every issue as if it were a crime to be solved. The pupils under her direction behaved like a squad of detective recruits, trained to be both sceptical and obedient, curious and dogmatic, believing that there was a logical answer and reason to every phenomenon. She taught geography like a book of clues; every earth feature was a piece of evidence for the inexorable march of evolutionary events; and so, each was to be carefully tagged, described, and assigned for appearance in examinations. Because of her teaching, the school had the best record of A's in Geography in the Senior Cambridge Exam and the geography departments in the country's universities were crowded with her ex-students.

Mrs Hong took leave for the rest of the day and went to see her brother immediately after the call.

Jubilant, the Form III A students spent the rest of the afternoon sketching dresses and faces because, although they wanted A's in their examinations, what they all truly desired were romances and fine clothes.

Teik Lock lived in 220, Jalan Dusun. The concrete single-story row house was one of a few hundred identical houses constructed cheaply fifteen years ago. The land had previously been squatter property, skewered by thatch huts and outhouse lavatories. An epidemic of cholera had forced the squatters out, the green rotting fruit trees were chopped down, the wells and wet duck compounds drained and two hundred and fifty houses built in the area once it had baked to a hard flat laterite where nothing, not even bacteria, could thrive. Even after fifteen years, Su Ann Hong found it difficult to recognize her brother's house. Unlike some of his neighbours, he had not attempted to plant a garden in the front compound. There were no curtains, light fixtures, or brightly painted door to distinguish his home from the other green, blue, yellow houses in his row. The different pastel colours were all unmemorable and tarnished with red dust from the soil.

When Lillian, her daughter was still living at home, especially when she was younger, Mrs Hong and her family visited Teik Lock and his wife frequently in the evening after dinner. Su Ann approved but could not understand her daughter's devotion to her uncle. What could a teenage girl have in common with an uncle already in his forties, she wanted to know.

"She enjoys my books, that's why! What harm can there be for Lily to read as much as she likes?" Teik Lock would reply.

Today Su Ann found him sitting in his bedroom at the back of the house with all the doors open.

"Hello," he said, hunching in his chair. His glasses were no longer on his face and, although his eyes flickered and groped, it was obvious that he could see very little.

As soon as she saw him, his face no longer shaded by the thick distorting lenses and now thin and empty of reflection, she began to cry.

"So, Su Ann. Why are you crying? I'm not dead yet!"

"The doctor called. He said that ..."

"Yes, I know what he told you. But why are you here now? You should be teaching."

"He called me in school. What happened? What's wrong with your eyes?" Even as she wept, she could not help throwing questions at him. The tears ran down her face and she licked them from her lips. "Why are you sitting alone here in the dark? You should be in the hospital. Why didn't you tell me earlier that you were losing your sight?"

"What good would it have done? Mother often said I would go blind someday, and how could you have stopped it?"

"She did not mean it." Suddenly confused, she stopped crying. Yes, there were times after their father's death when they were living with their great-aunt and their mother supported them by her sewing and by selling her special curry powders. Teik Lock always carried a book with him then; he read even in the outhouse, during meals, and while visitors were in the house. He did not seem to notice how wretched and hard life was. His nose was in a book even as he lay to sleep on the mat on the floor next to the sewing machine. Sometimes when she was tired and bitter, their mother had forbidden him to continue reading, warning him that he would go blind. Later, when she was asleep he would leave the room where they ate, lived, slept, and studied to read in the compound with only the light from the moon and stars. Su Ann had spied upon him in the evening peering into the pages of a book when there was not enough light to make out his features, and she had wondered if he were actually reading the words on the page or merely deciphering his own private longings as they took shape in the indiscernible print. Finally, it was a charitable teacher who found the money to have Teik Lock's eyes examined and to buy him his first pair of glasses, a square black-rimmed pair heavy with the powerful lenses which enlarged his pupils and gave him the hideous appearance of a frog.

Was that when he began to lose his sight? Su Ann recalled that his glasses became stronger and stronger in later years. The last time she had looked through them, they were blurred and fuzzy, seeming to hinder vision rather than to improve it. The world appeared as if one were seeing it underwater, and when she snatched the glasses away from her eyes, their power persisted in her own vision, pressing in on her eyes with a painful throb.

Recalling all these events she moved restlessly around the room. "I am going to put on the light," she said unhappily. The switch flooded the room with white light from three long fluorescent lamps. Teik Lock's gesture to his childless marriage was never to read in the bedroom; however, after his wife's death, he had the bright lamps installed and he stayed more and more in this particular room, reading the novels which he ordered from book clubs in Britain and drinking his small tumblers of Remy Martin brandy.

The white fluorescent light made a shocking glare as it bounced off the white undecorated walls and illuminated brightly the stacks of books and magazines on the floor. On the bedside table Su Ann saw only a tray with a bottle of brandy on it. Teik Lock held a glass of brandy in his left hand, and he put up his right hand as if to shield his eyes from the glare.

"I am not totally blind," he said, "despite what Dr Chen may have told you. I can distinguish between light and dark, and I can see people and objects, although not clearly at all."

"What can be done?"

"There is nothing to be done. He calls it a degenerative disease. The corneas have lost their elasticity, and, at my age, no operation to replace them could be helpful." His voice was calm and light, as if he were being ironical about the whole diagnosis.

Su Ann felt a sense of terror. "How will you live?" she asked, then was overcome by shame at the shamelessness of her question.

"I will live here as I have done for so long. Ah Leng will continue to look after the house and cook for me. Fortunately, I no longer have to work, and my pension is sufficient to provide for me. It won't be difficult for me to manage as I have always done."

She began to cry again.

"Ah," she wept, "if only your life had been different! If only you had a child! If only we hadn't been so poor!"

"Come ..." he said and took a swallow of brandy. "Su Ann, why are you crying?" He smiled in her direction and held his glass up. "Look! Although I may not see the object clearly, I can still feel its substance."

Because he seemed so cheerful, Mrs Hong decided not to inform Lillian about her uncle's condition yet. It was two weeks before the Christmas holidays. Lillian's letters spoke of excitement and joy at being in London, the fabled city of the world. Mrs Hong could not write and spoil her happiness. To her mother and her uncle, Lillian was still a little girl, for she had been the only child to both families.

That Saturday, Robert accompanied Mrs Hong to Teik Lock's house. He was a shy young man of twenty who had not been accepted into the university and who had taken over Teik Lock's position as a lawyer's clerk after he retired. Teik Lock had spent some weeks training Robert in his work; the transition of duties from the older to younger man had bound them firmly together. In fact, Teik Lock had given over his world without a sign of peevishness or regret.

It was a world dominated by a large wooden sign carved in red and gold with the names, Tan and Wong, Esq., Lawyers. It hung above the entrance to the building which housed the town's chief legal company. Teik Lock had started on the job before the sign was put up, twenty-five years ago, in a tiny room behind the four large public offices. The room was furnished with a heavy teak desk and a spin chair.

In twenty-five years nothing had been changed; the room had merely grown more crowded with filing cabinets, stacks of stuffed yellow manila folders on the floor, and an *almeira* which held the paper supplies. The room was seldom swept, and he rarely discarded any document that found its way there. A layer of light grey dust lay over all the accumulated and yellowing sheaves of folders and papers clipped together by rusting paper clips. The only light in the windowless room came from a solitary ceiling bulb of feeble illumination. Su Ann once asked why he did not have the bulb replaced by a stronger light and was surprised to learn that the bulb was an 80 watt. It was the dingy legal yellow of the walls and paperpads, the dark ochre of the old and shabby furnishing and the dusty crampness of the room which swallowed the light from the lamp and dispersed its rays into a subtle form of gloom.

Robert had taken to the work and to the clerk's office with good spirits, and he continued to display a meek and grateful attitude long after his predecessor had stopped coming to the office. Mrs Hong suspected that he was interested in her daughter and could not like him for it.

This Saturday afternoon he had come straight from work. He carried sympathy cards from his employers and from his own pocket he had bought half a dozen fine green apples and a dozen golden tangerines. Parking his bicycle by the gate, he did not enter the house but went in Mrs Hong's car directly for the drive to Dusun Road.

"How is Lily?" he wanted to know.

When the baby was born, Teik Lock had requested that she be named Lily, after the flower of purity and light, but Mrs Hong who had struggled through university on determination and little money and who had married a man securely in banking refused to name her daughter so sentimentally. They had compromised by naming the child Lillian; however, Teik Lock never called her anything but Lily, and Robert had picked this name from him.

"Lillian," Mrs Hong said coldly, "is doing very well in her studies."

"Will she be coming home for the holidays?"

"No, it is too soon this year. Besides, she says she wants to enjoy her first winter. She sent some photos of herself in Essex with her classmates."

"Will you send my regards when you write to her?"

"Yes. You know, she's at the stage when everything is so new and exciting, she has no time to miss anyone. I think she hasn't got the time to read our letters to her, even though she writes often about what she's doing there."

Mrs Hong knew she was not telling Robert what he wanted to hear. She resented his interest in her daughter. In a few months, he would forget her and would be thinking of other women in the town. She thought his visit to Teik Lock was nothing but hypocrisy. His shirt was stained at the cuffs with carbon and from his half-day at the office he still carried with him a whiff of the morning's aftershave cologne and a sweet brilliantine smell in his hair.

Lillian would never marry such a dull and unpromising man, she thought, but she was not going to write any news that would send her flying home and perhaps into the company of this miserable clerk.

Ashamed of her thoughts, she began to chat about Teik Lock's home in a friendly manner.

"I can't understand why he bought a house in this area, can you?

Oh, you've never been to his house before. I told him the place would never improve. You see, people bought houses here because they thought the centre of the town would move over. Of course it hasn't and these houses are badly located, so close to the squatter district. Look at the condition of this road!" she continued as the car turned and bumped down Dusun Road. Entering the house she averted her eyes from the lines of washing hanging in the neighbouring compounds. The front room was surprisingly cool, lined on every wall with glassed-in bookshelves. She felt herself full of dissatisfactions and sadness and could not sit in the bedroom with her brother and his visitor. Saying that she wished to tidy the rooms, she remained among the shelves studying the titles of the books for some understanding of the man who had read all these books and lost his sight perhaps from too much reading.

But the heavy-bound volumes of Rider Haggard, Arthur Conan Doyle and Rudyard Kipling which formed his prize collection only disgusted her. She knew they were second-rate literature. She herself would not keep them in her house where her English Literature textbooks from university days were displayed on her glass shelves. Lillian, however, had loved reading Teik Lock's collections. By the time she was fifteen, she claimed to have read every book in her uncle's house. To please his niece and probably because he enjoyed them as much as she did, he found a bookstore which carried romances, thrillers, gothic histories, and westerns. For years he bought every book written by Agatha Christie, Zane Grey, Denise Robins and Barbara Cartland. Mrs Hong despised those novels and tolerated her brother's and daughter's craving for that imagination of cheap and simple worlds. But this afternoon she could not tolerate the gaudily covered paperbacks, hundreds of them, which were arranged neatly behind the glass doors. It seemed to her that Teik Lock had used up his store of eyesight in reading, not what was the best or most beautiful, but indiscriminately, reading whatever was there in print between the covers of a book, as if the foreign visions which swarmed among the black and white letters were as enticing and as dangerous as the opium haze that had overcome their father.

On the way back she ignored Robert except to say goodbye with an air of angry finality which he could not interpret.

Her strange fit of anger persisted. On another visit, almost maliciously, she asked the blind man, "Do you miss your reading?"

He turned his lined, blurred face towards her and, squinting ironically, replied without hesitation, "Oh no."

"No," he repeated, and this time shook the glass of brandy almost defiantly, slopping the liquid on to the floor.

He was not usually eager to talk, and she would bring Lillian's letters with her and read them to him. Reading the letters aloud made them sound stilted and clumsy, but at the same time, as the sentences ran on to unconnected events or thoughts or ended abruptly and curtly, many suggestions of the writer's feelings and circumstances began to bloom.

In one letter, Lillian complained that he had not written to her. "Please remind Uncle Lock that I'm waiting to hear from him. I've found a reader's subscription for great mysteries of the year which I'm sure he'll enjoy. I shall send them to him as soon as I hear from him."

At this point, Mrs Hong stopped reading, but Teik Lock remained silent, and after a few minutes, she continued.

It was clear she had not informed Lillian yet of his disability, and as each week passed it became more and more difficult for her to do so.

"I'll write and tell Lillian myself," her husband said one evening as they came home from Dusun Road. Paul Hong, six years older than his wife, stared at her sternly. "What is this nonsense, the two of you pretending to Lillian that nothing is wrong at home." He raised his voice as he got himself out of the car. "Maybe she'll want to come home when she hears of it. He is looking very bad. Or maybe she'll decided to wait until her holidays. But I cannot understand why you haven't told her that he has gone blind." He wouldn't look at her as they went into the house and pretended not to notice her stubborn set of expression the rest of the day. But he did not write. He saw his brother-in-law's life as wasted and although he protested, he did not interfere now, just as he had never interfered in the past.

Teik Lock's life as a lawyer's clerk had been full and busy. Until he retired, he used to get up, dress, and be in the office by eight o'clock. He had breakfast in a coffee shop across from the building: sweet milky coffee, toast and *kaya,* or sometimes a sweet roll or cake. He worked in his little room until twelve, typing letters or meeting clients of his bosses who were sent to him to tell him their stories so he could write out their complaints. He ate lunch with one or a number of friends who worked in the municipal offices nearby. His best friend was an assistant superintendent of the town's police department, a tall swarthy Ceylonese named Pilleh who was usually dressed in a khaki uniform and who enjoyed narrating long cryptic accounts of suspected gang and communist activities around the town district. Teik Lock enjoyed especially the occasions when he had to leave the office to accompany a client to the office of justice, or immigration, or postal services, or court, or merely to deliver a summons or letter to someone. Many of the people who came to the lawyers' building in search of legal advice were illiterate immigrants from India, China, or Indonesia. Many others were well-to-do, respectable businessmen in their own town or country, but they were ignorant of the English language or were confused by the many changes that had occurred almost overnight in the legal requirements which allowed them to continue in their business without disturbance when the country became free of British rule. Teik Lock enjoyed tremendous esteem among the people he served since he knew all about the numerous forms, stamps, applications, licences, departments, courts, offices, fees, qualifications, requirements, testimonies, witnesses, certificates, documents, notarizations, cards, and what-have-you that made life difficult for the poor and unschooled in the town.

After he retired, Pilleh still dropped in on his old friend every evening. When his wife died, he went out more and more frequently with Pilleh to the bars on Winston Road. They drank beer and talked for long hours, Pilleh threateningly and coarsely about the bad elements in the nation and women he knew who plied their trade for soldiers and police. Teik Lock talked about the many cases of people whom he had helped.

Now that he was what he called 'slightly blind', he did not change his habits too much. He still got up at the usual hour, although he took a longer time to dress. The maid put his breakfast before him, coffee, toast, soft-boiled eggs. He would crack the tops of the eggs, carefully remove the splinters of eggshells, and suck on the whites before scooping the yolks out with his spoon. He had little difficulty in guiding the food to his mouth and he ate neatly. After breakfast he would take a chair out onto the front compound to listen to the children who were too young to go to school play in the neighbouring compounds. He could recognize voices and when they greeted him, he replied, "Good morning! How are you? Nice morning!" to the women as they went past the house on their way to the market. He also could recognize the sounds of the bells of various peddlers as they pushed their bicycles and tricycles down the road in the early afternoon. The vegetable, pork, and fish sellers would stop by the gate and greet him. He took great pleasure in buying the few items for himself and his maid for the afternoon and evening meals. "One *kati* of prawns," he said, then hefted the parcel in his hands as if to measure the accuracy of the weight given. "Ah, are you sure these prawns are fresh?" he asked, putting his nose to the package and sniffing loudly.

"Straight from the sea this morning," the fish-seller protested.

In the same manner he argued with the pork-seller. "What! Three-fifty for a *kati* of pork! I can get it cheaper in the market, you robber!"

"No, uncle, this is the best price you can find in the market. See,

I even give you a little over the weight because you are such a good customer."

The late afternoons, between one and four, were the worst hours of the day, when the children were busy at home eating their meals or having their naps and it was too hot to sit outside. It was so quiet on his road that he could hear the rustle of the washing next door as the sun dried the starch on the clothes.

The air would grow heavy if it was just before a storm; sitting by the front door, he listened to the rain drops as they rushed down the distance from the sky or as the wind blew a gushing cloud in his direction. He preferred rainy afternoons because of the changing multitude of sounds and scents. The loud plops of the first heavy drops and the clear sizzle as they hit the hot dry dust of the road soon changed to the monotonous general splash as the storm continued its force. Then there was the gentle rain, the drizzle which preceded the thunderstorms or which concluded a downpour; a wet cool breeze blew the sprinkles in a restrained rhythm, now diminishing like a cessation of water, now picking up again if a stronger wind should blow with a sudden patter of drops and renewed smells of clean grass and trees.

Many afternoons, he waited for the rain and listened to its fall and chatter as attentively as he used to read to himself. But it did not rain every day. During those afternoons when the sky burned a bright glaring blue with the flaming tropic sun which blistered his head if he ventured out of doors, on those long silent afternoons he sat under the ceiling fan in his bedroom and listened to the radio. The English station played popular western music: British rock groups howling like animals and drums, cymbals, strings crashing around his ears like a natural disaster letting loose all the bound-up bitter and lunatic noises of falling mountains, tearing waters, grinding abysses which opened up to swallow his loneliness into the absurd sentimentality of their being.

And in the evening he returned to his habitual existence. His sister and her husband came by after the evening meal. There were letters from his niece, his lovely young daughter-in-spirit, which gossiped of other young women, of parties and sights; hinted at young men, at meetings in colleges and restaurants; all her writing to reveal frankly her love of herself and infatuations with people and places in England. Her letters made him feel old and cheerful at the same time; her regular, ignorant correspondence seemed to reconcile him to his lonely afternoons. He drank while he listened to the letters. The brandy warmed his blood and loosened his chest. He listened to her chatter and recalled the warm milky smell when he first carried her in his arms and then that dusky flowery French-named perfume when he last said goodbye to that grown and glossy missy.

"And when are you going to tell Lillian of Lock's condition?" Mr Hong said loudly one evening. He spoke in his brother-in-law's presence with an unnaturally slow and emphatic voice as if the blindness had also made Teik Lock hard of hearing or had retarded his understanding.

"It's not necessary to tell Lily of my blindness. She may not understand and become upset." Teik Lock replied, as if the question had been posed to him.

"Teik Lock, are you so superstitious that you feel she should be kept ignorant of what happens at home?" In his agitation, Mr Hong had rushed into speech, but midway through the sentence he remembered his brother-in-law's infirmity and slowed awkwardly so that the last half of the sentence was delivered almost as a pronouncement.

"It isn't necessary," Teik Lock repeated.

"She may not want to return, but she may feel it her duty to do so. We cannot interrupt her studies!" Su Ann said.

"Nonsense! Lillian has too much sense to do anything foolish."

"Then, what is the point of telling her?" Su Ann asked impatiently.

"Because she may want to know. You know how attached she is to Teik Lock." Mr Hong directed his talk to his wife. He did not like looking at his brother-in-law whose eyes continued to discompose him with the suspicion that on their blank pupils may register still images and impressions. "Don't you want her to know?"

"It isn't necessary that she knows," Teik Lock repeated.

"Well, I leave it to you two to conspire. I will inform Lillian when she gets home that I had nothing to do with this silence."

Having expressed his opinion forcefully, Mr Hong said nothing else for the rest of the visit.

Later in the evening, Pilleh came by for his usual visits. He tenderly guided the blind man to his car, placed him in the passenger seat, and shut the door firmly for him. They would go to one of a number of bars where they would drink till eleven. Usually, at the bars were the regulars, or *kaki,* as they called each other. Goon Seng, sallow and small, with pretensions to a vast knowledge of world affairs culled from his reading of *Time* magazines, would nurse his drink for long hours while patiently awaiting the opportunity to debate on the state of international politics. He had a weak head for alcohol, and his views were seldom taken seriously, for, as his drinking partners told him, his interest in politics, foreign and domestic, was uncommon for a Chinaman. Raja, a chief clerk in the Education office, and Ramaswathi, stockier, blacker, and merrier than Raja, came in and left together; they were called R & R by the regulars, a nickname which gave rise to many jokes and salacious remarks when an Australian or British soldier or, more infrequently, an American soldier wandered into the bar. Other men, many of whom had attended the same schools as Pilleh and Teik Lock, were not as regular in their drinking of Tiger and Anchor beers. The five *kaki* knew the scandals and past romances of each other and shared a companionship based on their drinking habits and on their aging insularity. They were all single or widowed, unblessed by children, and enjoyed conversing about the larger world of England and America.

In the company of his *kaki,* Teik Lock spent the evenings. When he woke up the next day he would not remember the hesitant manoeuvres of his exits and entrances, the solicitude of his friends as they guided him into the car, the scolding complaints of the maid as she met him at the door and led him to the bedroom, or how, singing softly, he would fumble and undress himself before finally sliding down to the darkness of sleep.

One night, he could not remember what happened very well, his friends brought him to the hospital and he fell asleep in an iron cot in the free ward. Su Ann came as soon as the doctor reached her, but this time she did not cry. He had suffered a heart attack, the nurse explained. Of course, he would be put in a first-class room immediately. He did not request it when he was brought in by some men last night, and none of them knew what to do and had left all the arrangements to the hospital.

"It's not too late," Su Ann said. "I want him moved to a comfortable room."

Lying on the narrow bed, he looked as if he were ready to be wrapped up in funeral clothes and grieved over. His face had shrunk; the flesh was pale yellow and hung round his eyes and jaws in folds and crepes like unsmoked rubber. His yellow hands and feet stuck out of the hospital regulation pyjamas as if emerging from a bundle of faded sheets. He was weak and could not sit up.

"Hello," she said, raising her voice to reach him. "Hello," she repeated, and saw the blind eyes gleam as if they had recognized and responded. "Well, you're a mess, Teik Lock! The doctor says I shouldn't stay too long. Now you're not to worry. As soon as you're better, I'm going to make arrangements to bring you home with me." Seeing him shake his head, she could not tell whether to agree or disagree, she raised her voice even louder. "We won't discuss it now. By the way, I'm writing to Lillian that you're in the hospital, and that she should come home to see you."

"Ahhh," he said and beckoned her to his side. In a soft voice and straining intently as if to look at her, he said, "Tell Lily going blind has made no difference in my life."

He died the next morning before Mrs Hong had time to write the letter.

In writing to Lillian to tell her of her uncle's death, Mrs Hong could not decide what to tell her of the circumstances. Perhaps Teik Lock was telling the truth when he said that the blindness had made no difference in his life. On the other hand, he may have been lying in order to protect Lillian's feelings. If he had been lying, it would be wrong of her to convey his message to Lillian. Moreover, if he had been speaking the truth, would Lillian understand his message, or would she suppose that he had been lying? Besides, Mrs Hong pondered, if he had told the truth and if Lillian believed it, what then would be the purpose of the message? If his blindness had made no difference in his life, then it wouldn't be worth commenting on. At this thought, a tremor of horror confused her senses and she had to rise from her desk immediately, leaving the letter unwritten. When she finally wrote to Lillian, she told her that her uncle had died suddenly from a heart attack, but she made no mention of his blindness.

The Farmer's Wife

THE WOMAN came out of the door and stood a little way into the yard. She frowned, moving her lips from side to side as she turned her eyes first to the right of her and then to the left, then turned and stared ahead of her. A rutted path of hard packed earth rose between the swampy land, leading to the main road whose smooth flat surface she could discern faintly.

A scrawny cock strutted towards her with his neck thrust out. His cockscomb shook with each strut; he shook his long blue-black feathered tail, snapped at the dust and scratched the dry earth with his skinny yellow legs. A soldier, she thought. Look at his spurs, a true fighter.

The child who had been chasing the cock around and around the yard now stood still, observing the hard yellow bill snap at the upraised dust. He was brown from the sun and naked except for a small triangle of patched cloth attached by string around his neck and by another length of string tied around his waist. The child stood on one leg. He had recently learned how to do it and whenever he remembered to do so, he would stand perched on one leg with the other drawn up to the knee. He would stand in this position as if forever. But he soon tired and now the standing leg had lost its strength and he staggered like a drunken soldier reeling around the yard with his companion the cock.

The farmer had not returned yet although the sun stared high in the sky. It will be a good market day, he had said. Tomorrow was a big holiday, a Christian festival. The shoppers would buy much and would pay more. He had left before the sun came up in order to get a good spot in the market place and she had helped him load the large basket lashed to the back of the bicycle with cucumbers, greens, peppers, cabbages and four fat hens roped together securely by their feet.

She turned her eyes again to the left and to the right of her. The land was green and low where they had planted it with paddy, the two of them spading the hard earth, pumping the small waterwheel to flood the embanked area and stooping and stooping to firm the tender shoot in the wet sucking soil. Even then the work was not done.

There was no bicycle leaning against the wall by the door. The woman squinted towards the fields, moving her mouth from side to side, but she could see no one. She had thought he might have gone to the fields to examine the water level since there had been no rain for a week now. She would not wait for him to return, she decided, but she would take the child with her to pump the waterwheel and to turn up the vegetable beds where they planned to sow the pepper seeds.

It was a dry afternoon. The child picked up the large clods of earth she broke up with the spade and he crumbled them. Comfortably, he sat on the worked beds and pounded at the earth with his fists, impressed and pleased with his strength. From time to time she stopped the slow movements of thrust, turn over, thrust, to gaze around her. As the day grew later, her forward motion crept slower and slower; she rested longer and more often until finally she stopped altogether and stood quietly grasping the handle of the upright spade.

In this country, night comes quickly. She must cook the evening meal before it is dark and before her man comes home hungry. There was an unfamiliar urgency in the day's passing which till then had been so languid. Her thoughts which had followed the slow movements of her work, turning and turning, blanketed by the falling earth, suddenly shaped themselves. "I must cook the rice now," she spoke aloud, and, as if the sound of her voice released him from independence, the child began to whimper his weariness.

Ah, she had forgotten to feed him at midday. Now, sensing her sudden dismay and with hunger and weariness tumbling in his belly, he gave way to his grievance. Bellowing and staggering, he followed her home, until she picked him up and soothed him with her voice.

The child fell asleep immediately after he had eaten. He lay on the platform bed, naked from the waist down, his round well-formed head, newly shaven after his second birthday, twisted from the bedcloth. The woman sat by the table set against the wall and waited. Well, her man was complaining forever that she was slow, she had a trick like the buffalo, of looking ahead into the wind and standing still, but he was the slow one today. Shaking her head, she rose and returned the unfinished meal to the pot on the wood stove. She examined the lamp, lit the wick, replaced the glass cover, then set the lamp on the table. The meagre light flamed steadily.

She could not sleep yet. Perhaps, she thought, he had sold the hens for a large sum of money and had gone to Wong to offer for the land behind their house. But, no, it was low swampy land, good for paddy cultivation and it would cost more than they could pay for with some vegetables and hens. When he returned to his village in the mainland, he had looked for a farmer's daughter. He was not a gambler, nor was he a man for drinking foolishly. In this way the wife consoled herself for she could not sleep yet.

She had not slept without him for three years now, even when they were on the ship taking them from Canton to this country where he had a farm waiting. She remembered Canton still! A large city, and the people so busy and rude. Many cars, big buildings. They had gone to the park and walked along the lake and she had been afraid to talk to him.

There were some in her village who had said he made his money from piracy. It was true he was a strong well-built man who never spoke about his past. He spoke of the Japanese though, with hatred, and she knew he had fought them during the war. Otherwise he was pleasant and not too silent or too talkative. When she was carrying the child he had not allowed her to do the heavy work. When he saw it was a boy, she remembered, he laughed and bought wine for her to recover her strength. She sighed. The wick was burning low. She would lie beside the boy, she thought, and if he had not returned by midday tomorrow, she would go to the town and ask their clansmen where he was.

Outside, night had taken over the land. When the light in the house finally guttered out, the last outlines of the farm with its boarded coop and the low shapes of planted fields disappeared into the surrounding landscape as if returning into the swarming vegetation which had once stood there and which in daylight only had retreated a little way before the fields.

The cock woke her. Finding the door unlatched, he walked in and was roistering among the grains which had fallen to the hard dirt floor from the last evening's meal, wagging his comb in a fury of greed. The woman rose without waking the child. She went out to the well, dropped the tin bucket by its rope and stared down the rutted path towards the main road.

It was a pale morning. To the left of her, the cleared ground came up against a thick growth of jungle which, if she approached sufficiently near, was booming continuously with a wash of its populated world. There was the buzzing and ticking of insects, the rustle and snap of crawlers in the undergrowth and strange bird cries. To the right, the rice fields were embanked against a lower swampy area where the land was too sour to cultivate. It was an unhealthy place which gave out chills and fevers and from which, sometimes, if the wind blew the wrong way, foul swamp smells would find their way into the house. A long way down the left fork of the main road was the town of U.L., perhaps a four-hour walk away, or about fifteen miles.

The nearest acquaintance lived in the town itself. She frowned, thinking, "I will have to take the boy with me." Her heart began to knock against her chest like an animal in a cage. Slowly she hauled the bucket up, then set it carefully on the board over the well. It was as if she had lost her body's strength, she had become afraid so suddenly. It was strange she could hear no sound from the road which was travelled normally by trucks and clanking bicycles. There was absent too the familiar distant drone of the trains on the morning schedules, and as she pondered on the meaning of this desertion of sound in the world, it was suddenly important to be brisk. She could not tolerate the slow knocking fear against her ribs. No, she could not leave the child behind with only the cock for a companion.

By midday, she had washed and fed herself and the child. She had put on her best clothes, remembering he had told her it was a holiday. But it was a long way to the town, and when the car with the red-haired man in it passed by them, hours later it seemed to her, her neat blue *samfoo* was wet and streaked with dust and the child hung like a sack of turnips on her shoulder. The man stopped the car and got out to stare at the woman walking awkwardly along the dusty road with the heavy child slung on her hip. He had a red face, red hair and a uniform on, like a soldier's uniform, although he carried no weapon. He frowned as he watched them and she was afraid he would tell her to turn back since he stood so, obstructing her path with his large white-uniformed body. But he waved his hand, commanding her towards the back seat of the car, and with a sigh of fear, she obeyed and climbed in.

Clutching the child with one hand, she clung to the side of the seat with the other. This, she thought, may well be a missionary man, and now she wondered if he were also a devil who was taking her in order to eat up the child as she knew the missionaries used to do. The driver was bareheaded and thick red hairs stuck out of the back of his neck. The road was empty and the car flew down the smooth road with the wind flapping all around it, an evil sign. There was a stench in the air like a faint odour of disease. Terrorized by the speed and by the frowning stranger, she stared ahead and to the right and to the left of her in silence while the long-legged huts and crimson-blossomed bushes whirled around her, then dropped out of sight.

The car slowed down as it reached the town limits although the road showed as empty as before. On either side of the road the shops were shuttered. The stalls that had lined the sidestreets when she had come into town last for the New Year were gone. Above the red and black signs that read 'Coffee Shop', 'Barber Shop', 'Cloth Shop', the windows were shut. A bicycle lay on its side by a sidewalk. Otherwise the town appeared ordered. Only the uniform stillness in every street forebode anarchy. It was as if the Emperor of Heaven had died and had taken all the town people with him to the Underworld.

Misery, roared the car as the red-haired man gunned the engine. Misery, whimpered the child, pushing his smooth round head against her chest. Hearing the stranger grunt in reply to the whimper, she despaired. For the first time since she had left her village she mourned her coming away into foreign land.

Then they stood before the soldiers, waiting submissively while their guide addressed the sergeant. The boy clung to her as they walked up to examine the body laid out on the bench. The large grizzled head was twisted to show where he had been cut at the neck. She moved her lips from side to side and stared at the dried wound. There was the farm and the boy, she thought, and the cock pecking fiercely at the dust. The dead man's bony feet stuck out, brown, sinewy, with the dried mud still clinging to the soles. Frowning, she peeled a clod off the big toe. Now she had to take him and the boy home.

"Faugh!" the sergeant said to the Englishman. "These are truly foul-smelling, unfeeling, Godless people!" and he moved to eject the woman and her belongings from his station.

The Bridge

THE RIVER was only fifty feet wide, but a new bridge was being built. Gek Neo, on her way to visit Ah Koh, her father's sister, discovered that the construction men had already pulled down the wooden structure and broken the stone piles that anchored the ancient timbers. The unpainted boards, worn smooth and shiny by pedestrians and bicycle wheels, had been pried from their tracks, and black and white trestles now separated the site from the traffic flow.

No one was standing around idly watching. Gek Neo couldn't understand this, for in the town any minor event was an excuse for a curious crowd to gather. She herself loved to gape at any goings-on. On her brand-new Raleigh she rode everywhere, venturing to small corners wherever fire, accident, family tragedy or domestic violence was found.

No one was surprised at how quickly such news got around. The newspaper or bottle man carried it, or Beng the vegetable seller as he weighed a *kati* of *towgay* on his spring scales; the clerk dropping off her fat drooling baby with the wet-nurse next door; or the Ceylonese *roti* man counting change for two coconut buns. One of her brothers would hear of it at school, at the *mee siam* stall or by the ice *kacang*

120

cart as he sucked at the ball of sugared ice shavings in his frozen hand. Her father, introducing his mumbling immigrant clients to the proper big-shots in the Dutch-red government buildings, came home full of unofficial news. Sometimes, she simply came upon a crowd of onlookers and joined them, hanging back if it was a man beating a woman, and gawking at a mangled trishaw.

But here was the old bridge almost all torn down, and she hadn't heard of it! Pumping her pedals fast through Sulaiman Street, New Nation Road and Merdeka Bridge, she reached Ah Koh's house in just another ten minutes.

Ah Koh lived with her mother-in-law in a mouldering rubber-merchant's shop squeezed into a row of narrow houses. Kitchens and outhouses jutted over the dirty river. The front room where Ah Koh's husband bought and sold high quality pressed rubber was usually empty except for a scale and an impressive glass-topped desk. Today, leaning her bicycle against the tiled wall by the five-foot-way, Neo saw Ah Koh's husband sitting by the desk and staring out at the street. His figure was a heavy blob after the dazzling sunshine outside, and timidly she bobbed her head in his direction, not daring to address him in her faltering Hokkien.

Quickly she ran into his mother's kingdom.

Ah Mah was almost always to be found sitting or standing by the open-air courtyard, its marble floor stained with rain, among the enormous brown fired pots of dwarf bamboo. If sitting she had a leg up and foot tucked under, a string of prayer beads in her fat paw, for she was a very pious woman. If standing she was brushing her teeth, which Ah Koh told Neo she did at least ten times a day for five minutes each time. Prayers and brushing her teeth marked her day, hours that revolved around morning and evening offerings at the ancestral altar. Joss was always burning before the tinted portrait of her dead husband; and every evening the dead man was served a full meal of rice, soy chicken and whiskey.

Say 'Ah Mah', Ah Koh urged Neo each time she came to visit, and dutifully she dunked her head and called while looking away at the blackwood furniture, "Ah Mah!" The old woman spat out a mouthful of foaming paste on the grey marble floor. Gek Neo imagined her a powerful queen termite, pale, sluggish, squatting in a dark hole, vibrating as little bugs stroked and fed her. Ah Koh was terrified of her mother-in-law, for whom she fetched, washed, cooked, cleaned, mended, sewed, nodded and nodded, and Neo, who didn't admire her aunt at all, was just as afraid in her tomboy's heart.

So she visited Ah Koh just once a week, on Saturday, and then only from two to three, the hour after lunch had been cooked and cleared and before Ah Koh began preparations for the evening meal and altar services. It meant cycling in the most piercing heat of the day, when even the Chinese *kedai* dropped their cane and plastic awnings and the shopkeepers napped. Neo did not mind the open blazing sun. Her legs, arms and face had long ago darkened to a Tamil shine, and she cycled in the afternoons when all the townspeople snoozed under shade, with a delicious sense of freedom she did not feel at any other time.

The only reason she visited Ah Koh, Neo admitted to herself, was for her books. Hidden in the evil-smelling sooty kitchen Ah Koh kept a pure and simple heart. Given away to her husband's family at two, raised to be a proper daughter-in-law, married at fourteen, she had not been able to have a child. No one thought the fault was in her husband, for Ah Koh was a scrawny woman whose loose *samfoo* showed no sign of breasts. After six years the husband was encouraged to find a concubine. That was the end of Ah Koh's marriage. But even after the second concubine with whom he now lived in Bukit Kechil, there was no male child, and old mother-in-law finally adopted Ah Koh's nephew, one of eight boys, whose bright eyes and thick black hair marked him as particularly healthy and clever. How Ah Koh loved the boy! But now he was seven he did not want to have anything to do with her, for he had learned that Ah Mah controlled the coins, candies and fruits and that he could play outdoors all day after school and never have to say hello to Ah Koh as long as he gave Ah Mah his sweetest smile. Neo knew all this and despised Ah Koh for loving Chang who pinched her when she tried to kiss him and kicked her in the calf when she didn't get him his iced drink quickly enough.

"Look!" Ah Koh said lovingly, pulling up her black trouser leg to show mauve bruises. "Look what the *samseng* Chang did to me today. How strong he's growing!"

Neo did not admire Ah Koh, but they shared a secret vice. Ah Koh had a small allowance for clothes, soap, powder, hairpins, the little possessions women accumulated like their body scents. But whereas most women hoarded their money to buy gold chains and jade amulets, Ah Koh spent it recklessly on romances. In her tiny private bedroom above the kitchen with just enough space for a *kang* and *almeira,* she saved stacks of paperbacks and magazines. She kept her life pure reading and re-reading romances in which the heroine struggled through hurricanes, deserts, crevices, faceless masses, to fall into the arms of a lord, a millionaire travelling incognito, a handsome passionate stranger. Ah Koh loaned her romances stingily, counting them out and eagerly welcoming them back. After the first greeting, they retreated to the bedroom, pushed the pillows and blankets off the *kang,* and sat down with copies of her collection.

"Tell me what you think of *The Dark Deliverance?*" Ah Koh asked, her bony face beaming.

How had she learned English in the first place, Neo wondered, for Ah Koh had never been sent to school.

It was love at first sight, Ah Koh told her. When she first saw a *True Romances* magazine clipped to a rope among comic books and newspapers in Kutty's stall, she had fallen in love with the cover that showed a slim girl embraced by a distinguished gentleman. She bought the copy, carried it home, rolled up discreetly, in her shopping basket, and somehow, she had learned to read it.

"How?" Neo asked.

But Ah Koh could never tell her.

Neo knew she was not as simple as her aunt. She didn't really believe these romances. They were like eating peanuts, an addictive pleasure that she put away, three books at a sitting. Real boys were nothing like the heroes in *True Romances*. They were poor, shy, scruffy, when they weren't bossy and mean-mouthed about easy girls. Life was not at all like romances, and was perhaps preferable. It was topsy-turvy, you could lead it where you wanted it to go, like on a bicycle, and the laterite lane might end in a friend's house, the garbage-strewn path at the cheapest and most delicious *rojak* stall, just as in Ah Koh's little cage you found the largest stacks of romances in town. There was nothing common between life and romances as there was nothing common between herself and Ah Koh, she thought, as she turned to wave goodbye one last time to poor Ah Koh's miserable face before pedalling off toward the wooden bridge.

Neo ran in breathlessly hardly acknowledging Ah Mah seated in her grotesque blackwood armchair and clicking her prayer beads. Usually Ah Koh would be resting upstairs, but today she was in the kitchen stirring a giant *kwali* in which chunks of chicken bobbed in hot oil. All four *dapurs* were smoking, and steam rose in miniature clouds from the bubbling pots. Ah Koh's face was more pinched than ever, and her normally flapping *samfoo* was stuck to her back with sweat.

Surprised, both stared at each other.

"Oh, Neo, sorry, I don't have time to talk."

"Today a special feast day?"

"No," Ah Koh lowered her voice, "I'm cooking for the workmen."

"What workmen?"

"The men building the bridge." Ah Koh pushed her hair back into its bun with her left hand, and stirred the meat in the black wok with the spatula held in her right hand.

"But why are you cooking for them? Are they paying you?"

124

"Neo! How can say that! I am not servant. No, two days ago the *kapitan* come to see Siew, very frightening man. He say we must give something to his men, otherwise bad luck come to us and the new bridge. Siew say workmen very bad men, not Chinese or Malay or Indian. Maybe Siamese or Bugis or what not. All very fierce, carry *parang,* and have bad *datuk* to protect them. What to do? Siew say we must do what the *kapitan* want, so we promise to give men their *makan.*"

Ah Koh flipped the frying chicken expertly, covered the wok with a steamer cover, and picking up two pieces of rags, picked the wok off the *dapur* and set it, wobbling slightly, on the concrete counter that ran along one wall. "There, all done." The fire in the clay stove hissed and steamed as she poured a handful of water over it.

"How long are you cooking for these men? Are you going to do all the work by yourself? Ah Koh, you'll fall sick." A throb of indignation banged against Neo's chest, and her eyes stung from the steam and anger. "You know, this is corruption. The *kapitan* has no right to extort food. You should report this to the police immediately."

"Shhhh!" Ah Koh looked at the doorway. "Don't say anything." She pressed her lips tightly together and shook her head from side to side.

"Well, look at you, you look sick already. How long can you go on like this? It's bad enough you have to slave for your family, but these men are not your responsibility, I don't see why your husband …"

"Stop!" Ah Koh gripped her hands together in front of her face. "You will get me into trouble, you bad girl. You don't live here so how you know what is like for me? Is my fate, my mother-in-law very strict, and I have to follow old ways, but what can I do? Soon they will finish building the bridge, and I can stop cooking."

Neo swallowed hard. Perhaps Ah Koh was right. She was a schoolgirl, she knew nothing about selling rubber, she couldn't even cook. But again, the sting of indignation! It came from nowhere unless from her heart. Her head felt heavy as if a metal hat had been set on it. She tried to think through the weight of the hat.

"Ah Koh, why didn't your husband offer the *kapitan* something else? Why do you always have to do the work?"

"But what else am I good for? I only know how to cook and clean. Anyway, Siew has no money. Business very bad nowadays, everything slow down. Maybe he bring second family to live here also. If he give money how to manage the rent? Don't think we are the only ones who are caught. Everyone on this street also have to cough up. Ong Yin Chin, the big *towkay* at end of street, I hear he give few thousand dollars. Even Mrs Wan, she got no money, she give her jade earrings. We lucky the *kapitan* see Siew's business not doing well and take *makan* only. Everyday only few dollars extra."

Neo thought of Mr Blake. her school principal. He was an Englishman and she was sure he would not agree with Ah Koh. This wasn't bad luck, this was unfair. How could this happen now, when in school they learned about justice and democracy, when Mr Blake himself picked the strictest and most unbending student for prefects and himself punished every student who stole or cheated? Surely, if the police knew about the matter, they'd put a stop to it.

Ah Koh must have read her expression, for she said in a low vehement voice, "You mustn't tell anyone about this, you know nothing about wicked men, what they can do. Swear before Tua Peh Kong you won't tell anyone, you must swear." Gripping Neo's shoulder, she turned her toward the corner where the figure of Tua Peh Kong in thickly outlined robes sat spread-kneed, drawn on red paper and pasted to the wall. "Quick, put your hands together and swear."

"I won't," Neo muttered, twisting easily out of the grasping hand. "Besides I don't believe in Tua Peh Kong, so what's the use of making me swear?"

"You are too modern, Neo, will get you into trouble." Ah Koh couldn't keep up the fight long. "But you better stay away from bridge. You know, every time they build bridge they make sacrifice to the *datuk*," she whispered, "human sacrifice."

"How can, lah? This is modern times, even in New Guinea no more headhunters. The *kapitan* is a gangster, extorting money. How can you read books and don't know the world has changed? Everyone has to obey the laws now. This is 1959!" Angrily she added, "Here, take back your books."

"Wait, wait, my hands are oily," Ah Koh cried.

Neo picked the books up from the greasy floor and wiped the stained covers remorsefully with her school skirt.

"Never mind, don't dirty your uniform." Ah Koh took the books away from her. "Always so untidy, I don't know why your father won't remarry. Why be a widower so long? Not good for you without a mother, running around like wild girl. Black like Indian, who's going to marry you when you so wild?"

For a moment Neo was abashed. Ah Koh never minded her rude talk; there was sometimes an orange saved for her or a handful of offees secretly taken from Chang's store. Sometimes Ah Koh would fumble with her beaded purse and find a twenty-cent coin. Neo usually left with more than borrowed books. Before she could retort that she was not interested in marriage, Chang was shouting from the courtyard, "Ma, Ma, I want ice water," and Freddie de Cruz was laughing in crazy jerks.

"Sorry, Neo, no time today," Ah Koh said as she fetched a glass of water from the flowered thermos.

"Where's my water?" Chang yelled. "Ma, Ma!"

"Get me some too," Freddie said. Although a Eurasian, he was Ah Mah's favourite because he spoke Hokkien to Chang, and Ah Koh waited on Freddie because Chang and he were inseparable.

Neo glared at Freddie as she passed him. "No manners," she muttered, but he only stuck his tongue out at her. "Eurasian you!" she said and was immediately ashamed. Freddie rolled his eyes, and continued to buzz around the courtyard.

Neo cycled to the library, furious with the streets for being dull and empty. There was nothing she wanted among the shabby, dirty one-story shopfronts whose iron gates were now pulled to the sides She was the only person in the library except for the librarian writing in his ledger. She found a novel about a woman rescued from a shipwreck by a Tuareg sheik that she had read last year. The librarian wrote her card number on his ledger and stamped the date with a bang.

Once home, leaning the rattan armchair back with her feet planted on the wall, she could not enjoy the novel. In place of the astonishingly blue-eyed hero, descendent of Crusading knights washed up on the Tunisian shore, she saw small dark men in tattered shorts, bare torsos shining with sweat and coconut oil. The short muscular men shook their *parangs* menacingly and pointed to their mouths. They encircled her, her hair crinkled from the heat. Then she felt a sudden relief. The fire was coming from a *dapur,* and she was not going to be burned. She was only cooking a meal, gratefully, in exchange for her life.

Her legs slipped off the wall as the chair righted itself and she woke up. The dream worried her, she couldn't hold on to the images. The dark men danced around in her mind then faded till all she could remember was the terrible fear of dying and the relief at understanding she was saved. She knew the dream had something to do with the bridge. She would have to do something to help Ah Koh, but what? Her father was in the government offices every day, handling forms in triplicates, paying stamp money, and translating English rules and laws to his Chinese clients, but he was only a petition-writer and a Straits-born Chinese whom no one paid any attention to.

But Mr Blake had blue eyes and a white skin, like the Tuareg sheik. He was the only white man she knew. As a white man, surely he would be able to do something about the *kapitan's* extortions.

The next day she waited for Mr Loh's history class to be excused. Mr Loh, barely her height, had a fine sensitive face in which doubt, frankness, hurt and delight showed so clearly that all his students believed themselves at liberty to bully him. He never remembered their wrongs but saw them as children to be pitied for the poverty of their society. Neo knew this about him, that he pitied her, and she took advantage of him whenever possible.

Instead of heading for the girls' toilets, she took the corridor to the principal's office, a room no one entered except for bad news, punishment or signatures. She didn't stop to ask for permission from Mutu, Mr Blake's clerk, who was at the filing cabinet.

Mr Blake was sitting at his desk behind a stack of papers. Seeing her, he reached for his pipe, surprised, and asked calmly, "What do you want?"

She broke straight into the matter. "I have an aunt who lives near Ho Seng Bridge."

Mr Blake sucked on his unlit pipe. Driving to work he had watched the old bridge being torn down. In just a few days the gang of half-naked men had constructed a new frame. As for the pupil, the form master had brought her to his notice earlier that year. She behaved as if she had certain rights, quite forgetting she was only a student, he had complained. Recalling the conversation, Mr Blake banged his pipe against the ashtray.

He had once debated at Oxford for independence for the colonies. He had been twenty-six when the war began, and after the killing stopped he decided to teach in Malaya to help the people prepare for home rule. But in the ten years he'd been in the Malayan Civil Service he'd met many Malayans who didn't seem comfortable with him. Everyone jumped when they saw him, peons, form masters, gardeners, policemen, the barman at the Club and the Cold Storage manager. He decided to listen to the child who had come into his office without a please or excuse me.

"The workmen are extorting money and food from the houses near the bridge."

"Were you asked to tell me this?"

"People are afraid to complain." She knew she was lying, and imagined Ah Koh's hand shaking her shoulder. Was she wrong to tell him secrets no one wanted talked about? As he struck a match and held it to his pipe, she said quickly, "May I go now, sir?" and when he nodded, she jumped out of the office and trotted swiftly back to class.

Three days later John Leung told her during recess that a bridge worker had drowned. "He was carrying a stack of rods, you know, and when he fell off the beam, the rods fell on top and knocked him unconscious."

Neo's fried *mee hoon* stuck in her throat.

"The strangest thing, the workmen didn't even stop for half-an-hour. Someone fished him out and took him to the hospital. Too late, lah, but the men went on working. Just like that!"

"What do you expect they'd do, say a Mass for him?" John was set to attend a seminary after sixth form, and Neo's wild jibes showed that she, at least, took his faith seriously.

"I don't know, perhaps they could have taken the rest of the day off?"

"Silly John!" Neo was unsettled. She remembered Ah Koh's hiss, "Human sacrifice!" and refused to be softened. "Accidents happen all the time."

"But the man died!"

"Go say a Mass for him," she sneered, knowing she was being wicked, and left the table to sit with Jenny who only talked about boys and make-up.

After school she bicycled to Ah Koh's house. Ah Koh was upstairs reading a newly arrived paperback, *The Dark Mills,* and Neo laughed nervously when she saw it.

Ah Koh got up hurriedly from the *kang.* "Neo! I'm resting before cooking *makan.*"

"Where's Chang?" Neo asked, not wanting to appear to know more than she should.

"So sad, Chang went to Port Dickson for a week with Freddie's family. Old mother-in-law refused, but he begged and begged, so she said yes, and now he won't be back till Monday."

"How can he leave school like that?" Neo felt a faint envy. She never missed school except once when she was too young to remember and had the measles.

"Freddie's grandfather's eightieth birthday. The family has a house in Port Dickson, so big family reunion. Uncle from Ceylon, two aunties from Portugal, and so many cousins from Penang. Even one from Medan. So surely school excuse Freddie."

Neo didn't ask why the school should also excuse Chang. "Why you're not cooking today?" she said, coming to the point.

"Eh?" Ah Koh was puzzled.

Neo thought impatiently that Ah Koh's sorrows were as insubstantial as the romances in her room.

"You mean the workmen?" Ah Koh lowered her voice and reluctantly put the book down. "The *mata-mata* came one day asking everybody if got complaint against workmen. Siew talk to *mata-mata*. Don't know how they find out about *kapitan*."

Neo smiled. She knew but she wouldn't tell anyone. It was a secret between Mr Blake and herself. She had the power to change things, not like John with his Masses or Ah Koh and Jenny with their dreams of romances.

"So?" she prompted.

"So no one said anything. Siew said no complaint, Mr Ong said no complaint. No one want trouble with the *kapitan*."

"You mean everyone was afraid!" Neo exulted.

"No, but why make trouble? Bridge almost finished. Soon the men will leave. Very difficult to build a bridge. Got bad spirits in the river try to stop people from breaking nature. Nature say river must flow. *Datuk* angry if we break the river flow. Bridge is not nature thing, so we make sacrifice to keep *datuk* happy."

"I didn't know you believe all this *datuk* superstition! You *pai-pai* for mother-in-law every day, have no life of your own!"

"Never mind, we respect our ancestors. If we don't, how our children respect us when we dead?" Neo was astonished to hear the pity in Ah Koh's voice. "You too young to know right. Right is very difficult, like the bridge. Old ways hard, but if don't have them, what can have? You have luckier life, learn to be doctor or teacher, but all same work. You will learn to *pai-pai* some day."

Fancy Ah Koh preaching to her when she had saved her from all that work! "Well, how come you're not cooking today?" she asked contemptuously.

"After *mata-mata* come, I think the kapitan got warning. Two days they never come for food, so much wasted, *sayang!* So Siew say today no need to cook, *mata-mata* stop them."

"Aren't you happy about that? Now you don't have to slave every minute."

"True, true," Ah Koh stretched her arms above her head. "Today catch up my reading, feel like *towkay's* wife, can shake leg."

Ah Koh has no idea, Neo thought, her life is nothing! Chang will throw her out of the house like a piece of rubbish as soon as he is old enough, which is all she deserves.

"But why you come today?" Ah Koh took her hand affectionately. "Something wrong at home?"

"I forgot to borrow books the last time." Neo willed her hand to be cold and still.

"Yes, yes," Ah Koh went eagerly to the *almeira*. "Which one you haven't read? I got new ones, from Picadilly."

Neo regretted her excuse. Now she would have to visit Ah Koh one more time to return the books. But she didn't want to see her again. Ah Koh was never going to change, she would always remain a wretched reader in her smoky old bedroom.

Turning to leave, she asked casually, "Did you hear about the man who drowned?"

"Shhh!" Ah Koh sat down with a thump on the *kang* and clutched her blouse near her heart. "Some things never talk about!"

132

"Oh, O.K." As she climbed down the steep stairs she said over her shoulder, "I have School Sports on Saturday, so I won't come then."

Although she wasn't athletic, Neo loved School Sports Day. There was free Ovaltine, ice-cold from a tapped barrel, and she ducked in and out of the ropes that held back the spectators. Sports Day ended at five with the presentation of trophies. Mr Blake stood in starched white shirt, a grey and maroon striped tie, and long pants, and introduced Puan Fatimah Hashim, the Deputy Minister's wife, soft and dumpy in red and gold *baju kurung* and white jasmine in her hair, who gave away the prizes. It was the best School Sports Day ever, Neo decided. Mr Blake had respected her speaking up. It was true, life belonged to people who stuck to the race, ran the fastest and acted on what was right. Next Sunday the Chief Minister would cut the ribbon and declare the bridge opened and she would ride over its smooth tarmac.

But the morning before the bridge ceremony the wet nurse next door, cradling a baby over her half-opened *samfoo,* said that a decapitated head had been found under the bridge. "No, I tell you it's true, a coolie unloading a boat kicked the gunny sack and the head rolled out."

Neo's head ached. It was too horrible to be true, like a Hitchcock movie, when frightful things happened just to scare you. But here was fat Liew Seng placidly describing the decapitated head while the newest baby was trying to get her nipple into his mouth.

"Everyone saying the head offer to *datuk* to keep bridge standing. Wah, so many superstitious people still, so many still worship *Syaitan.*" Liew Seng jiggled the baby as he squirmed, then let him turn his face to her breast. "I don't believe but *bodoh* people all crazy." She patted the baby's buttocks as he began to suckle greedily. "This baby grow up to be leader, can find milk all time."

"Blind and superstitious like everyone else!" Neo thought of the New Government School, how busy yet orderly it was, of the School

133

Sports Day prize ceremony, of economics and the laws of demand and supply, things known and mapped out. Surely one couldn't believe in demons nowadays.

As she pedalled past Sulaiman Street and New Nation Road to Ah Koh's house, it seemed to her that the town was filled with mumbo-jumbo, with Masses, *pai-pai,* joss-sticks, ancestors, *datuks,* romances, sacrifice. Pushing the pedals hard, she thought, it may be someone I know, Ah Koh's husband or Chang. Or Ah Koh. Oh God, she thought, Ah Koh with her romances and ancestors, the perfect victim! Her eyes pricked with tears. But of course she was being sentimental. Who would hurt poor simple Ah Koh?

She slowed down as she came into Ah Koh's street, half-expecting a mob at her house. But the street was in its usual Saturday torpor. Leaning the bicycle against the wall, she ran in through the empty courtyard. "Ah Koh," she said with relief as her aunt came out through the narrow kitchen door.

Ah Koh held a handkerchief which she rubbed against her eyes, red puffs of wept-out holes.

Neo heard sounds like an engine stalling, ugh, ugh. "What happened?"

"Chang, he …" She stopped to rub her face with the balled-up handkerchief.

Neo imagined Chang lying in a coffin, his head resting on a raw neck. Briefly she thought of Mr Blake, what he would make of her aunt, a bag of bones more soft-hearted than any English Romantic, among sesame oil and soy bottles. What could be right for her? Chang was first in her life, the baby she never had, and now he was dead. What was right against what was needed or simply given?

"Freddie got in accident, broke his leg. The doctor say maybe many months before can walk, and Chang crying so hard …"

"Oh thank God!" Relief flooded Neo's hot perspiring body. "I thought the workmen had killed Chang." Then, understanding the cruelty of her words, she began to cry, gulping sobs, for herself, for Ah Koh, for Chang and Freddie, and for the poor body severed from its life.

Thirst

JAMES THAMBY MCNAIR was tired. When he was tired he wanted a drink, preferably a foaming glass of Anchor. But his second daughter had just returned from Leeds last Tuesday and she was waiting for him. He wasn't in a hurry to meet her. Fleur had always been a proud girl, and he was afraid she would find him a disappointment after all the English gentlemen she'd met. But he knew his duty, so he told Mohan, the estate lorry driver, to drop him off at the house.

Five houses stood at the end of the rutted laterite lane. Here, in the common compound, Saturday afternoons were like market days. The Wong family next door had its mahjong party going, four elderly men banging plastic tiles on the brown-paper-covered table on the front porch for all the world to hear. The Cantonese family on the left was swarmed with a litter of relatives; some pop-song blared from the uncurtained windows and half-a-dozen children screeched and clambered over the verandah railings like wild monkeys.

James preferred the two-room cinder-block shelter Mr Watson, the estate manager, had given for his use. Hidden among tall mango trees behind the big house, it looked like a concrete bunker, cool with the sweltering cool of stone under leaves, and quiet. Mrs Watson's two children were seldom around, the older girl away at the Convent boarding school, and the four-year-old, shepherded by the *amah,* allowed to play only in the front garden which was planted with purple bougainvillea, fancy golden canna, and white climbing roses adapted to the tropics.

Mr Williams, the previous planter, had settled the back clearing with guava, mango, papaya and banana trees, but it was now overgrown; the *kebun* said he had found snakes, scorpions and giant poisonous spiders there. It was no use telling Mrs Watson that the *kebun* sold the fruit to the Chinese *kedai* in town, she never ate local fruits. It was no use giving newly arrived English any local knowledge, they never understood one's reasons for telling.

James bore no ill-will toward the Watsons. They were nicer than Mr Williams who drank too much. Mr Williams yelled at him every time a tapper got sick and couldn't work, as if it was his fault there was malaria in the estate. Or that a viper had bitten Valasingham or that Balakrishnan had slashed Sulu almost to ribbons for fooling with his daughter. He was sure Sulu was done for, he hadn't wanted to take him to the hospital to save the doctor the trouble of stitching up a dead man, but Tamil tappers have the constitution of elephants. You couldn't kill them if you tried to, and now Sulu was married with a new born daughter. Pity.

That was two years ago. When he felt the thirst he could only fight it by brooding on his past.

"Why don't you pray, Daddy?" Rosa had pleaded, challenging him with her grave brown eyes. Among his five children she was the one who made him most uncomfortable and whom he loved best. Sweet quiet Rosa, silent as a mouse when it came to complaints. Yet she was the only one who questioned him while the others nagged and yakked at his faults, his shortcomings and his sins. "The trouble with you is ..." Miriam said, and he felt a weariness, not sorrow or remorse. But when Rosa asked, "Why don't you pray, Daddy?" he wanted to weep, to apologize for being such a hopeless fool, and an unbeliever.

Rosa prayed for him. Every night, squeezing her eyes shut the better to concentrate on the Virgin Mary standing in the corner of the living room in blue and white plaster robes, she prayed intently for him. When she was five and hadn't learned to pray silently he'd hear her pipe, "Please save Daddy and make him believe." He knew she was still making the same prayer. So when she overcame her shyness, her delicate hesitation in fear of hurting his feelings, to ask, "Why don't you pray?" he felt the tremble of an answer on his lips.

He could tell her he didn't believe in a great white god in the sky. That, although he was supposed to be some kind of medical man, he was, like all men, a fraud. The powders, lotions and ointments he gave out were like talismans the Hindus tied around their wrists or the disgusting bugs the Chinese dried and boiled. He was cheaper than doctors, and in proportion to their salaries, he knew much less than them. Salve, iodine, aspirin, cough mixtures, any pair of hands could dole them out. The dispenser's place in the estate was that of a medicine man, to reassure the tappers the planter cared enough to pay someone to dab their cuts and bandage their wounds. He was a fraud, but he would never tell Rosa this, for it would break her heart to think of her father bound for hell.

Today the anticipation of Rosa's angelic smile didn't raise his black mood. The dispensary had been busy all morning, the estate children were down with some kind of flu, and he had only aspirin to give out. Mr Watson had called the hospital. It had supplies of antibiotics, but a doctor was needed to prescribe it. Mohan was to fetch Dr Kandiah after he dropped James home. All over again the memory of his hopes as a medical student returned and taunted him, like the doctors he had worked for, in their white coats and black stethoscopes coiled around their necks, ordering him to fetch, sweep, weigh and measure.

Throwing himself on the sagging cushions of the rattan settee, he said to Miriam, "I'm home."

She was sitting with crossed feet on the cane lounge, humming softly to herself. "Hello, dear," she smiled absently.

"I'm home," he repeated and waited for her to tell him the week's news. The crashing of mahjong tiles came in through one window. Screams and sobs as if someone was having his head bashed in came through another. "Where's everybody?"

"Oh, Fleur took them for a drive with Manikam," she smiled, even more pleased with herself.

James felt sour. He hadn't had to hurry home, and Miriam, being so pleased about something, wouldn't have minded a little beer on his breath today. "Who's Manikam? First time I've heard of him."

"Sixth Form teacher at the Government School. B.A. Economics."

"What's he doing with our Fleur?"

His daughters were too religious for James. There Lily was, a Carmelite nun in some barren bog in Ireland, forbidden to write to her parents except once during Christmas. And Rosa, his lamb, dreaming of entering the novitiate. Fleur was less prayerful, but even she had shunned boys. He didn't know if he approved of her taking up with a teacher so quickly.

"Did Gloria go with them?" Forgotten Gloria whom they had not really wanted. After three girls, Miriam prayed every Novena for a son. But Gloria came instead, and Miriam had named her not after a flower like the others but after God, who knew better. "Glory be to His name," she had said through dry lips when the midwife brought the fourth daughter to her bed, and quickly crossed herself as if to ward off an evil wish.

"And John?" John, Beloved of the Lord, who finally arrived twelve years ago. James felt the usual pain when he said his name, for it was John who had severed Miriam from him. Lying in the rumpled bed with the acrid smell of afterbirth and carbolic soap, she had told him, "That's enough now."

He'd thought she meant enough childbirth and he heartily agreed with her. The cry for a boy, a boy, was mad. Five children in thirteen years. She was too old for the last one, over thirty-five. He found she'd meant it was enough of bed. The passionate yielding girl he'd run off with against his parents' wishes, leaving behind his medical studies, to come to the Malayan jungle to labour as a lowly dispenser, was a mirage of his youth.

From their first coupling had come pale devout Lily, studious, painfully shy, wanting only silence and the white god. To marry Miriam he'd signed a contract that their children would be raised in her faith. After the first-born it was easy to say goodbye to all the others. Every single one of them had been her child, and her faith had guarded them against him.

He hadn't been angry over their separation. When she refused him the right to her bed after John's birth, it was as if he was saying goodbye to yet another thing in his life, beginning with his goodbye to his mother who had lifted her head up high with no tears when he left with Miriam on the boat for Klang.

"Is this the way to treat a hard-working blighter?" he roared. The thirst swirled in him like dust. He coughed, trying to make it sound bad and deep in his chest. "Slave all day with a flu epidemic, and come home with no one to say hello to their father."

Miriam repeated, "They've gone for a drive. Manikam has a new Opel."

"Who is this Manikam?" he repeated petulantly.

"Oh, Holy Saints! I told you ..."

"I know, Sixth Form teacher, B.A. Economics. But what is he doing with my family?"

Miriam glared at him and he felt much better. She gathered her *sari*, a pale green flowered nylon, much better than the old torn *saris* she usually wore around the house, and shook the upper folds. "He's been seeing Fleur."

"How can he be seeing Fleur when she's just come back from England?"

"Not just come back. She's been back for almost a week." She gave another smile, settled back on the lounge chair and looked

140

happily at her feet.

"I see, they must have been seeing each other for a week." The sarcasm caught in his throat so he had to cough again in a pitiful manner.

"Her old teacher, Mrs Chan, gave a tea-party for her on Tuesday and she and Mani got along very well. He's been visiting her everyday." She smiled some more.

"It's Mani, is it? Every day for the last four days?"

"I'm sure if you saw them together you'll know what I mean." She hummed an old Indonesian lullaby, and as she didn't know the words she kept repeating the first line. *"Nina bobo ... oh oh ni i i na bobo ..."*

James got to his feet. "I'm going for a drink."

Miriam looked happily at him. "Why don't you wait for them to return? Then Mani and you can go for a drink."

When they'd first married he'd been too busy making a living to think about drinks. He'd worked for his father's cousin as an orderly. Although his family had disowned him, his father had written to a cousin, Winston McNair, M.B.B.S., to consider James for his medical office. Dr McNair was only too pleased to train him for his dispensary. As Miriam often said, where else could he have found such a brainy orderly (almost a M.B.B.S. himself if he'd finished his medical studies) for so little money? After Rosa, Miriam grew more devout, so devout he spent more time listening to family prayers than enjoying her body. He discovered a few beers could make him feel almost as good as Miriam used to. But how she'd fought over those bottles, sometimes enough to welcome him back to bed.

The tickle in his throat grew stronger. Fumbling with the change in his pocket he walked down the hot red-stone lane, past the mahjong clashes and children's wails, towards the corner coffee shop by the main road. He didn't hear Miriam's yelp of disapproval. Leaning on the grey marble tabletop he poured an icy golden stream out of the sweaty bottle and drank it thirstily. The tight grip on his Adam's apple loosened. He breathed deeply of the sweet malty air. How easy it was to feel good about oneself. He'd go home when he'd finish the bottle.

Miriam was furious when James walked out just like that, but she was a fair woman. He'd hurried home for Fleur and was disappointed to find the children gone. She'd told Fleur to wait for her father, but Fleur wasn't to be reasoned with, not with the dazzle in her eyes that saw the world in only one light.

Manikam had been done for as soon as Fleur had seen him. Two years in England had done that to her, the men who had chatted her up but stayed away because she was dark and because she wouldn't give herself away. She was always proud and choosy, always careful who she'd spend time with. She had filled out in England, breasts and hips and calves, but the men hadn't come to her. The hours she'd spent alone in the cold library or with the plain old maids in the cinema or washing her nylons and drinking a cup of tea by herself in her bedsittingroom, all because she was dusky. A child had told her that her skin was like the brown shiny shells of garden snails, and she almost slapped her.

No wonder once home she fell immediately for the first man who didn't think twice about her colour. She fascinated Manikam, and not only because she had just returned from England. There was the red curl of her mouth, the faint muzzy hairs that grew on her upper lip, the bony sweep of her jaw. He told her on Friday how much he liked her. Her eyes shone like a steady signal, then she dropped them, but he'd seen that she'd returned his feelings.

Fortunately, Mani's family was in Penang; he could spend every free hour with her. Not that her mother was careless about Fleur. She wasn't like his Hindu parents who kept his sisters away from a man's passionate glances, but Aunt Miriam was a strict Catholic and she made sure they were never alone for long. He'd made a big thing about meeting Fleur's father, for he was certain he would be asking him for permission to marry her.

142

It was almost an hour before the children returned. The three younger ones were flushed with the wind that had blown through the open car windows, and Mani and Fleur were slow and heavy with an equal rhythm of something ripening under the lid of a bin, like yeast, making them smell richer and stronger.

"Where's Daddy?" Rosa asked.

"He went to the coffee shop." Miriam gave a helpless shrug.

"Oh no!" Rosa knew what that meant.

"He waited and waited for you," Miriam said to Fleur as if to deflect Rosa's disappointment from herself.

But Fleur wasn't angry. She felt energetic and heavy all at the same time. She couldn't be angry with her dad, she was too full of the milk of human kindness, she thought, and wished she were still in Mani's car smelling the new vinyl interior and watching the red hibiscus bushes and thick Malayan trees flash by. All the while she'd been aware of Mani's strong dark arms beside her, his large spread of hands on the wheel, with the black hairs springing up on the backs and the pale pink palms deftly spinning and spinning the wheel as the engine hummed.

"Let's have tea," she offered, wanting to reward those hands that had brought her all the way to Tanjong Bidara to look at the fishing boats.

"I'll fetch Daddy," Rosa offered.

"Yes, he'll want his tea." Miriam opened her purse quickly. "Buy some *kaya* and a loaf of bread, we only have stale bread from yesterday." She flashed Rosa a warning frown.

"I'll get him." Manikam was at the door. "Tell me where the coffee shop is. And I'll get some cakes for tea."

As Rosa shook her head, he appealed to Fleur, "I could do with the walk, not enough exercise, you know, after getting the car. I really want to meet your father, man to man, you know."

Fleur knew what he meant. A few beers on Daddy's breath wouldn't affect Mani's intentions, it might even put him at ease. Besides he was sure to like Daddy's looks, for Daddy was tall and fair, almost like an Englishman, and his face, except for the light brown colour, was exactly that of an Englishman's.

Daddy took after his grandfather, Andrew McNair, a Scottish planter who had married a Sinhalese girl from an aristocratic Buddhist family. Daddy's father was as white as could be, but he'd married a Tamil girl whom he'd met at the Anglican Church. Not too many Ceylonese were Anglicans, Daddy said, which accounted for the fact that Great-grandfather McNair took to the Thamby family. But when Daddy fell in love with a Catholic Sinhalese, his father wouldn't accept the match. Daddy couldn't understand why not, since there was every other kind of religion in the family. His father said Buddhists and Anglicans shared a common civil spirit, but Hindus and Catholics were outside the pale. Daddy was only nineteen when he ran away with Mommy, and the Medical College wouldn't take him back. Grandfather sent them off to Malaya and never saw them again. Daddy was funny about his life in Ceylon, usually he wouldn't talk about it at all.

"Oh tell him where the coffee shop is," Fleur said carelessly. "Daddy wouldn't want a girl calling him home." Her dazzling smile and moist breath promised Mani a welcome when he returned.

James was pondering whether to have a fourth beer when Manikam came out of the afternoon sunshine.

"Mr McNair!" he chirped, and wrung James's damp hand. "Your daughter has told me so much about you." He was struck by James's gloomy solitariness, so different from his children's gregarious company.

"Have you been sent to bring me home?"

A surge of protectiveness reminded Manikam how much in love he was. "No, no, I came to introduce myself, I'm Manikam …"

"I know."

"I promised to get some cakes for tea, I'll just ask the boy …"

James took the opportunity. "Have an Anchor while he brings the cakes."

Manikam didn't drink in the afternoon, but he grinned. "Good idea, I'll buy you one."

James relaxed. A cold glass. He drained half of it in one swallow. Manikam paid up and sipped. The bittersweet liquid made him nervous. "Mr McNair, you have a wonderful family," he ventured.

"Yes, pretty girls, especially Fleur."

Manikam swallowed his beer, speechless.

"I was young once, also. Ran away with Miriam when I was nineteen, she was pretty then."

Manikam swallowed again.

"I'm forty-five. Do you think that's old? I was old long before, became an old man when John was born."

"Umm," Manikam murmured, pretending interest.

"Well, how old are you?" James asked challengingly.

"Twenty-four, sir."

"Don't sir me. Never got a college degree. A labourer, that's what I am, no different from a common tapper. Did Fleur tell you I work in an estate? What did she say, medical man? An orderly, dispenser, giver of pills and syrups, a drone. My wife's the queen. Do you know what she does all day?" James drained another mouthful of pity. "She prays. Never seen a family with more prayers. Every one of them a prayer."

Manikam picked up the package of teacakes and stood up. "Better be getting along, they're waiting for tea."

James wove as he walked down the rutty lane and muttered each time he stumbled over a tuft of *lallang*.

Almost in sight of the houses, Manikam spoke up. "I want to tell you how much I admire Fleur. I've become very fond of her. I mean she is so good ..."

James stopped and looked around.

Manikam hurried with his speech, "I'm asking your permission to ... to visit your daughter."

James felt a sharp annoyance. The dark Indian was repulsive. His face seemed overlaid with black grease and his thick pink lips grossly effeminate. Manikam's complacently plump features appeared heightened by the high mound of oiled hair. "What d'you wanna visit her for, eh? Being a teacher makes you alright to everybody? She's come fro' England, what'd she wanna someone like you?"

Manikam's white Dacron shirt was stuck under his armpits. "Actually, Uncle McNair, I have honourable intentions. Fleur deserves the best …" He'd sometimes wondered what it would be like to propose to a girl. Now he was overcome by a giddy silliness. "I'm proposing to an old man," he thought. At the same time, heroically, he was seeing his duty in life, risking his life on a tightrope. He imagined Fleur's breasts round as oranges under her pink nylon blouse. "I want to marry her." There, it was said. He shrugged his shoulders to unglue the shirt from his back.

James had foreseen weekends of Manikam taking tea in his house and driving his children all over town. He hadn't been prepared for Manikam walking Fleur down the church aisle. He saw poor Fleur pouring tea for the fellow and waiting in bed for him in her prettiest lace nightie, and he was sorry for him. "You're a fool," he mumbled.

"What?" Did the old man disapprove of him? But Fleur was getting the better match. His position, his degree, his family background and money (father A.A. Dorisamy, owner of Dorisamy Store in Penang Road, brother barrister-at-law). Also, his savings, his new car, his youth. Naturally, Fleur returned his feelings. He was a very good catch.

"You're a fool, Fleur will have you for life."

"But that is marriage!" Manikam protested. "I will be a completely faithful husband, I assure you, I'm not the type to play around."

James didn't want to stand arguing with a fool. He'd been up since four-thirty and busy all morning with flu cases. He coughed and staggered a little. "It's no good arguing." Holding on to the doorpost, he smiled at Rosa waiting by the door and headed for the back room where he lay fully clothed on the old queen bed he shared with John and fell asleep.

No one understood it, although no one discussed it. Mother wouldn't talk about it with Rosa. Rosa ended every discussion with the suggestion they say a rosary to the Virgin Mary. Fleur told Mother about Daddy's no. Mani was so fired by Daddy's opposition that nothing now would stop him from marrying Fleur.

James woke up at six as the blue-white sky was cooling to the purple half-glow before the black tropical night took over. The inside of his mouth was mouldy, his eyes burned from alcoholic drought, but he remembered Manikam's old-fashioned request, which was more than he had asked from Miriam's parents. "Bloody fool, why can't he run off with her! Posing like a *lawyer buruk!*" He hid from Fleur as long as he could, reading the newspaper in the outhouse, taking a long time over his bath. She found him in his bedroom tying his sarong and hugged him happily.

"Daddy, daddy pet, you're up," she hummed.

"Umm, umm, so you're back." He was pleased despite his misgivings. "How was England?" Again he felt the glow of proprietorship that moved him so in Ceylon during the Anglican services. "England, umm, has it changed?" He did not know what England was like before it was supposed to have changed, but the B.B.C. which he listened to every night was forever going on about changes, England going to the dogs.

"Has it changed? You wouldn't like it anymore. All my English friends want to come east. I told them we have a cook, they were green with envy. No one can afford a servant in England now, not unless you're a lord or lady."

James turned gloomy. After John, Miriam couldn't do without someone to wash and cook. He had to take the job at the Dunlop estate, fifty miles away from home. It paid more than Winston was willing to, enough for the family and a servant. "We can't afford a servant either," he said, but Fleur pecked him on the cheek and continued.

"We live like lords and ladies here compared to England. None of my friends' boyfriends can afford a car, they have to take the tube, noisy dirty things. Come have dinner. You missed tea. Mummy's invited Mani to stay."

"That fellow," he muttered

"What's wrong with him?" Fleur asked. "He's the most decent person I've met here."

"But you've been home only a few days," he pleaded uncertainly. "Give yourself time to settle down."

"I've been on my own for three years Daddy. I was sending money home from Alor Gajah. You didn't pay a cent for my studies in England, the government bond ..."

"Money, everything comes down to money. I suppose because you don't have a dowry you're going to throw yourself at the first man who comes along."

Fleur's eyes were lighted. "I'm not cheap, not like some women."

"What d'you mean? I've never looked at another woman since your mother." James was truly shocked. The quarrel was going further and faster than he knew what to do. He wished he'd brought home some beer. Manikam would drink with him at dinner, Miriam couldn't object to it.

"You're not standing in my way," Fleur whispered. Her chin squared as she glared white and black-eyed at him. "I'm not going to end up with a good-for-nothing." As James averted his eyes from the Medusa in his bosom, he thought he heard her say, "Like you!"

His heart thumped violently. He was at once light-headed, empty like a husk or the smallest feather falling, and warm, as if a tight coat was pulling around his shoulders. "What d'you mean, what d'you mean?" He could hardly say the words.

But Fleur had left him. She was in the kitchen, saying loudly, "Curry chicken, Mummy, oh I love curry chicken. And lady's fingers and brinjals." Rosa giggled nearby and Manikam's deep laugh echoed with her, "Ha ha ha ha."

James held out his hands and looked at them. Iodine stains edged his stubby fingertips. His nails were raggedy but fresh pink, the colour of a young girl's. Rosa called from the kitchen, "Daddy, Daddy, come and eat." His hands shook. He put them behind his back and went into the kitchen.

The next morning he waited for the children to leave for nine o'clock Mass, then said to Miriam, "I'm returning to the estate."

"Why?" She was annoyed. "Even your day off you cannot spend with your family. How you expect your children to love you like a father? What's wrong with you? Last night you like a monster, won't talk to Mani, won't talk to me." Tears gathered, and she spoke more rapidly. "I've been a good wife to you, five children, never enough money. I have to pinch here, pinch there. Luckily Father Francis helps us, otherwise where to find money for the milk powder, margarine, Lily's novitiate clothes? But you are never grateful, oh no, won't go to church to thank Father Francis. Your daughter does so well, teaching diploma from Leeds, how many fathers can boast about daughter going overseas, earning $500 a month now, making more than you. And Fleur is going to give me $200 every month. We can move to nicer house, at least three bedrooms. What's wrong with you? Other fathers give Mass for thanksgiving but you ..."

"Shut up, shut up before I beat you!"

"Oh my Lord!" James had never struck her. Miriam gaped at him with mouth ajar. "Oh Holy Saints! What has happened to you?" She became delighted. "You have no feelings for me, all these years I've suffered, never complaining, just to make you happy. Now you want to beat me. Beat me, beat me!" She jumped from the settee and thrust her face up at him.

For a moment James thought she wanted him to kiss her. It was so many years since they touched in passion that he was confused. He stared at the expectant face, crumpled with frown lines and greyish rice powder. "Aaww," he said in disgust to the mousy eyes and ratty nose, the sharp feral cheekbones. He left her standing among the framed pictures, Jesus with flowing golden locks pointing long-fingered to his scarlet heart pierced by arrows, the Lady of Fatima clutching her sky-blue robes with one hand and blessing the rosy-cheeked shepherd children with the other, and the black cross brought down, the pallid half-naked corpse beside it, and two weeping women embracing the body, faces white as the exposed torso, and cheeks as red as the colour of the wounds on the forehead and bony chest.

He drank two beers while he waited for the Muar bus. In Muar he walked to the toddy shed behind the bus station. The shame he felt went away as soon as he entered the shade of the *nipah* roof. He had gone to Coomarasamy's shack only twice before, protesting, dragged in by tappers to celebrate a wedding and a birth. To his surprise he'd liked the milky sour-sweet palm drink. It didn't taste as sweet as an Anchor, but it cost about a tenth as much.

After three toddies, the body felt strong, the breath steady and the spirit clear with happiness. He wasn't expected back at the dispensary till ten the next morning, and Mr Watson had said he could be a little late if his family needed him. New planters know nothing about Malaya, James thought, drinking he'd forgotten to count how many toddies, because the air smelled sweet and pungent in Coomarasamy's shed, the trestle on which he rested his glass was scrubbed clean with sand and well-water, and he could drink without having to talk to anyone.

It was late afternoon when he walked back to his place. He was careful to skirt the Watsons' front lawn and he walked from tree to tree for their protective shade, hanging briefly to each crumbly trunk. He saw he had left the door unlatched. Pushing hard he stumbled through the semidarkness and fumbled for the narrow bed against the wall.

Ouff! he breathed as he fell onto the thin mattress. Closing his eyes he imagined his breath coming out in great white steamy curls, like smoke from a giant cigar. He heard his own tired chugging from his aching throat. He heard a laugh like a mouse squeak. Leaning on an elbow he turned his head.

The *kebun's* daughter, Lai Neo, stood by the doorway, giggling. "Uncle, you drunk," she said softly.

"Shhush, shhush, wha' you doing heerrsh ..."

"Every time you not here I come rest in your house." The *kebun's* daughter, James knew, was at least twenty years old. He had heard that the *kebun* beat her and wouldn't let her marry. He'd beaten her with a bamboo pole last year. James had dressed the cuts on her arms and legs (she'd refused to let him examine her back) and threatened to report the matter to Mr Watson if he ever had to treat her again.

"You better leave," he said, suddenly sensible to his drunken state. "Go away."

She drew closer. He squinted and a blue flowered *samfoo* wavered, unfocused. A dim pale face hovered above him. Squeak, squeak, went her soft giggle.

"Uncle, you want something, you need something?"

The pale face breathed on him. He smelled the sour taint of toddy. Two hands touched his chest. A spasm of yearning shook him. Yes, he wanted to reach up, to take the blue lady down on his foam bed, he wanted what he needed. He opened his eyes and stared into the dark eyes shining in the dark room. He saw Fleur's eyes, smiling, narrow, heated. He pushed her away with the full force of his arms and began to hiccup, his face to the wall. Then he felt a warm hand stroking his hunched shoulders. Slowly his hiccups stopped and he reached towards it, unthinking.

PART 3

Woman

Keng Hua

THE CREAMY BLOSSOMS hanging in a cluster from the centre of the broad-leafed plant looked like human flesh, the flesh of an expensive woman, smooth, hairless, with the lightest tint of pale yellow showing through ivory. She had been told since she was a child that the Keng Hua flowered only once a year, often unseen at midnight, and the appearance of the blossoms presaged some stroke of good fortune if one knew how to take advantage of it. That was always the problem, knowing how to take advantage of a situation which presented itself unexpectedly and urgently. 'Opportunity knocks but once,' she had learned as a schoolgirl, and here were the blossoms in the bright morning light, leaning against the kitchen window seemingly as heavy as the damp dust-mop, their companion, leaning its grey head against the same glass.

It was Friday, and, tomorrow, she would be thirty-six years old. She touched a smooth clear petal; it looked healthy, as if the print of a fingertip could never mar the pearly finish, but a faint purple bruise immediately materialized on it like a grimy shadow. "Oh my!" she said.

She had taken to talking a little to herself and recently had begun repeating certain short phrases aloud, "Oh my!" "Oh no, it can't be!" "Where, oh where?"

She picked the heavy pot up with both hands and moved it to the living room. With its long straggling leaves and bunched-up blossoms, it was too large for the rattan table, but it made an impressive show. The neat room with the faded batik cushions and skinny rattan armchairs suddenly took on a glow of luxury. It reminded her of the time when she was sick and her colleagues had sent her a bouquet of orchids through Interflora; the ostentatious tawny blooms imparted exactly the same exciting shine of money to the room.

Well, she thought, at least Peter will notice this.

The men in her life had been many, yet, lately, it seemed to her that she had never been anything but a spinster. It was hard to know what to do with her life which ran smoothly and successfully, so sufficiently that it was months sometimes before she became aware of neediness, and then, of course, she would immediately go about trying to answer the need as efficiently as she went about doing her work.

She was at her desk writing up a list of items to get from the market when the phone rang.

"Weng, what are you doing today?" Siew knew she didn't teach on Fridays, but she never openly presumed to know.

"Nothing, I have to do some shopping for tonight."

"Yes, lah! I'm dying to meet him."

"He's nothing special," she warned in her flattest voice. "Big and clumsy." It was Siew, she thought, who had the better life. Two daughters, pretty as can be, a Mercedes, and enough money to run around the boutiques shopping for American jeans. If it wasn't that she would have to take short pale Chong Lee with the rest, she could almost envy her. Siew, she knew, envied *her,* the men coming and going, the promotions, raises, and independent decisions.

She gazed out of the window to the parking lot below, not listening to Siew's chatter. Only three cars were left in the lot this morning.

She didn't enjoy her Fridays when all the world seemed occupied with work and love while she stayed three stories high, neither up in the clouds nor down among the men and women.

"I'll meet you at Hassim's for lunch. No, don't dress up for tonight. It's only for drinks and chitchat, for God's sake!" She felt like a man next to Siew. Irritability, a crude desire to hit and revile her when she ran on and on in a sentimental gush: she controlled these impulses more when she was among men, or, perhaps, she felt them less. But it was women with whom she spent more time.

"A spinster," she thought as she looked at the Keng Hua. "Perhaps, a spinster is a woman whose life has remained constant to women."

She was careful not to touch the flowers again. A slight unfamiliar scent lingered in the room, almost pleasurable except for a faint smell of something corruptible, like dank earth or barely rotting lettuce leaves. She would have to do something about the smell. And she still hadn't decided what to do about the Keng Hua flowering.

"You must buy some lottery tickets!" Siew cried fretfully. "You may never have the chance again."

"If you are sure it means anything so certain, why don't you buy the tickets for me, instead of having me waste my money?" she replied mockingly.

"Oh, that's no good. It must come from you."

Hassim's, being a Muslim restaurant, did not have lottery tickets for sale. Siew was insistent that they drive somewhere and buy them, but she resisted.

"There must be other ways of being lucky than striking a lottery. Let's think of some original things I can do to make luck come to me."

"No, no, you don't understand. It all has to do with money. The good luck means making a lot of money."

"Well, then, I can gamble."

Siew stared at her suspiciously. "Have you really been gambling?

I thought you don't like mahjong."

"Silly, there are other forms of gambling than mahjong. Cameron Highlands has a big casino now."

"Oh, oh, let's go! What fun it will be. I can leave the girls with the servant, and Chong Lee won't mind if I'm going with you."

"I'm pulling your leg. Don't you know when I'm not serious?"

"You're the silly one," Siew said, puckering her mouth. "If you won't be serious about this once-in-a-lifetime chance," she raised her voice, "you're a big fool."

"No, I'm serious about it. I like the idea of being lucky, especially just before my birthday and I go over the hill. But I want to use my luck carefully. I keep thinking there's something I want more than money." She knew she had said the wrong thing. Siew's silence was more irritating than her stupid chatter. Was that what she really meant, that she wanted marriage, a family? What was there left to want in life if not money and if not this? "I don't mean marriage either." She turned her head away and stared at the two flies dancing above the remains of their lunch.

She didn't feel old, and she didn't feel not old. Siew frequently said she was young at heart, as if she were already a grandmother instead of a young mother who looked and behaved like a girl given to giggling and jeans. Weng could not be accused of such silly behaviour, but then, her appearance was neither as attractive nor as ridiculous as Siew's. She had been excited over the Keng Hua this morning; now, after the heavy lunch of curried prawns with the Coca-Cola fizzing uncomfortably in her stomach, she was bored with it.

"I tell you, Weng, maybe we ask your friend Peter to suggest something. Americans are very smart."

"I know you. You're hoping Peter will marry me. I told you we hardly know each other. He's been in the college for only three months and we've had lunch together twice."

"Never, lah! Why should I want you to marry an *ang-mou-kau* and

158

leave me?" Siew shook her head violently and laughed with her mouth open. "But it would be nice if he falls in love with you."

Love interested Siew, Weng had observed. Siew saw love emanating from every presentable male she met. Discussing the men she knew with faithfully married Siew usually made whomever it was appear more desirable, the consequences more pathetic. When Siew talked about Weng's affairs, they became love and interesting rather than something else and tediously painful.

It was after eight o'clock when the four of them paused before the entrance of her building. Despite Peter's tremendous height and bulk, he let her lead the way up the stairs. She was aware of how closely he followed after, with Siew surveying the two right behind them and Chong Lee a distance away.

"Drinks," she had said gaily when he made his approach late Tuesday afternoon.

"Hey, wanna spend some time together after work?" he'd said as they found themselves leaving the library together. She had heard that invitation in various forms so often through the years that it seemed like a memory or a dream to hear the big, brown-haired, red-skinned man who had a roll of fat above his trousers and thickly coiled dark hair over his bare arms, springing up from the backs of his hands, and who was walking casually beside her turn to her with the same proposition.

"No, I don't particularly want to ..."

"No, I'm not the kind of woman who would ..."

But she turned towards him instead, smiling. "Drinks?" It wasn't till later she told him over the phone that Siew and Chong Lee were also invited. They had a car and would drive him.

When she saw him standing by his door, she was angry. It was clear he had been drinking. "Hallooo," he said as he bent over and got into the car beside her. An acidic smell of beer and sweat came from her body. She remained angry through the drive, although Siew was obviously amused.

"All white people smell," Siew had told her. "It's the meat they eat. Big plates of red beef with the blood still dripping. Ughh!" Most of the men she had gone out with had masked their body odours with perfumes: Old Spice, Yardley, English Leather. She could tell Siew honestly that they smelled more like women than men. Peter had not bothered.

Sweating like a distressed giant, he apologized all through the ride. "I've had some booze earlier. Mannika took me out to an Indian restaurant, and the air-conditioning wasn't working, so we drank a lot of beer to cool off. Hey, I hope you don't mind my beginning early. That Tiger Beer really fooled me; it's got more kick in it than moonshine." Walking up the stairs to her flat, she could sense his efforts to move steadily.

She knew something was wrong as soon as she saw the door ajar. "Wait!" she said. "Someone's in the flat."

"Do you mean there's a burglar in there?"

"I don't know, but I locked the door before I left."

"Move over, honey," Peter said, and pushed the door wide open with one huge paw. There was no one in the room.

She felt her pulse slow down, then race again. "Oh no! There was someone here! The Keng Hua's gone."

"Gone?" Siew cried from down below. "Someone's stolen it!"

"What's a Keng Hua?" Peter asked, walking swiftly past the bare coffee table. He peered into the kitchen and moved purposefully down the corridor towards the bedroom. He paused by the office door, slid open the doors of the built-in cupboards, then stood surveying the bedroom. "Your typewriter's here, and your record-player and T.V. Doesn't look like anything's been touched. Wanna check your jewelry?"

"I don't have any," Weng said. She didn't like Peter knowing so much about her so quickly. It didn't seem right that he could just walk in and look over her rooms and tell her what to do. At the same time, she felt reassured by his tall hulking figure. There were only the two of them in the flat at that moment, and it made her feel both uncomfortable and safe. "All right, you can come in now," she said, beckoning to Siew and Chong Lee who were waiting by the door. "We're …"

Siew was stammering with disappointment. "You see how valuable your Keng Hua is? The thief wanted the luck. Chong Lee, don't you agree she should have bought the lottery tickets today? It's too late now. Your luck's gone."

"So that's a Keng Hua," Peter said as he sat wedged in the armchair between the two women. Chong Lee and Siew were politely sipping tall tonics with a little gin in them, and he was having his second glass of Scotch. "You Malaysians are superstitious." He laughed. "But it's worked out for you. The burglar could have taken something really valuable, and the Keng Hua sacrificed itself to save your material goods."

"We Malaysians? What makes you think you know us?" Weng barely tasted the Scotch Peter had poured for her. She felt a nervous throbbing behind her eyes.

"The trouble with Americans is they spend a few months in a country, and they think they're experts about the people." Since Chong Lee had been promoted to an assistant vice-president in the National Bank, his views on American influence had grown more outspokenly critical.

Peter laughed again. "I don't pretend to be an expert on the economy or even on the politics," he said with an embarrassed wave of his huge hand. "We've made a big enough mess at home, so I don't care to interfere with someone else's messes. It's because I love the country that I make these observations."

Weng was surprised at how easily he had said the word 'love'. She could see that Chong Lee was also unsettled by it.

Siew leaned over towards him. "What do you love about Malaysia?"

"Well, there's one thing I don't love. That's the climate." He slipped a finger around his open-necked shirt as if to unbutton it, then stopped. "Actually, I don't mind it so much when I'm at the beach. You have beautiful beaches. Good fine sand and clean water. And no tourist hard-sell yet."

"Is that all, the beaches?"

"Siew believes 'love' is a very important word," Weng said. "She's the only person I know who believes in love at first sight."

"So do I." Peter took her hand.

She flushed and pulled away, but he held on tightly. "He's drunk," she said to Chong Lee and Siew.

"I am," he agreed and let her hand free. "In my past life, I was a priest. Roman Catholic. Never married. You know, women are forbidden to priests. Not liquor, however." He tried to hold her hand again, but she moved it out of reach. "What do I love about Malaysia? I love the women. Beautiful women. Slender, petite. Sharp as knives. I bet you're happily married," he said, motioning to Siew.

"Yes," Chong Lee replied.

"Married to a woman who believes in love at first sight. Yeh, you must be a happy man. I can never forget women. That was my problem as a priest."

"Were you a bad priest?" Siew's eyes were bright with scandal.

"We were talking about the country," Weng interrupted. "What have you found out about Malaysians?"

Peter gave her a quizzical look. "You were offended when I called you superstitious, but that's what I like about Malaysians. Intelligent and hard-working, but still irrational. You believe in devils. That's simpler than having to come up with some other explanation. I like the simplicity here."

"Siew believes in love, not devils."

"They go together." He got up, walked over to the kitchen, and came back with a fresh glass. He weaved as he walked. His shirt had worked itself out of his belt, and a narrow expanse of his back was exposed. There were dark hairs on his back.

"Listen," he said, squatting awkwardly beside her chair. "You're a beautiful woman. I really go for you." His hand was like a big damp mop on her cheek.

She felt her breath stop with pity. Something in her chest twisted at his loneliness, his ungainly size. She wanted to rest her cheek against his hand, to take his drink away and make him sit still.

Siew giggled. Turning her head sharply, Weng caught Chong Lee smiling. She slapped his hand hard and said, "You know nothing about Malaysian women. I think you should leave now before you make a bigger fool of yourself."

He got up and looked at his hand. He was so big and abrupt that she was afraid he would hit her. But he only looked sad, as if this had happened to him before, and moved away from her silently. He didn't say goodbye as he left with Siew and Chong Lee.

Alone, she stared at the table where the Keng Hua was supposed to be and where only the glass half-filled with whiskey remained. She could still smell his strong sweaty palm on her face. Her neck ached as if she had been holding it too rigidly for too long a time. She wished the evening had never happened, that it was morning all over again and she was watching the Keng Hua as it secretly unfurled its flowers petal by petal through the tranquil rhythms of an unending morning. She knew she would see Peter in the college. He would shamefully avoid her eyes, and they would continue to chat as strangers.

It was only later, after she had washed the glasses, dried them, and put them away in the cabinet and was lying in bed remembering she would be thirty-six tomorrow that she cried because she had lost the Keng Hua and her good luck.

Another Country

WHEN SU WENG regained consciousness, she was alone. Her head was helmeted in a swath of bandages, her right arm and hand disappeared into a roll of white cotton, and her left leg was raised by a pulley above the bed, the foot encased in a large wrap. Her bed was screened on two sides, and at the foot of the bed was only a blank white wall. A fat plaster sat on her right cheek partially blocking her vision.

"I say, you look like Pharaoh's mummy! I think you surely die when they bring you in. You look really terrible, lah!"

Su Weng painfully adjusted her aching neck towards the left from where the cheerful voice was coming. Dimly she was aware of a shapeless figure in a loose white gown half-hidden by the screen.

"What's your name, eh?" The white shape approached her bed.

"Mrs Hashim. Mrs Hashim! What are you doing here? You're not allowed in this room. The doctor is coming and he will be angry if he sees you here."

At the sound of this brisk voice coming from somewhere out of sight, the shape turned and vanished. Su Weng kept her neck strained waiting for someone else to appear, the nurse or doctor or some more

164

familiar visitor. But no one came and soon she was drifting off into dark emptiness. At one point she woke at hearing voices and saw a group of men and women standing around the bed, then she must have slept again. When she woke up, it was three days after the car her father had been driving had gone off the road and crashed into a telephone pole and she, the sole passenger, was thrown a hundred yards onto the five-foot way.

"So, you finally woke up," the neat little nurse said, pushing before her a white enamelled cart loaded with vials, bottles, rolls of cotton wool and gauze, metal cups, sponges, trays of syringes, scissors, knives, and other gleaming steel utensils. "We're going to clean you up today. Your bandages need a changing." Out came a large pair of scissors. Snipping deftly she dropped masses of gauze into a plastic pail. The gauze was clean, then stained with yellow ointment, then brown with dried blood. The last layers were stuck to the body and whenever the nurse peeled a piece, it left the wound freshly raw and bleeding. It took an hour to peel the dried gauze off and Su Weng, exhausted, had stopped screaming by then. It was apparent there wasn't much whole skin left on her. The nurse was sweating and trembling as she washed Su Weng with a cool liquid and re-applied the ointment; this time, only a light gauze was taped.

"Eh, can hear you ten miles away. People think you're being murdered, lah! You got a lot of pain?"

The dim grey shape shifted, focused, and coalesced. Su Weng stared numbly at the woman who was surveying her, it seemed, in close-up.

"You're in Ward 4B. My name is Fadzillah Hashim, I been in 4B for one month already, so, you wanna know anything, just ask me. Must have fun in this place, you know. Otherwise, can die, lah!" She giggled and hopped on one foot. Su Weng became aware that the giddy motion of Mrs Hashim's shape was not because of her own dizziness but because Mrs Hashim was constantly fidgeting. She was in a continuous dance and the white hospital gown swayed and bobbed as her head and shoulders weaved and her arms swung. "You come and see me in room 10. I know everybody in 4B. Can introduce you to some nice boys. You're not so bad. Cannot see your face anyway, so doesn't matter if you're not pretty, eh?"

"Mrs Hashim, Mrs Hashim, visitors for you," the call came from somewhere. She ducked around the screen and Su Weng found herself alone and finally wide awake.

Loud confident voices were walking along the corridor outside her room. Concealed by the screen, a patient groaned to the right. A nurse came and removed the left screen; the bed on the left which was by the door was empty. Su Weng gazed eagerly out through the open door.

Her mother and brother came. He sat on the metal folding chair next to the bed and said nothing. Her mother stood by the side and explained that her father had not been hurt in the crash, but he would not be able to visit because hospital sights and smells upset him. Su Weng's eyes filled with tears. She was her father's pet, and she knew he must be distressed by the accident.

A clatter and heavy smell of boiled vegetables and rice reminded them it was dinner time. Her mother waited to see the kind of food served to Su Weng: watery potato soup, a bowl of rice, a plate of pale cabbage, and a saucer of stringy beef. "I will bring liver and spinach tomorrow. Hospital food isn't nutritious. You must promise not to eat anything with soy sauce in it. Soy sauce will scar and blacken your wounds." Su Weng thought of the numerous stitches on her face, arms, legs and back, and of the white and pink flesh that the nurse had stripped, and she nodded.

She was studying dismally the rejected tray of food which her mother had left on the chair when Mrs Hashim appeared at the door. "Visitors gone? Nuisance, eh? Always make you feel bad. Never mind, I'll get a nicer visitor for you." She disappeared and returned a few minutes later pulling a young man along behind her. "This is my friend, Chun Hong. He's a very bright boy, in university in Australia.

But cannot take the pressure, eh, Chun Hong? Come back home because got stomach ache all the time."

"Actually, I have ulcers," he said.

"Really cute, eh? Like elephant nose," Mrs Hashim said, waving her hand at the thin plastic tube which was clipped into his right nostril and which dangled down his pyjama shirt.

"I can't eat solids. This tube drips liquids into my system." His face was sallow and melancholy; thick black hair sprang, uncombed, straight up from his forehead. His expression of reluctance and embarrassment changed to curiosity. "I heard you had concussion. Do you remember anything about the accident?"

Su Weng shook her head.

"Nothing about coming to the hospital? Perhaps you're better off not remembering. Mrs Hashim has been telling me all sorts of things about you. You're on your way to the university in Kuala Lumpur."

Su Weng nodded and began to cry. She was supposed to leave for the campus in a week when the car went off the road. Now she wouldn't be there in time for the beginning of the first term.

"Hey, hey, no crying allowed here!" Mrs Hashim said with a wild jump. She did a little dance. "Tomorrow you ask the nurse if you can get up and we'll have a party. Chun Hong and I must visit other people now." She grabbed his hand and pulled him out of the room. He smiled and winked as he left.

Su Weng stopped crying immediately. Her left foot was hot and throbbing. She tried to sleep, but the pain flashed every few seconds like the beam of a lighthouse sweeping through a dark ocean swell. When the nurse came to give her medication, she swallowed a sleeping pill and slept fitfully. Now and again she woke and listened to the woman in the next bed moaning. The fluorescent lights outside cast a pale glow in the room. Half asleep through the night she heard the nurses' murmurs as they passed each other and their footsteps hurrying up and down the long corridor.

The next morning, as the nurse changed her bandages, she gripped her pillow hard and didn't scream. The gauze came off more easily this time, and, besides, she knew that somewhere, Mrs Hashim was listening. "No, you can't get out of bed," the nurse said as she turned her over and slipped a fresh sheet under. "You can't put your foot down yet. The doctor thinks you may have blood-poisoning." The cut on the left foot had left the white bone showing, the nurse explained, and even with twenty-two stitches, if the infection got out of control, she might lose the foot. After the nurse had tucked the grey blanket in and bundled the soiled linen out of the room, Su Weng sat up in bed and reached over and touched her bandaged foot. It had ballooned to twice its normal size.

"Must stay in bed, eh? Never mind. Your foot won't drop off," Mrs Hashim said. Su Weng blinked back her tears. "You know how to play poker? I got cards here." Mrs Hashim waved a pack of worn pink-backed cards. "No money involved. Cannot gamble, you know, but just for fun, eh. We pass the time like good friends." She perched on the bed and dangled her slippers with her toes. Swiftly she dealt and laid the cards on the uncrumpled sheet. Su Weng picked them up painfully; her right hand was taped up and only her fingers were free to manoeuvre. They played for a while, Su Weng silent and Mrs Hashim laughing and calling out in excitement. "*Ada nasib!*" she exclaimed as she won a hand. "Oh, oh, dangerous, lah! Must watch out for you."

"Mrs Hashim, Mrs Hashim, where are you?"

"Sshhh." She put her finger to her lips.

"Mrs Hashim," the nurse said, standing at the door with her hands on her hips. "You know you're not supposed to be out of bed. Doctor's orders. CRIB, remember!" Mrs Hashim picked up her cards and waved them unpenitently. "You must stop disturbing the patients."

"She wasn't disturbing me," Su Weng protested, waving back with her left hand.

"She's probably got you overexcited, your temperature's gone up," the nurse said, putting her hand to Su Weng's forehead. "Lie back and go to sleep."

"What is CRIB?"

"Doctor's orders for Mrs Hashim. Complete Rest in Bed. She's not supposed to get out of bed at all. The same for you." She frowned down and left.

Mrs Hashim was back many times and the nurses' cries of "Mrs Hashim, CRIB!" became commonplace to Su Weng. In a week her foot had healed enough for her to hobble to the bathroom down the corridor. "Eh, you," Mrs Hashim said as Su Weng emerged, damp and flushed from a tortured shower. "Come and meet Uncle Tan." She took Su Weng's towel and dripping soapbox in one hand and supported her at the elbow with the other. Dancing and hobbling, they walked down the length of the dormitory-style second-class area. It was a section for patients undergoing surgery. In some beds men and women slept like grey stones; in others, they were reading or gazing ahead of them or sitting by the sides of the beds bent over. Mrs Hashim stopped by a bed. A heavy man in his fifties was sitting up in it, propped on his pillow and reading *The Straits Times*. He was wearing the usual hospital pyjamas for men, grey and white striped shirt and trousers, and he had his legs stretched out with the ankles crossed. From his neck downwards he appeared massive and inert, but when he looked up, his brown face flashed with life and intelligence. His smile lifted his eyebrows and crinkled the skin around his eyes.

"Aha, Mrs Hashim! Have you come to cheer me up?"

"Oh, Uncle Tan, you are the one with the good jokes. This is my friend, Su Weng. Under the bandages she is a pretty woman." They laughed while Su Weng smiled bitterly. "Uncle Tan is a very smart man," Mrs Hashim said, taking Su Weng by the hand and guiding her to the bedside. "He's a philosopher, you know, a lover of wisdom. Uncle Tan's been married, eh?"

"Two wives," he replied. "Two big mistakes."

"Don't say that," Mrs Hashim exclaimed. "Mrs Tan will be very sad to hear that."

"In the first marriage, my wife was the mistake, but now, I am the mistake," he responded.

"Come, come, uncle, a clever man like you! You are a big prize for any woman."

"Ah, yes, an expensive prize, and Mrs Tan is a poor woman. So, have you come to wish me good luck?"

"*Nasib*, you're asking me for *nasib*? Cannot, lah, uncle, I got too little. What you want good luck for?"

"I'm going for the operation on Wednesday. You think I will come out all right?"

"Very hard to kill a big man like you. You come out of the operation with less, but don't worry, your wife won't miss what the doctor take away."

Mr Tan suddenly looked sad. "I don't know …" he sighed as if he were tired.

Mrs Hashim rose up quickly from the bed. "Must leave you, eh. You need rest for the big day. Cheer up, uncle." She was bobbing down the long room before Su Weng could gather her towel and soapbox to leave.

Mr Tan had closed his eyes. His face was now a grey mass of wrinkles and unhappy droops, and Su Weng limped away without saying goodbye.

Su Weng had few visitors; her friends had left already for the start of the term in the university. The patches of flesh from where the skin had been torn were healing slowly. By the second week, only her mother came to visit regularly. Every evening she brought a triple tiffin carrier, the lowest dish filled with rice, the second with fried liver, and the top dish with watercress soup. The blood lost, she said, was best replaced by eating the freshest pork liver, and the shock to Su Weng's spirit which was causing her to droop her head and cry each evening was best treated through a potion of bitter bark and ginger steeped in rice wine and masked by sprigs of watercress. She would get up to leave only after Su Weng had eaten a satisfactory meal. Su Weng thought the tears which involuntarily rolled down her cheeks every evening were caused actually by her strong distaste for the slices of grey liver and the pungent soup, but she concentrated on her mother's hope for her recovery and swallowed each spoonful silently.

One evening, her mother had to attend a relative's funeral and Su Weng was alone during the dinner hour. Rejecting the hospital meal, she decided to see what Mrs Hashim was eating on her Muslim diet. As she approached Mrs Hashim's first-class room, she heard a loud chatter of many voices. Around Mrs Hashim's bed were clustered a number of women dressed in bright *baju kurungs;* on the bed with her, children were lying, some clinging to her arms and some sprawled by her feet. By the window sat an old woman with a baby on her lap. A handsome man stood by the head of her bed observing the activities with a broad smile.

"Eh, my friend, Su Weng. *Marilah,* and meet my family."

Su Weng stood shyly by the door, conscious of the coarse faded gown in which she felt like an abandoned orphan. Mrs Hashim was also dressed in a similar gown, but, surrounded by children, she appeared like a mother goddess robed in flowing white.

"These are my children, Ibrahim, Ahmad, Norina, Nazir." She tapped them gently on their heads as she named them, and they each adoringly tried to capture her swiftly moving hand. "And there is my youngest, Fatimah," she said, gesturing towards the elderly woman by the window. "And my mother-in-law."

"*Masuklah,*" the woman smiled, showing her toothless gums, and the baby stared at Su Weng with round solemn eyes.

"My sisters and sisters-in-law," Mrs Hashim continued, motioning towards the women who (with the same solemn gaze as the baby's) had all stepped back to observe Su Weng. "And my husband, Abdul Hashim."

The man shook her hand courteously, said in an indifferent tone,

"How do you do?" and turned back to his wife. The women began chattering again, the children tugged at Mrs Hashim possessively with cries for attention. Su Weng waved goodbye to the mother-in-law who was still smiling sweetly at her and walked away; there was clearly no room for her in there.

"Do you know Mrs Hashim has five children?" Su Weng asked Chun Hong. They were standing by an open window along the corridor watching the cars and vans drive up the hill on which their building was situated. When they tired of visiting each other's rooms or playing cards or reading, they would stroll down the corridor and lean over the windows to look enviously down on the traffic and pedestrians hurrying below, seemingly full of purpose and health. Chun Hong no longer carried tubes attached to his body and he would be leaving in a week if his ulcers healed by then.

"Why are you surprised?"

"Well, I never thought of her having a family outside."

"Don't you have a family outside?"

"What do you mean?" Su Weng was offended.

"You're angry," he replied calmly. "Do you think I have a family?"

"I don't know. I suppose so. Everyone has a family somewhere."

"Most people do. It depends on what you think is a family. I used to think I didn't have a family. I read too many Western books. When I went to Adelaide, I discovered what family was. Actually, the reason I got so sick there was that I was depressed for a long time. I was lonely in Australia. The moment I got home, I felt better. I'm not close to my parents, you know. They're Chinese-educated, have a bicycle shop in Tampin, but with a family, you take what you have. I don't ask to be different from them any more." Chun Hong spoke slowly. There was a suggestion of sadness in his voice. "But you haven't decided what you want to be yet. You are still in conflict." He held her hand diffidently. Su Weng felt sorry for him.

Mrs Hashim found them playing cards that afternoon. "Sshh," she whispered. "I'm CRIB. Come, I've found a secret place." They walked through the ward in which every bed seemed inhabited by a prone figure suspended between lunch and teatime. They passed the first-class section, through a heavy fire-door, into a large room with windows on three sides, cushioned rattan chairs, lounges and low bookcases. "This is the doctors' rest room," Mrs Hashim said with a throaty laugh. "But no doctors come, lah. So far, always empty. We can talk here till teatime."

"How did you meet your husband?" Su Weng asked. His broad handsome face and good eyes still intrigued her.

"Ah, another woman interested in Mr Abdul Hashim!" Mrs Hashim replied in a sarcastic manner. "We met in college. He was a *kampung* boy, never dated until he met me. I was an Arts Freshie, he was a senior in Engineering. We got married the next year because he was going to Manchester to study."

Su Weng was confused. "You went to England?"

"Oh, yes. What's so wonderful about England? Just another country." Mrs Hashim's voice softened. "Three years in Manchester. No children yet, no mother-in-law, no sisters-in-law, Abdul has a heart. We went to London a lot, lots of trips, parties." She began to bounce lightly in her seat. "That was a long time ago. Now Abdul is head of the Municipal Waterworks, very important job." She began to speak in pidgin, tripping the words like a simple melody. "Life funny, eh? Now I'm Mrs Hashim. Yah, the doctor say I stay two more weeks here. Must watch my blood count."

"I'll visit you," Chun Hong said.

"Oh, you visit your girlfriend, eh, Su Weng?"

But Su Weng had taken a *Reader's Digest Condensed Books* volume from the shelf and pretended not to hear.

It was Friday, eleven a.m., a time when orderlies, nurses and doctors had completed their morning duties and the men and women in Ward 4B, bandaged, medicated, and tranquillized, were left alone amid the sharp ammonia scent of mopped floors to contemplate time passing before the clatter of lunch carts and the smells of food, like the smells of wet cloths steaming before a fire, announced that time had, indeed, passed. Mrs Hashim took Su Weng to visit Mr Tan who had an emergency operation that morning, two days after surgery for a hernia. His bed was screened all around and in the shadowed quiet of the small enclosed womb, Mr Tan was lying motionless. They stood silently observing him sleep. His face was drawn and quite peaceful. Then he opened his eyes and looked at Mrs Hashim. For a moment, a recognition flickered in his eyes.

"Uncle, *ada baik?*" Mrs Hashim leaned over and spoke softly with her face close to his. "We missed you, eh. Where you been?"

Mr Tan said distinctly in a hoarse whisper, "In another country." He moved his hand as if to reach for her and closed his eyes.

Mrs Hashim leaned by his side for another moment while his eyes remained closed. Then she walked away without her usual dancing motions and went to her room to lie down.

Chun Hong visited Su Weng on Monday morning to say goodbye. Dressed in a white shirt and khaki pants he looked ordinary and dull. Only the pallor of his complexion and his long uncut hair indicated that he had been ill for some time. "I'll ring you when you come for the holidays," he said as he shook her hand.

"Aren't you coming back to visit Mrs Hashim?"

"No, there's no point."

"No point? I don't understand." Su Weng felt a shock of anger. Her face was sullen as she stepped back and sat on her bed.

"You like Mrs Hashim," he responded, his thin face unmoved and still friendly.

"Yes, she's the happiest person in the ward."

He shook his head. "If being crazy is happy, she's happy."

"She isn't crazy!" Su Weng said violently. "She just can't stay still."

174

"She's a manic-depressive." He began to walk up and down by her bed, turning occasionally to give her a quick look. "Besides, she's never going to get well. She has leukaemia."

Su Weng pressed her fingers into her palms. Her eyes were pricking with tears and she stared at him hatefully. She didn't want to hear what Chun Hong was saying.

"You don't know what these words mean, do you?" he asked.

Su Weng could only repeat, "She's not crazy."

He stopped pacing and took her tightly fisted hand. "We're all crazy. I'm crazy. I'm depressed all the time. Mr Tan is crazy. He's dying and doesn't know where he is. You're crazy also, but you don't know it." He said all this calmly as if he were instructing her.

She remained silent and allowed her hand to remain in his.

"It's different here. Things are normal here that are crazy outside. When you return home, you'll find that you've changed. You won't be normal any more."

Su Weng didn't believe him, but she didn't wish to argue. "All right." She pulled her hand gently away from his grip. "I hope you'll be okay in the future."

He suddenly appeared embarrassed, mumbled some words, and left abruptly.

She stayed in her room the rest of the day, reading and waiting for her mother's visit. Mrs Hashim didn't appear. On Tuesday, she went to look for Mrs Hashim and found that she had been moved to the isolation room at the end of the ward and wasn't permitted any visitors except for her family. Su Weng was leaving the ward the next day; she had already missed two weeks of study in the university.

Before she changed out of the hospital gown into the dress that her mother had brought, Su Weng sneaked into the isolation room to say goodbye. Mrs Hashim was sitting up in bed reading a Penguin paperback on art in the Muslim world. She had grown perceptibly thinner in the last few days, but she gave a gleeful grin when Su Weng slipped through the door. "Getting lonely, eh? What to do!

Nurses make sure I stay in bed all the time."

"I'm leaving today, Mrs Hashim," Su Weng said, drawing nearer.

Mrs Hashim's eyes were full of grieving. "So soon going away? Good luck, eh. You looking beautiful today."

Su Weng felt her mouth dry up. She thought she had never loved a friend like Mrs Hashim, but she didn't know what to say. "I hope you'll be all right," she whispered.

"Oh, fine, fine, I'm doing fine. The doctors say, maybe two more weeks, then I can go home also." Mrs Hashim had dropped her book and was waving her hands elaborately. She jiggled up and down as if impatient and the metal bars on the bed creaked.

"Oh, Mrs Hashim," Su Weng exclaimed, alarmed, "Complete rest in bed, remember! Please don't get excited. Goodbye!" and she left hastily, vigorously waving goodbye.

Walking down the hill with her mother, Su Weng turned back and looked up towards the windows of Ward 4B. She wondered which was the window that Chun Hong and she had leaned over these past weeks envying the people walking below. Someone was leaning out of a window on the fourth floor, and, for a moment, she thought she recognized Mrs Hashim's face, but, of course, it was too far for her to be sure. Briefly she pondered on the misery in Mrs Hashim's eyes earlier, then she looked up at the trees which lined the hospital road and at the great green stars springing from the branches, and she felt a tremendous happiness at being alive.

Haunting

TUESDAY WAS LIKE EVERY OTHER DAY. The sky above the sea was a taut blue which broke into ragged cumulus at the edges near the horizon. Blinding sunshine poured like sheets of burning rain into the compound where small trees of lime, papaya, prickly pear and custard apple were striving to grow. Only the slender areca palms were moving, their dark green fronds serrated by the breeze and tossed up and down, alternately shadowing and revealing thick clusters of orange nuts. They reminded Jenny of crab eggs, those sweet round clumps which suddenly glow bright orange as you break loose the shell. The smaller the female, the larger and sweeter the egg clusters. She was surprised to feel herself hungry; it was weeks since she had an appetite.

Dressing quickly and carelessly (already she could taste the sharp black coffee brew on the tip of her tongue), she didn't stop to note, as she had done every morning before, how much weight she was losing. Her thighs were flat and straight like a boy's. Her stomach was stretched so tight it pulled inwards between the pelvic bones which stuck out like switchblades. She had always been slim, but since she and her husband had moved into her mother-in-law's house, she had grown gradually more slender, then thin, then skinny, till now there was a skeletal quality to her frame, almost as if the flesh left on her body were becoming translucent and letting in light. As her dresses began to hang on her and she had to borrow Jong An's belts to keep her jeans up, she felt her mind, like her body, being stripped, tightening, turning hard and sharp and self-sufficient.

From somewhere deep in the house a clock was chiming ten. Picking up the car keys, she ran out of the bedroom, through the verandah, and across the compound to the Austin-Mini parked under the *angsana* tree. Su Weng and she had arranged to meet in a coffee shop off Royal Flower Street at ten to eat *dim sum*.Shutting her mind off from the anxiety which was still nibbling in the corner of her consciousness and concentrating on the empty knot of hunger in her belly, Jenny drove quickly through the narrow crowded streets.

As usual, leaving the house, she had seen no one. Her part of the house was always empty and soundless. She never got out of bed before nine, long after Jong An and his younger brother had left for work and school. Her mother-in-law and the ancient family servant, Toh Peh, never came into her rooms when she was present. Since she and Jong An moved in three months ago, she had woken up each morning to the golden empty sunshine in the garden and the utter dim silence in her rooms.

At first, Jenny had been pleased to give up her life of work. After the relentless routine of waking every weekday at six in order to drive fifteen miles through traffic whose fumes combined with the oil-soaked tarry smells from the macadam roads would give her a sick headache before she began teaching at seven-thirty, after the scramble to shop, cook, launder, and clean house in seven years of marriage, Jenny was pleased to lie back in bed, to stroll along the beach, to catalogue the various trees and plants in the large garden, and to sit and eat whatever was placed on the table. At first, she liked being treated like a guest in a first-class hotel. When she made the bed in the morning, she would find it re-made that afternoon with fresh, unwrinkled sheets. Forgotten panties discarded in a corner of the bathroom would appear washed, folded, and smelling of Ivory soap on top of her bureau. The faint sprinkle of powder over the mirror was gone by the time she was ready to make-up again; her lipsticks, perfume bottles and combs were wiped clean of fingerprints, spills, and stray hairs. At first, she enjoyed having these unseen assistants who seemed to anticipate her needs and to surround her with a vast sense of unaccustomed comfort.

No one, however, had said she was to do nothing. When she heard of Jong An's transfer to his hometown, she had immediately written to the State Education Department to request for a job in a school in town. The reply arrived a week after they had moved; there were no foreseeable vacancies except for positions in the outlying rural areas. They had discussed the situation, and Jong An suggested she take a break from work till a teaching post in town came through.

During the first month, Jenny luxuriated in the long stretches of time between Jong An's disappearance in the morning and his return at six when the sunny days rolled before her like a carpet of blue and gold. Hidden from the house by the wild plum bushes, she walked along the beach and gazed at the calm rippling waters of the Straits. It was fun to pick the pink and mauve shells, tinier than her little fingernails and no more than hardened curlicues gleaming among the fine white sand. She would spend whole mornings watching the sand crabs like bleached ants barely an eighth of an inch in length scuttling from cave to cave. Hurrying on pale spindly legs, almost transparent in the sunshine, they moved in and out of their watery tunnels, rolling before them pebbles almost half their size. She had lived all her life inland among the low hills and gravel of Selangor, and now, the shore which curved behind the house was an unknown kingdom in which Jenny felt all at once and strangely a child whose inheritance had finally come.

Her mouth full of *siew mai*, Jenny described those first weeks in her new home.

"Your mother-in-law must think you're nuts!" Su Weng laughed. "You mean you do nothing but stay out on the beach?"

"I sit out in the garden and read a lot."

"Don't you go shopping?" Su Weng asked curiously.

"Well, she goes shopping with Toh Peh every morning. They cook the meals and clean the house." Jenny hesitated, then added with a trace of irony in her voice, "They seem happy to leave me alone."

"Lucky you! A perfect mother-in-law. So, you're not going to find your own place?"

"How can I suggest that to Jong An?" Jenny thought her voice sounded disconsolate. She stopped eating and forced a smile. "It's his home. Besides, it's a large house. We have three rooms to ourselves. And we don't pay rent."

Su Weng grimaced. "Some people have all the luck. That's why it's taken you so long to look me up. You've been living the good life."

"You know, when I found you were back in town for term holidays, I felt relieved?" Jenny glanced around the coffee shop and lowered her voice. "We were such good friends at college, and I was hoping you would be exactly the same after all these years." She leaned forward and touched Su Weng's fingers. "I have to talk to someone. I think I'm going crazy."

"No one has her head more on her shoulders than you," Su Weng replied, squeezing her hand reassuringly. "But I can tell something's bothering you. You look like you've been starving for weeks. Are you having problems with Jong An?"

"Oh no," Jenny said, surprised. "It's the house."

"You don't get along with your mother-in-law?"

Jenny shook her head. "It's not that either. Actually, we hardly talk to each other. She's *Nonya,* you know, and she only speaks bazaar Malay. She chatters like a magpie to the servant and to Jong Teik, Jong An's brother. I think she likes me; anyway, she smiles at me when we meet. It's uncomfortable living with a mother-in-law one doesn't talk to, but we stay out of each other's way. No, it's the house. I think it's haunted." She caught Su Weng's sympathetic eye and waited, but suddenly impatient, she began to speak rapidly. "I can hear it. They leave me alone, oh, who knows why. Perhaps I was shy or uninterested. If you can imagine being alone all day with two old women. There's absolutely nothing I can say to them. You know how rotten my Malay is. It's embarrassing speaking like a child or, worse, an idiot. And they don't understand English or Cantonese. Then, I began hearing noises; just little house noises, you know—creaks and pings. It's an old house, built in eighteen something. You can see the age in the wood. Then ..." She put her hand to her mouth. "You're not going to believe me."

"Why shouldn't I?" Su Weng responded. Placing a dumpling in her mouth, she chewed placidly.

Jenny understood by this that her friend accepted the reality of her report. "Come over," she said intently, "and see for yourself. There's something about the house. I hear it, especially in the afternoons. The sound comes from deep inside. Sometimes I think it's coming from the mother's bedroom or from the kitchen, but when I track it down, it turns out to be only the mother and Toh Peh talking."

"What do they talk about?"

Jenny felt a flash of anger. "Who cares? Anyway, it's all in some mumbo-jumbo Malay. They shut up as soon as they see me." She was eager for Su Weng to visit. This would be the first time she was bringing a friend into the house. Till then, she had thought herself too much a stranger, a guest, to extend the house to another. A recognition was breaking through which she couldn't yet understand. "Come on," she repeated. "Spend the afternoon with me and tell me if I'm imagining things." She couldn't decide if the urgency with which she hurried Su Weng out of the shop into her car and headed towards the house was caused by her delight in finding a familiar friend to confide in or by the anger which seemed to have replaced the anxiety that had been probing at her self-confidence like a nagging voice.

She drove slowly, almost reluctantly. Once out of town, the road widened and followed the gentle curve of the coast. The shambling brick buildings along Old Beach Road gave way to rickety thatched shacks, and these flimsy huts in turn led to stretches of open shore interspersed by large stone and tile houses set back behind gates flanked by Foo statues or lotus sculpture or giant granite balls. There were at least thirty or forty such estates along Elephant Carriage Road. Her mother-in-law's house, as Jenny persisted in thinking about it, was about ten miles from the town, situated between the fenced grounds of a once-rich-man's mansion converted into an Association for Tin-Traders and an overgrown property, once a coconut plantation, but now a tangle of morning glory vines and wild *lallang*.

Jenny supposed the house was impressive. When Jong An first drove her through the long sandy driveway which circled the compound, she had felt a stab of possessive pride that this was now to be her home. The house was visually wide; it had wide stairs and balustrades centred between two wide sweeps of rooms and outhouses. This was the original building, constructed wide and narrow in depth to make the most of the sea breezes. Then the children and children's children had built more rooms, two wings of rooms in single file stretching back from the original facade towards the sea. Long shallow steps leading up to the verandah were tiled with green and blue porcelain painted with flowers and birds. The verandah, shaded by bamboo awnings, ran the whole length of the front and by the left wing. The floor was planked with teak and sandalwood. When she first stepped on it, it felt impossibly cool; the awning, smelling pleasantly of damp bamboo, creaked in a slight sea breeze. In the shade striped with the light falling through the bamboo slats, Jenny could almost imagine that she was on board a junk with the salty sea air stirring lazily on her cheeks and the hard wooden floor almost slippery under her feet.

She never recovered that first emotion. As she stood in the front hall with their five suitcases and numerous packing boxes by her feet listening to Jong An's mother, the mistress of the house, jabber in the singsong rush of *Nonya* Malay, she thought she would never feel at home. The rooms were such an odd jumble of impressions that they left no clear mark on her memory. Even now, as she paused before the steps with Su Weng, she could hardly bring them to mind. The main hall, which was never used, was crammed with an assortment of furniture, tall heavy glassed-in cabinets, high carved tables and awkward square armchairs fashioned out of teak. Each seemed a curious nineteenth-century piece, more at home in a museum, but together, they were indistinct, unusable rubbish put into storage. To the left of this large room stuffed with vases, out-of-date encyclopaedias and lacy doilies, which was always meticulously dusted and swept and which seemed to harbour echoes and puddles of darkness in its niches, was the major portion of the residence, the shared living room with a record-player, television, and cushioned rattan furniture, the dining room with cupboards full of flowered china and old tobacco tins which Jong An's father had collected, and a sunroom with a wall of louvred windows to let in air and light. The kitchen, the last room on that wing, was a primitive, poorly-lit room; it contained no modern appliances, only some charcoal clay burners and a cold water tap in a concrete sink. It was as if the men who built the house had given no thought to their women and had provided them with only walls, a roof, and a hole for a window, from which they expected the most delicious and nourishing food to appear.

Su Weng murmured appreciation of all she saw. She, unlike Jenny, seemed to enjoy the antiquarian charm of the furnishings until they came to the kitchen. In the bright shaft of sunshine which beamed through the solitary aperture in the back wall, they could see two old women dressed similarly in loose cotton *kebayas* and brown sarongs squatting on the wet kitchen floor. One was pounding a pestle in a stone mortar, the other was picking through a tray of dried peas. They formed a harmonious composition of brown shades and yellow colours, and they were talking in a continuous stream, first one, then the other, in an effortless mingling of voices.

As Jenny and Su Weng paused by the open door, they stopped chattering and the woman with the tray stood up and smiled. She nodded as Jenny said, "My mother-in-law." Pounding a red paste in her mortar, Toh Peh looked up indifferently. Even in the half light, her grey hair netted in a bun on the nape of her neck gleamed like an oiled nut. Her face was netted with wrinkles and expressionless.

"Let me show you our rooms," Jenny said uncomfortably as the two old women continued to look at them in silence. As soon as they were out of sight, she whispered, "Did you notice anything strange?"

"No."

She was disappointed. They were now in Jong An's and her private rooms, the first one being a sitting room with a modern sofa and two lounge chairs. Jenny swung her feet up, stretched her body the length of the sofa, and closed her eyes. Perhaps she was too sensitive. She could see that Su Weng had been unmoved by the tour. She had been so sure that another woman, a stranger, would have immediately sensed the disturbance, the air of tension; would have picked up, with that alertness to feelings underlying the surface of the ordinary, a certain distortion of senses, a disarrangement apparent in the main wing.

"You were right in calling this an old house. I would call it old-fashioned."

Jenny opened her eyes and sat up. Su Weng's tone indicated an empathetic warning that cheered her. "Tell me what you've observed."

"It's no place for you, Jenny! Everything's too old. Not that it's falling apart. In fact, when I saw that verandah, I thought we had moved to another country. The house is certainly solid and well looked after, but it doesn't belong to this century."

Again, Jenny was disappointed. There was a time when she would have agreed that she didn't belong there. When Jong An and Jong

Teik were home in the evenings or during the weekends, it was fun, like visiting. The three lounged in the living room, listening to noisy American music, dancing, watching a television program, or reading, relaxed in the others' companionable silence. The mother and Toh Peh kept apart; they would meet them only during meals when the two old women would serve them, but they took their meals separately. Jenny supposed they ate in the kitchen or in the mother's private wing which ran parallel to her rooms separated by a sandy path and low spiky pandan bushes. However, when Jenny was alone, the effervescence and ease she felt in the company of the two men disappeared. She had begun to feel more and more like an unwelcome intruder whose presence was banished by the mother's and servant's silence. She tried on a few occasions when she met them in the garden or when she lunched alone in the dining room and brought the dishes to the kitchen to say something pleasant to the mother or to Toh Peh, but their blank or smiling nods made it clear they didn't understand her. It was then that the thought that she should be somewhere else pricked her. Recently, she had begun to rebel against the domestic arrangement. That was when she heard the whispers from the house.

No, she no longer felt that she didn't belong here. The voices she had been hearing, although they made her anxious, didn't frighten her. They seemed to be whispering a kind of suggestion which she still couldn't grasp. She wanted to place their physical source in the house, the whisperers in their room; and this curiosity, the desire to track down the corner, the shadow, the hole, from where the voices emanated, gave her a goal, a claim to being in the house.

She re-stacked the magazines on the coffee table and attempted to keep her voice light. "Well, it's going to be my home for a long time."

Su Weng shrugged. "It's sort of impressive, in an old-fashioned way. They once had a lot of money." She glanced at Jenny's nervous hands rearranging the magazines. "You haven't been eating. Doesn't that tell you something?"

"I don't like *Nonya* food," Jenny responded. She circled her left wrist with her right thumb and middle finger and jiggled it to show the slack. "I've lost over twenty pounds. It's having to eat alone. Every morning facing the cold coffee and eggs, and every lunch sitting alone to rice and leftovers from yesterday's dinner. Jong An thinks his mother and Toh Peh are wonderful cooks; he eats plates of rice and *sambal*. You know, the two women spend the whole day shopping and cooking. Every evening there are about five or six fresh dishes. But I can't stand the taste."

"Have you tried cooking for yourself?"

"It's impossible. You saw the kitchen. Besides, the two women would never let me cook."

Su Weng shrugged again. "Doesn't that tell you something?"

Jenny sprang to her feet impatiently. "Tell me, tell me. Are you trying to tell me I'm crazy?"

Su Weng was startled. "No, no. Only, it seems to me if you don't like living here, you should find your own place."

Jenny shook her head. "I told you the house is haunted. Didn't you feel anything as we were walking through?"

"Feel?" Su Weng repeated, and as Jenny nodded her head, she said, "The house felt old." She looked at Jenny who was clearly waiting for more and continued, "It was sort of quiet, like it was empty. Or like it was waiting for someone." Then, as Jenny sighed, she stopped and shook her head, "But it doesn't mean anything."

"Listen!" Jenny said, lifting her head up and back with a faraway expression in her half-closed eyes. "Do you hear it?" She turned to her friend.

"No."

"Shhh. Listen carefully." She held on to Su Weng's fingers.

Su Weng's fingers were firm and warm. Jenny could feel her own hand vibrate as if on the steering wheel of an accelerating car. She was sure the tremor was passing like electricity between their two hands, the nervous humming of the blood in her responding to the faint humming in the air which she had just picked up and which her friend must also detect, if not of herself, through the steady thrumming of her fingers. Su Weng's eyes widened. She seemed to turn her head towards the shut door, then she wrenched her hand away from Jenny's grip. "You aren't well!" she exclaimed. "You should see a doctor before you fall quite ill."

Jenny pressed her two hands together to silence the sound. She could hear it clearly, an audible whisper which blew in from somewhere and filled her head till the short hairs on the nape of her neck stirred anxiously. The sound was a light howl, an oooohh which could almost be the wind whistling through a crack except for its insistence, its resemblance to human calling. "I'm all right," she said faintly. "I'll drive you home." A dark nausea rolled over her eyes and she began to heave. Then she was sick all over the bathroom floor, too sick to be embarrassed or apologetic. She found herself lying in her darkened bedroom, listening to Su Weng clean the mess next door, then she fell asleep and woke up to hear Su Weng and Jong An talking outside her door. She was fresh after her sleep and hungry all over again.

"Hello," she called, and was so pleased by their prompt appearance that she laughed out loud. "What a good friend you are, Weng. I'm sorry you had to clean up. That's the first time I've thrown up. I'm hungry. Can we go out for supper?"

She knew she would not be able to tell either of them what had become suddenly clear to her as she slept that afternoon, when her helpless body, void, her mind had listened, gathering the eddies and ghosts of sounds and sifting through them for their significance, for she had recognized the whispers. They were saying "You," "You," "You." It was the house giving voice to a welcome for her, despite the mother's remoteness, Toh Peh's coldness. Like a child with a mind of its own, it was calling. If the house was haunting her, Jenny thought, it was only a playful and tender tug for her attention.

She sat up in bed and repeated with delight, "I'm hungry."

Su Weng hurried to her side while Jong An lingered by the door. "Good thing you are!" she said brightly. Lowering her voice, she looked down with concern on her friend. "I called the doctor this afternoon. Have you thought you may be expecting?"

Jenny knew at once that she was right.

The damp evening breeze was tossing the long leaves of the palm trees outside the bedroom window. A delicious sense of calm and ease seemed to breathe from the darkening blue sky in which the broad strokes of pink, purple, lavender and gold were gradually being extinguished. "Of course," she said and turned to share the pride that was swelling in her throat with her husband, when she saw that he had been weeping.

"Toh Peh had an attack this afternoon," he said, his face sullen as the light left the room. "We're burying her tomorrow."

The rising night wind blew around the house. "How awful!" Jenny cried. Through the window, she could see the first fireflies spark up in the compound. The phosphorescent glimmers caught, died, and caught again. "But she was old, Jong An," she added consolingly. "We'll find a new servant soon."

Conversations of Young Women

AT THE FAREWELL LUNCH we gave her the day before she left for London, Meng told us about a shattering thing that had happened to her when she was a child. Her confession made a confusing story. I thought then that she had nothing to do with the main events, that it was not she who was the heroine in the story, if such a story could have a heroine.

Meng was maudlin that afternoon. She was especially sentimental when she was depressed, and I avoided her then because she became a different person in those moods, not at all likeable. We had been celebrative over lunch. It was the first time in almost a year that all six of us had gathered together, and we felt we were saying goodbye, finally, to the kind of life we had enjoyed for the last five years or so, a carefree student intimacy which, now, with Lois and Ai May married and Meng leaving for London, was over. Endings are events to celebrate, and we drank beer as if the afternoon marked the end of a final examination we had sat for.

"If it wasn't for the rape," Meng said, "I wouldn't be leaving the country."

"What rape?" we wanted to know. Meng's confiding moments,

even when unwelcomed, had often provided us with curious subjects.

"Well," she replied, "you didn't know me then. I was thirteen, probably shy and stupid. I knew little about life, you know, boys and all that." She touched her bright dress as if to reassure herself of her present female wisdom and continued above our laughter and hoots, "It was difficult for me to learn about women since I didn't have a mother. I have a stepmother you know, but she is no relation to me, just a total stranger."

"What happened when you were raped?" Ada prompted her. We had heard of Meng's motherless condition before and it was no longer an interesting subject.

"Oh, it didn't happen to me, but it was a shocking experience still. It left me feeling for a long time as if I were a cripple or a hunchback."

"No," we said, unbelievingly.

"It was my friend, Mary, who was raped. I was in Form Three at the Convent of the Immaculate Conception. Mary had finished school the year before. She was two or three years older, I'm not sure, but she seemed much older than me. I met her on Chinese New Year. I had woken up that morning feeling I was missing something. My stepmother was entertaining relatives; my first aunt was in the house with the children. She was very poor; her husband had died, and she was taking in babies for a living. She visited us often, with different babies each time, all ugly and dirty and always wet. It was Chinese New Year, and the walls were crawling with wet, drooling babies. First aunt was helping my stepmother to pluck the chickens, and when she saw me, she began to talk under her breath. It was a dirty habit she had, muttering under her breath every time she saw me, but this time I heard what she was saying. "Aiyah, poor child! Not to have a mother." I tell you it was a revelation for me. Suddenly I knew she was telling me something."

"Yes, that's sad," Ada said impatiently. "But what happened next?"

Meng stared at us morosely. "You want to know what happened to

Mary. She was a reporter for the T.A. newspaper. T.A. is a very small town, you know. I thought she was an important person because she covered all the news in the town. She took me along to some strange places, The Hawkers' Association Building, the Welfare Home for the Old, the Methodist Church Community meetings, a Hindu funeral, and after that a Hindu wedding. I found out that T.A. was not such a small town after all. Mary told me that T.A. was like the Batu Caves; the town had many caves and each cave had its own community and its own skylight. I learned some strange things about T.A. Some of the old men in the Welfare Home, well, I wouldn't be left alone with them for any money. There was this old man, brown and wrinkled like an old shoe that's walked all over the place and is no good any more. He ate porridge and salted egg for every meal which was all he did. If he had any life before he was put in the home, it didn't show. Talking about food, the Hindus I met never eat beef; some eat nothing but vegetables. It's not an important fact, but there are people who remain Hindus all their lives. And the nuns in the Cheng Buddhist Temple remain nuns all their lives; they seldom even leave the Temple. I used to wonder if they were curious about the outside world."

"They are who they are," one of us said. "It isn't necessary for them to know everything in the world."

"No-o-o. But it is necessary for us to know that the world is not a cave."

"Not all of us are adventurous," Lois said impatiently. "I like living in a nice home with orchids in the garden and an *amah* in the kitchen."

"I'm not criticizing you. I only want to explain myself to you. Or perhaps I am apologizing for something of which you have no idea. Besides, my story is about Mary. I had met her that New Year's Day. I was cycling around the town aimlessly, and, as it was the New Year, there was nothing in the streets; no people, no cars, all the shops were shut. Nowhere to go and nothing to do. Then the bicycle wheel went flat. I was sitting on the roadway about to cry when Mary found me. She brought me to her home and gave me an aspirin. I lived by her side after that day, like a sister. Until she was raped.

"Because of her job, it seemed everyone in T.A. knew her. There was a magic circle around her because she was so glamorous. She wore tight pants and cycled from meeting to meeting, asking questions and taking notes for the newspaper. Through her, I learned who the important people in T.A. were. She told me everything runs by favours; you pull the right strings and meet the right people. The world is webbed by influence. T.A. became a strange place to me, a riddle of tunnels running from cave to cave. While some people sat in their caves and never left them, others, like Mary, ran like messengers through the tunnels.

"Then, one morning, in school, my friends were whispering about something scandalous that had happened in the cemetery last night. They wouldn't tell me about it, but I read about it in the papers when I got home. She was out in the park with a boy when two men pushed her into a car. They were friends of her father who were taking her home, they said, because she was out with an Indian man. She was too wild, so they punished her. They took her to the cemetery and raped her."

"That's depressing."

"But there is more to it. She lost her job. The paper reported the trial and all the sordid details of the medical examination. The cemetery was crowded with sightseers. The men pleaded provocation and were given six months. No one in the town would go near her."

"And you?"

"I was going to be brave. I went to the pictures with her the next week, but it was different; I couldn't see that she was the same person anymore. I couldn't go through with it, the friendship. I never went out with her again." Meng began to cry.

"You shouldn't feel guilty about it," Ai May said. "You were too young to know better, and, perhaps, she did provoke the men. After

192

all, she was out late at night with an Indian man."

"That's just it," Meng said, blowing into her napkin. "We women are the first to turn against ourselves. I met her again once, accidentally, on the street. She had grown fat. She said she was married and was going to have a baby."

"It looks like she came out all right in the end," I said.

Meng stared at me for a long time. "You don't know what you're talking about," she said finally. "None of us do."

Meng writes chatty letters from London where she is studying interior decoration. Sometimes, when I read her letters, I remember our last conversation and wonder if she, among us six, knew most what she was talking about.

Transportation in Westchester

I HAD JUST BEGUN TEACHING in a junior college in suburban New York. The college was in a small town, one of those arbitrary settlements which bead the numerous highways of the United States. The epithet 'suburban' could not be applied to the campus itself, for the municipality had set aside two hundred acres of grasslands for the gratification of its few thousand lower-middle-class students. The college's ungated fieldstone walls enclosed pastoral exurbia, and to that place I quested forth daily.

I was living then in a crumbling nineteenth-century brownstone, dignified in real estate advertisements as a townhouse, in the deeps of Brooklyn. Brooklyn is nothing like a little town by a brook. Its decaying wharves and buildings cover like an irremediable fungus the western half of a once-verdant Long Island, from the East River to the Atlantic Ocean. Although signs near collapsing railway tracks still boast to its being the fourth largest city in the United States, it was incorporated in 1897 as a borough into the conglomerate known today as New York City. In attractiveness, wealth, style, and suitors, Brooklyn is the stepsister to the profligate good-time bitch, Manhattan. From my raunchy and Hispanic-spiced 'block', as the New Yorker calls his community of buildings, I headed every morning for the rustic academe in Westchester County.

The college was a good fifty miles away, not as a crow flies, which is, I imagine, in gentle dips and sweeps, but as the superhighway 287 speeds in lines of berserk automobiles, each gnashing at the other's fenders. Having refused to learn to drive all my life, at the anxious age of thirty-one, I had no desire to master a 100-horse-powered machine of steel and plastic; thus, lacking the courage to rush the merging lanes, I took the coward's way out. This way was by subway, by train, and by bus, which then unloaded me onto the carparks of the college from which I wended my way through barriers of metal, six-cars deep, to my office.

I spent three months, from September to November, commuting by track, rail, bus, and foot, a journey which accounted for 550 hours of my life or almost twenty-three full days. During that period I became schooled in American divisions. I should add, at this point, that I am an Asian woman, still youthful in appearance, still genteelly shabby—this being my pretension to simplicity—and then, although no longer so, still insensible to class distinctions.

On my first day at work, while I waited for the train home at North White Plains, a middle-aged black man tried to pick me up. He was a railway maintenance man, he told me; he asked if I were a schoolteacher, praised me on my pretty handwriting as I was marking a student paper, and so continued to hold a long conversation with me, although I didn't say a word in reply. "See ya tomorrow evening, honey!" he said as I boarded my train. This incident surprised me. I had lived in the United States for seven years, five of them in the racial free-for-all of New York City, and I had never before this evening been paid the compliment of an advance by a black man.

On my second day, I waited for a train home at White Plains, having discovered the free bus which ran from the campus gym to the White Plains Railroad Station. Here again I found another sociable stranger, an elderly black woman who carried a large brown shopping bag and dispersed advice as I limped past her towards the station platform.

"Soak them in hot salt water, honey! I always buy Epsom Salts an' I jus' sits and soaks them tired feet. Never fails."

Her name was Mrs Callaghan, as I later inferred from the course of one of her monologues. Mrs Callaghan was a small woman whose head barely came up to my shoulder. It was a finely wrinkled head, coloured like tanned leather luggage, and she wore a brown nubby suit that must have been custom-ordered to match.

The first evening of our acquaintance, I thought her odd, whimsical, wise even. She reminded me immediately of Tiresias appearing in the disguise of a brown knit; it seemed apt that she should materialize, friendly as can be, in the darkening evening, to me, a weary traveller ignorant of the train schedule, suffering from blistering feet, and lonely for a companion.

Her speech took the form of slow, lengthy monologues. It reminded me of the epic and heroic style of the *Odyssey*. As she spoke, I noted with fascination how she slipped one sentence into the mouth of another; the thought would run up one track and end up at the start of another indistinguishable from the first. Like the blind poet of the *Odyssey*, conventions governed her narratives; thus, as she moved from one story to the next, she would lick her lips with a quick lizard-like movement and add in the wet trembling pause, "So it goes."

"No point hurryin'. The train jus' done gone by. Won' be 'nother till seven. I could of caught it, but I warn' 'bout to hurry. Used to hurry when I was younger, but no more. Makes no difference when I git home now."

I perceived the depth of her experience and thanked her humbly for sharing it. "It's my first day at this station," I confessed. "I will have to get used to missing the train."

"If you don' git this one, you'll git the next. They comes along, one after the other. No use hurryin'."

Finding ourselves alone on the waiting platform, we settled our separate bags at our feet and sat together on the bench. I was eager to learn of the vagaries of the Harlem/Hudson line and pressed my guide for information.

"Oh Lord, yes. Thirty-seven years I've taken the train. Never make a date with a man for the evenin' for you never know when the train is late. You be waitin' here and he be waitin' there with his tongue sticking out. No use makin' a date. Never know when you'll be late. So it goes."

She slipped her little pink tongue out and tugged at her hair. I noticed then that tufts of yellow-grey were sticking out under her ears and at the nape of her neck and that her straight black hair was only a short wig which, like a winter cap, did not cover all her head. This revelation of human vanity warmed me. She could have been seventy years old under the incongruously adolescent wig. I suspected she knew immeasurably more than I did; the figure of my grandmother stood by my shoulder in the company of all those selfless and loving grandmothers spoken for in children's tales.

"I'm so hungry," I whispered in a rush of confidence, hoping that perhaps she would produce a biscuit from her capacious shopping bag.

"Don' they feed you there?" she asked, lifting her eyebrows. Then she worked her lips as if to chew reflectively on the lunch that she had been fed.

" 'nother hot day tomorrow. You can tell by the sun."

"Can you really? How do you tell?"

"Why, it's a red sunset. That mean 'nother hot day. Oh Lord! The summer wen' so quick. I never saw it go so quick. An' no hot days, such a nice pleasant summer."

"It was terribly hot last week."

"Well, that's summer. You got to see some hot days. It wen' so quick. So it goes."

Her tongue leapt out swift as a newt swallowing her pause; she pulled at her shiny black wig, dislodging more of the grey curls under her ears. "You better do something about those blisters. When you have to be standin' on your feet for the whole day, you gotta watch out for the feet. Standin' on your feet the whole day, they gotta be good."

I wondered why she thought I would be standing on my feet the whole day. It occurred to me she might have mistaken me for a salesgirl, someone who was fed in her company's cafeteria. Not wishing to tell her she was wrong, I smiled and kept silent.

"Yes, thirty-seven years I've bin workin' for the same people. My boss, he don' mind me and I don' mind him. They be nice people. Live in Harrison jus' a little way from here. The boy, he's grown now, he calls and says, 'Are they treatin' you right?' They better treat me right, or he come down and tell them what. He calls and says, 'Come visit me for Christmas.' He lives in California now. He says, 'If you pay your fare over, I'll pay your fare back.' An' know what? I jus' might do that."

By this time, disappointed in Mrs Callaghan's powers as a guide or even as a surrogate grandmother, I had taken my students' papers out of my schoolbag and was making a studious pretence of reading them. She glanced at me, faced the broad orange glow of the evening settling over the flat roads and scattered buildings of White Plains and said, "Know a funny story? My mother had a friend told a lie on me. Said I did somethin' when I didn' do it, and my mother, she came home and smacked me for it. I was mad. Isn't that somethin'? To tell a lie on me? It wouldn' of bin so bad if I did done it, but I didn' do it, and, boy, was I mad! An' know what? I never forgave her. No, my sister called me and said she was dead an' would I come to see her. An' I said, no, I wouldn' see her when she was alive, an' I wouldn' see her now that she's dead. No, I never forgave her, comin' or goin'."

There was a moral to this tale which rushed into my unprotected ears like the smooth beat of a tide. I could not ignore the flow, and, bowing my head over my papers penitentially, I smiled. Mercifully, the train pulled in. I followed Mrs Callaghan to her seat, then

198

walking past her expectant face, I hid in a seat two cars behind.

Guilt and pleasure at shaking her loose chilled and warmed me alternately all the way through to Brooklyn. Riding the F train home that night, I missed the desolate hollowness of solitude which, like a strong drink after a hard day, usually saw me reeling through the front door punch-drunk, filled with second wind, and frisky as the life of the party. I was depressed that I had not read the signs correctly; the blind poet, Tiresias, my guide, was nothing but an old windbag of a lady. As I dropped into a black sleep of dejection, I recalled distinctly the twenty themes still to be read for the next day.

The next morning was cool with washed skies and creamy sunshine, less autumnal than like a mild spring morning. With no thought of last night's encounter, for a good night's sleep works like a bleach on my conscience, I read my students' papers on the train to work. Texts emerged, resounding like prophecies and impressing themselves on my memory:

> *Laura lives in White Plains. She is saving for a car so it will be easier for her to get to the college. She has been saving since December and hopes to buy a car this year.*
>
> *John has just been in a car accident. A woman hit him from behind. Luckily, he wasn't hurt, but the car was wrecked.*

The leitmotif woven through the themes was the automobile as dominant force, the coilspring of a world presented as mechanistic with all the objective mute terror and charm that attend such a system. The themes did not speak *ecce homo* nor of a universe *sub aeternitatis;* they spoke naively, instead, of a world tigerish, unstable, expressed in images of the cougar, the wild cat, the fury, the thunderbird of change, naturally obsolescent, and beautiful in chrome and vinyl. Not the Great Wheel of Being unified humanity, but radial tires spinning in loops of superhighways hummed as suburban experience. I began to know the nature of the beast: private transportation, as my students spoke to me in their writing, was of a nature wholly material, but it also symbolized a state of mind, a state of nature in which the grace of middle-class mobility sanctified the awful killing separation of driver from driver and the senseless consumption of precious and irreplaceable energy whose burning fumigated the earth's sweet air.

Waiting for the bus home that evening, I pondered these thoughts. Around me some ten or more black women students sat talking, in their inimitable dialect, of school and 'what they do here'. I noted five lanky black males behind me; they sported sweatshirts and jackets emblazoned with various logos and insignias of the college. These men spoke exuberantly, their voices penetratingly loud and jocular. Their speech was colourful, sprinkled with profanities, and, finally, it struck me as hostile.

I had taught for three years previously in the South Bronx, a ghetto which intrudes into the present like the American nightmare of its urban future. The South Bronx is a condemned country of burned-down buildings, a war zone where junkies and the unprotected poor crowd each other in abandoned tenements and where abused children and rats as large as Australian hares scrabble together in the debris of vacant lots. But those students in the South Bronx who studied in unwindowed classrooms, bumping shoulders and knees, writing illegibly and incoherently of their experiences, never raised their voices in profanity so frequently nor so aggressively as the young black men waiting for a bus under the green branches of an oak tree.

These youths, who had just emerged from a gymnasium equipped with an Olympic-sized swimming pool or from a towered library, threw their four-lettered words like javelins. What were they scoring, I wondered. All I saw were a few uncomfortable white students; two brunettes, earnestly hanging on to their conversation as if they were on telephone lines, and three males whose flared nostrils, like foals scenting danger, registered disgust and sullen superiority. Having drawn up a list of obscenities in the English language when I was sixteen, I found the words that flew in the air unimaginative, repetitious and altogether forgettable, except for the peculiar musicality of their pronunciation. But my presence in this murky blue air implied my participation in their game; I began to wonder if some administrator passing by would approve of my 'hanging out' with the 'dudes'. Besides, surely an Asian woman who had cause to feel a historical hostility in this idyllic American campus should not herself be subjected to such hostility?

Perhaps I was overreacting. After the first week of public transportation, I took stock of my bearings: I was tense, irritable, nervous, depressed. Mrs Callaghan's evening appearances were beginning to irk me. That Friday evening as I was smiling numbly through another of her monologues, I had a sudden insight to her character. Mrs Callaghan was a domestic! A small polite person inside said to me, "She takes you for one of her own." And why not? Every morning the train stopped at 125th Street where dozens of blacks climbed aboard for work in Westchester County. Every evening other black women nodded familiarly to Mrs Callaghan and me. What else would I be taken for, bound for Westchester in my mild-mannered skirts and worn-down heels, my black Chinese hair tied back in a bun, and carrying an old schoolbag?

That Saturday I went shopping and bought a silk blouse. It cost me fifty-nine dollars and ninety-nine cents plus tax, but the extravagance paid off on Monday night when I met Mrs Callaghan.

"Nice shirt you have there," she said with her mouth open in consternation.

"It's an old shirt," I replied politely, then turned firmly to my newspaper behind which I shut my face and ears till I boarded the train and dodged into the smoking compartment.

The next evening she was waiting for me in an elegant lace suit and white wrist-length gloves.

"Oh, it's an old dress," she said as I unwarily raised my eyebrows. "So it goes. Did I tell you 'bout my dog? Ten years I have him now an' jus' the sweetest poodle you can see ..."

The oppressive sensation of being a victim to victims hung over me each evening on the trip home. I began to resent Mrs Callaghan, the black males, their eager friendliness, and their penetrating speech. One evening after a particularly heavy teaching schedule, from behind the bus where the tall black youths sat came a whiff of marijuana. The pungent smoke soon filled the bus and, I suppose, my lungs. I grew nauseous, giddy, and a little hilarious. The impulse to stand up and deliver a lecture on culture and anarchy, decline and fall, the wasteland, was difficult to suppress. I wanted to say, "Why do you sit at the back of buses? Your fathers and mothers were forced to sit at the back, to suffer segregation, but you choose to segregate yourselves. You are the image of the victory of racism—now you are free, you cannot lay down the burden of your history of slavery." What would have happened if I had spoken so?

The bus lurched by the railroad station, and I climbed down trembling and close to tears. I waited for the train by the steps to the platform. I was hungry, exhausted, and my feet hurt. Memories of early years floated through my mind.

I am ten years old and home from school in a letdown and patched uniform. My brothers and I are waiting for father to come home from work. He will carry home a package of rice and greens from a foodstand, and he will share the food, our only meal for the day, equally among his seven children. What will I grow up to be, I think then, being too young to be a mother to my brothers and too old to be a child. I will grow up to be a servant to a rich family who will feed me all their leftovers, and I will never be hungry again. I will carry home brown paperbags full of leftovers.

As the train roared past the station, I examined my dingy brown skirt smeared with chalkdust. Ah, no, Mrs Callaghan, you will not trap me so easily.

The next day I applied for a driver's permit and a bank loan for a new car, and now I drive to work in Westchester County in a brand-new automobile.

202

A Pot of Rice

IT WAS RAINING HARD when she got back to the apartment. Stepping over the letters on the hallway floor, she headed for the bathroom and sat fully clothed on the toilet. A mouldy smell from the cold walls tickled her nose: she sneezed sharply and shivered under the green sweater, sodden as her hair. Between the subway stop and the apartment door was a good fifteen-minute walk and even running pell-mell she was soaked. She wrenched the matted wool over her head. The pink shirt beneath was wet also except, for some reason, around the buttons. She tugged at the vinyl boots. They were too small to begin with and now the wet calluses stung, rubbed raw by the thudding sprint on cracked pavements.

Plump Steve Katz's face wobbled into view when she closed her eyes. Pinned to the grey sheet behind her lids, his pink adolescent head trembled prematurely bald. She wished she could like him more. He was one of the few students to show some curiosity about her, and, if that large round body were expressive of feeling, she could almost believe he had a crush on her.

How her neck was aching!

The bus was half-an-hour late and the waiting passengers had backed up around the block. She stood all the way, mashed in the middle of the bus between two silky blonde girls and a bulky woman in a nursing uniform who stared hard at her and leaned their bodies away distinctly because her clothes were already quite wet by the time the bus pulled in. That half-an-hour wait meant catching the Lex. at Forty-second Street at 4.50 p.m. at the precise moment, it seemed to her, that thousands of offices, banks, stores, hospitals, schools, libraries, businesses, luncheonettes, and other containers of people burst their doors and leaked their smelly, twitching, tightjawed, black-edged-under-fingernails contents into the avenues and underground tunnels. All the way home she had shrunk herself as small as a centre in a music box and now her body hurt.

Only the sad students liked her: the fat or short or stammering. She didn't care to think of them as she rode the subway. These students liked anyone who paused to smile. They stopped to smile themselves, perhaps because they had nothing better to do. Steve Katz, Bertha Willard. They hung around her after class, walked her to class from the office. Perhaps she never showed them she had anything better to do, although often she had nothing to say and nothing to share except understanding that they all alike were missing something.

A student like Robert Healey said nothing all the time. Yet he took up a whole corner of the classroom, his legs tightly encased in greasy blue dungarees sprawled wide and his handsome torso positioned boldly to face the open door. She didn't dare throw him a question, for it would have fallen on his thrust-out groin and twitched shamefully there.

The papers he handed in always on time were dull. She wrote back, "You can do much better work than this. C+.", but he didn't care and never came up to complain. He was like Susan Krammer, Jack O'Hagen, Donna D'Agostino—almost all the students in two sections of Introduction to Composition. They came to class on time and waited for the end of the hour before leaving—thank God for middle-class conformity—but their faces brooded above the open textbooks like those of hardened young criminals planning a jailbreak. She felt exactly the same way. Finally stripped naked Su Yu dried her damp arms and chest with a rough faded purple towel. To teach in Queens, to live in Brooklyn—she hadn't bargained for the jolting two-hour commute each way or for the dreary piles of compositions to be graded each week. It was like slogging through endless mud slides, the composted heaps of a city's garbage, while fluttering the girl-guide's bandana.

Robert Healey sprawled in a corner of her mind, relentlessly bored by her.

She slammed the refrigerator door. Already she knew she would serve rice for dinner. Mark would make a face. And she would make a curry, very spicy. The heat from the cloves and chillies and the white steam from the rice would warm her and spark the brown lonely kitchen with fiery scents.

Wrapped in the old navy-blue bathrobe she trudged old-womanish and barefoot across the kitchen from refrigerator to sink to stove. Through the window she saw the backyard still light in the early November evening. Large drops left over from the afternoon storm gathered on the drooping branches and fell steadily from the Ailunthus which thrust out of the glass-spangled earth to suck up half the open sky. Holding the pot full of rice and water she stopped to look. Light and sky. A slight catch in her chest yearned for the white space not yet consumed by the tree or by the evening. Soon, she remembered, the cold will lock up the yard again; the ground will freeze into a solid black sheet, and she will begin all over again to hate the landlady when the hot water runs out.

Her father had died last year. He had been dead for two weeks before she knew of it. Her brother wrote to tell her of what she could no longer help days after the funeral. Mark had been terrified by the crying jags which overtook her in the middle of sleep, but they gradually grew fewer, less uncontrolled. With her father's death there was no longer any reason to leave the city from whose harbour the Statue of Liberty seemed to gaze across the oceans to Singapore as if towards a giant Chinatown ghetto. Remaining in New York with Mark, she felt she was merely choosing to remain in open water, having left behind the narrow concrete island crowded with socialist housing developments.

Su Yu watched the water boil over the lid and the milky starch sizzle on the gas flame before she lowered the heat. Mark could not get rice to cook to the sticky texture she preferred because he did not allow the water to boil over. She could not eat the gritty grains he served. Their food habits made them strangers to each other while most Americans, she thought sadly, held hands over slices of toasted Wonder Bread.

When grandfather died, his massive mahogany coffin on the back of the estate truck was hidden by mounds of white and yellow frangipani. Houses almost three feet high with green and yellow translucent paper windows were massed on top of the truck. There were even paper and bamboo garages and paper cars—the latest in sporty convertibles—and skinny men in black suits and top hats: effigies burned at the grave site to keep grandfather company in the other world, together with mountains of gold and silver paper which the women, staying up the whole night in grandfather's house, giggling and gossiping, had shaped into bricks. Sons, daughters, grandchildren, uncles, aunts, cousins, second and third cousins, in-laws, employees, debtors, tenants, strangers also—half the town walked in the procession behind the truck which rolled slowly behind a trail of wailing trumpets, moaning oboes, banging cymbals, and rattling drums. Bare-chested gangsters leaped from the truck to herd away cyclists and rickshaws. Young men carried banners of bright-coloured cloth emblazoned with laments and old men pushed carts loaded with water pots for the family who stumbled in the heat behind the truck. Her black dress had just come from the dyer's and smelled sweetly of faded flowers. She wore a hood of gunny sack and grass sandals tied around her shoes. Everywhere women were crying and waving their arms helplessly.

What a splendid display of mourning that was, she thought, and felt tears of self-pity prick. This is the time of prayers for father, she remembered. Her mother would have the altar freshly dusted and a clean red prayer cloth hung in the front. She would place bowls of rice and soy chicken and cups of tea and brandy before a large photograph of her husband. Was his appetite for good food and drink lost merely because his body had died? Su Yu stared at the pot of cooked rice. In its steam she saw her father's greedy smile appear like a sudden daydream.

Mark found the dining table set for worship when he got home after his late meeting. A blurred machine-made snapshot of Sue's father was propped before a candlestick which stood behind a cereal bowl filled with cooked rice and a plate holding a whole boiled chicken. The rice was ashy—was it from the candleflame or from the mould in the air? The chicken's boiled skin was discoloured, dotted with pink and black feather marks which showed garishly under the fluorescent light.

Sue, wearing a red dress and with gold barrettes in her hair giggled when she saw his face. "We mustn't eat until he has finished his meal," she warned.

"What's all this?"

"I'm mourning the first year of my father's death. This is the ritual of ancestor worship."

"Well, how do you know when your ancestor has finished eating? I'm hungry."

"You throw two coins." She held up two quarters.

"And then?"

"Oh, I forget! It's either two heads or two tails."

"What will you do? You've forgotten! Does this mean I don't get to eat tonight?"

Su Yu smiled. "I know my father, I'll know when he's finished eating."

Mark went to the bedroom and turned on the television. He wasn't hungry any more, not for cold sticky rice anyway. And the chicken looked more like a dead thing than a meal, as if the essence of food had left it and only the material stringy flesh remained. "This is the first time," he said loudly, hoping she would hear in the kitchen, "you haven't served me first."

Two Dreams

SHE WAS SITTING on the carrier of her brother's bicycle while he cycled fast on the beach. On one side of them the sea frothed in little breaks and wetted the wheels as they veered effortlessly by the contours of the embankment. On the other side, the grassy and rocky bank rose steeply to the road and to the interior houses screened by trees and bright flowering bushes. "Only in Malaysia," Martha said, "do people take you on pleasure rides." Then she laughed and woke up immediately at the sound of her laughter.

February in New York was cold—a clouded and snow-sooted month during which Martha dreamed repeatedly of her hometown and of the warm salty sea of her childhood, like embryonic fluid, she thought, to which she returned in her sleep. Finally in late March, she borrowed money for a return ticket from her husband and boarded a TWA 707 home.

At London, she left her winter coat behind in the waiting room and shivered until the plane landed in Calcutta. There the airline personnel arranged for the London Office to hold the coat for her until she could pick it up on her return flight three weeks later. Released from the worry of her loss and from the European winter, she slept for the full six hours it took the plane to reach Kuala Lumpur where she disembarked to be greeted by her family.

She slept also, through the first few days at home, on a narrow twin bed directly beneath a slowly rotating ceiling fan. Then, as she adjusted to the moist clinging heat, she slept on the wood floor, with the window shutters closed and the door shut. Her breathing was slow, audible, and exhausted. She timed it to the turns of the fan and all the while she dreamed of New York's Grand Central, of dark menacing faces, and of hurrying down long deserted streets shadowed by crumbling buildings. Now and again she pressed her ribcage against the cool hard floor as if to escape the sunlight which filtered through the shutters.

During the second week she put on her bathing suit and went to the beach where she lay quietly and half-asleep. April was a good time to return home. It was the season of ripening fruit, and trees of reddening rambutans shaded the village houses on the road to the beach. Lured by the putrefying smell of durians, she cycled around the town, buying mounds of the globular spiked fruit from the wayside stands. The casuarina trees and royal palms on the Esplanade, no longer familiar, were like fragments of her dreams shimmering in the hot sunlight.

Her old college friend, now a professor of economics at the university, invited her for dinner to meet his brother, a student at the Massachusetts Institute of Technology, who was home from the United States for the spring intersession. Absorbed in arranging for an apartment in Cambridge, Harry's brother talked for most of the evening with a Communications instructor who was leaving for a three-year doctoral program in New Haven next month. Martha listened while they discussed race and crime problems in American cities; although she had lived in both Cambridge and New Haven, she had little to say about them. She avoided talking about New York; instead she tried to befriend the lone Australian who had just arrived in the country that day. Mr Checkers, who had signed a three-year contract with the university to replace the Communications instructor, however, merely offered that he was staying in the E & O, the island's best hotel, for the night, consumed the prawns, dumplings and cake silently, and then said goodbye and left abruptly. The others stayed on after the food: an American with a Malay wife, an Indian from the History Department, a German from the World Health Organization, and a computer man of indistinct nationality. It was a pleasant evening filled with talk of campus personalities and agreeable stories. At the end of the evening, Martha accepted Harry's invitation to accompany him to the political rally the next day.

The rally was to honour the Prime Minister, Tun Razak, who was returning from a politically significant visit to the People's Republic of China. Early next day, Martha waited by the radio to listen to his homecoming address. He spoke in a slow, deep voice which made everything he said of peculiar emphasis, as if the resonance of the voice box captured the emotional vibrations of the actual event; it was the voice of a statesman, dignified, accustomed to respect, and assured of being heard, a thread of air which penetrated through open houses. She felt she could respect him as she could not respect those American politicians of whom Nixon, sweating and incoherent before the microphones as her husband in New York wrote to her, was the arch-representative.

A sense of the historic occasion began to fill her. That morning the five years she had been away seemed like a period of sleep; the scene had ceased during that time, and she was awaking now to a country as busy, ordered, and safe as a story-tale kingdom read by a child. When she got to the rally and saw the strings of buntings in the *padang,* the brightly-lit town hall, and the buses of people from the nearby *kampungs* already waiting along the roads and in the field, her satisfaction increased. Like these people, she thought, she also had come for the exotic festival which made politics common and constitutional in their country: the ten-foot banners and coloured palms, the turbaned carriers in silver and blue sarongs, the drummers and lion dancers, and the suited party men forming a solid cadre at the road entrance.

An excellent guide, Harry found her a place close to the driveway. As they waited for the entourage to appear, they exchanged wry notes on the confused, excited, and noisy crowds around them. She told him of the St Patrick's Day parades on Fifth Avenue when thousands of New Yorkers would wait the whole morning to watch a spectacle whose purpose seemed only to satisfy their watching. Then, unexpectedly, a long black Mercedes cut swiftly past, led by four pairs of helmeted and goggled guards mounted like insects on shielded motorcycles. The vehicles swung past the welcoming party, the troupe of drummers, and the carriers crazily waving their pink and green palms; the crowds broke and ran into the field, racing for the front rows before the stage on which the town's dignitaries would sit with the Prime Minister.

"Now we must find a good seat where we can see him," Harry said, pulling her across the field and towards the stage ringed by armed guards. More uniformed men stood behind a single row of chairs to the right of the stage.

"The Chief of Police," Harry said, pointing to one of them. "He's a good friend. There are seats up there for officers and musicians. We can get away from the crowds."

"Could we sit on the grass? Those chairs look like they are meant for important people."

"Yes, it's the VIP row. Wouldn't you rather be with VIPs?"

"Not really," Martha admitted self-consciously.

They found a space beside the stage from where they could observe the masses of people to the left of them. On the right, the field was bounded by the coast road. A smell of petroleum, oily and heavy, drifted in from the gunboats anchored off the shore. Martha counted a dozen boats on the near shore; she could make out the dim outlines of many more larger boats further out to sea whose searchlights were scanning the black night sky. The gunboats reminded her that although there was no menace in the rally that night, perhaps elsewhere in the town, or in the island, or in the larger region, the Communist threat was still being confronted by armed forces. She felt acutely that that moment in the field waiting for the Prime Minister to report on his triumphant tour of the People's Republic was a consequence of the history of the Emergency and of the victory over the terrorists. Perhaps, she thought, Harry and herself, like fellow Chinese Malaysians, were saved equally with citizens of other origins by exactly those forces which patrolled the sea that night.

The town's Chief Minister spoke first, at length, in Malay and with alternate translations into English and Mandarin. After half an hour, the crowds became distracted and began to mill around. Martha listened intently to a group of young women behind her who chattered constantly throughout the address about themselves.

"Ai!" said one, "if he goes on this way, everyone will give up and go home. I come to hear Tun Razak, not the Chief Minister. I say, I like working in the factory! At one time, what can you do with an L.C.E. certificate? Now we can work in the factory and make one hundred and seventy dollars a month. And we have Saturday half-day. Now we are independent, we can improve our lives. I vote for the Party all the time because it gives us good job opportunities."

Suddenly Martha noticed a *kereta* boy darting through the crowd. The town had many such *kereta* boys, strays who slept under shop fronts, begged for money, and ate scraps from the foodstalls. Martha had seen many of them swimming and fishing every day on the beach. Like the others, the boy wore only a torn pair of khaki shorts. Flashing his large white teeth, he had pushed his way to the front of the crowd and was trying to dodge under the restraining rope to escape from a pursuer, when the guard, a commanding person in jungle-green uniform and a gun in his belt clinched tight around his burly waist, feeling the tug of the rope, turned around, raised his stick and swung it twice, hitting the handsome dark head once and the bare shoulder once. The boy dropped silently to the ground, then he scrambled frantically through the legs of strangers until, at a safe distance from the guard who was glowering and gesturing fiercely still, he whimpered, put his hand to his head, and cried with pain. On the stage the Chief Minister was completing his address; Martha turned in protest to Harry, but he turned his head away. He did not look at her, and she, in turn, could no longer look at him.

Finally, the Prime Minister rose to speak. The boy was hidden for a moment among the surging bodies. With few gestures and in a slow and halting voice, the Prime Minister said, "The leaders of the People's Republic welcomed me warmly. They wish our country well and they promise not to interfere in our internal affairs and to respect our independence." There was nothing grand in his speech, but, as he continued, the slow deep voice seemed to draw the crowds ever closer to the stage. Pressed by the movement of the crowd, the guard turned to face the people, and seeing the *kereta* boy, like the others, creeping closer to the rope, he reached out to push him back.

"*Jangan pukul!*" the women behind Martha shouted out.

The guard hesitated and drew back. The women's shouts could be heard clearly above the mechanical boom of the loudspeakers.

"*Jangan pukul! Itu budak kecil.* I will report you to your commanding officer."

Slowly he turned his back to the crowd and moved forward a few feet, allowing the eager people to move with him.

"Yah!" Harry yelled. "*Jangan pukul atau saya buat report!*"

Hearing this, the guard turned around, put his hand on the boy's head and patted it clumsily.

That night Martha dreamed of war and fighting. She was in a classroom in New York. Harry was giving a lecture which had many numbers in it, but all his students were leaving because the police were beating them on the head. Harry continued to speak through the microphone from the rostrum above the noise of blows and crying and she was the only one left in the audience when she woke up.

She told Harry of her dream while they were waiting for her flight to New York.

"What a funny dream," he said. Then he seized her hand and shook it. "I am sorry you won't be coming back. It isn't really as bad as you think."

"No," she replied, "it isn't as bad."

But she was already wondering about finding her winter coat in London.

Glossary

ada baik?	are you well?
ada nasib	I've good luck!
Ah Mah	grandmother
almeira	a tall cupboard for storing clothes
amah	traditional female servant
ang pow	gift of money wrapped in a traditional red envelope
ang-mo-kau	white man
angsana	a type of large tree with yellow flowers
apa buat?	what's up?
Baba	male Straits-born Chinese
baju kurung	traditional Malay long skirt and tunic
bak choy	a type of Chinese vegetable
belacan	dried fermented shrimp paste used for flavouring food
bodoh	stupid
brinjal	eggplant
bunga tanjung	sweet-smelling beach blossom
cencaluk	fermented shrimp
char siew	barbecued pork
ciku	small tropical fruit with sweet brown flesh
dapur	wood-burning clay stove
datuk	spirit
dim sum	Chinese savouries
ikan bilis	anchovies
Itu budak kecil	He's a young boy
Jangan pukul!	Don't hit!
kacang	beans
kampung	village
kang	a built-in platform used as bed and seating area
kapitan	foreman

kati	a measurement of weight, about two pounds
kaya	egg-custard jam
kebaya	Malay blouse with long sleeves
kebun	gardener
kedai	grocery store, shop
kerbau	buffalo
kereta	car
kerosang	broach
klong	mine
kong-kong	grandfather
kongsi	association
kuih bulu	a traditional Malay cake
kwali	wok
lady's fingers	okra
lallang	a type of tall coarse grass
lawyer buruk	a pretentious and pompous person
macam bunga	like a flower
makan	eat; food
mamak	Indian-Muslim food peddler
mari	come
marie-piah	crackers
masuk	come in
mata-mata	police
mee hoon	vermicelli
mee siam	noodles served in a spicy, sourish soup
na' makan, 'mak?	Do you wish to eat, mother?
nenek	old woman, grandmother
nipah	a type of palm tree whose leaves are used for thatching
Nyonya	female Straits-born Chinese
orang jakun	aborigine; country bumpkin
padang	field
pai-pai	pray; observe ancestral worship
parang	long curved knife

pontianak	a type of female demon
pulut	glutinous rice
rojak	a cold dish of sliced vegetables and fruits seasoned with a sauce
roti	bread
sambal belacan	piquant sauce
samfoo	traditional Chinese buttoned top and trousers
samseng	thug
sari	traditional Indian dress
sayang	what a shame!
Serani	Eurasian
siew mai	Chinese savoury made from pork and flour
sini boleh	here will do
sirih	betel nut
sundal	prostitute
Syaitan	Satan
ta' malu	shameless
towgay	bean sprouts
towkay	merchant
Tua Ee	Eldest Aunt
Tua Peh Kong	Supreme Deity
yau soo	cursed